Chapter One

Pannonia Province, Roman frontier 166 A.D.

The morning was pleasant, and the chatter of birds filled the forest, providing a melodious backdrop across wide stands of oak and pine trees. The collections of wild timberland and dense underbrush stretched into the far distance, making for a sporadically untamed atmosphere.

Bountiful shadows filled the interior of the woods, contrasting the patchy open meadows with a tint of darkness that evoked a forbidding atmosphere within the tall thickets.

Above, collections of feathery clouds moved silently across a backdrop of blue skyline, offering a sort of eternal openness to the accumulation of vibrant nature below. Far into the sky, arching shapes of migrating birds worked their way through undulating air currents, flapping and gliding without care for what lay underneath their routes to distant destinations.

In this isolated area, an energetic creek wound between the green forest cover and grasslands. Neither excessively wide nor deep, the bubbling waterway flowed over elongated and weathered rocks as it wound between soggy earthen banks. The twisting outlines of the stream were as chaotic as they were gentle, combining noisy rapids with occasionally deep pools in long stretches on its inexorable path eastward.

After a series of particularly raucous rapids, an area below the strong current became a calm basin. Spreading out into a large and open area, an unobstructed view into the deep waterhole became possible as the creek slowed to a gentle pace.

To the side, several large and flat-topped boulders were arranged along the creek's bank. Two children stood on the sturdy stones, transfixed and appreciative as they gazed into the stream's dreamy depths. The trickling water soothed the siblings and magnified their moment of calm as they absorbed the peaceful surroundings.

The youngsters, Thaddeus and Severina, had not yet reached ten. Though beyond the age of toddlers, the lively children still held close to the blind innocence of early youth. Dressed in simple tunics tied with corded belts, they each gazed at flitting minnows in the water, as if not wishing to miss even a single wonder from nature's entertaining display below them.

"Father, can I be first to catch a fish?" asked Severina, her face expectant. "He got to go first last week."

Thaddeus, a bit younger and equally excited by their view and location, scrunched up his face. "I didn't get to, Papa. I only caught a crawdad—no fishes."

Stepping from tall reeds behind them, Appius hopped onto a rock to join his children. Smiling, the squat and powerful man was also dressed in basic clothing, with a clean tunic pulled tight and held in place by leather straps. Meticulously tied sandals covered his feet, showing the image of one accustomed to careful dress and preparation. With dark skin, the middle-aged

Praesidia

by

Timothy Bryan

"The mind becomes accustomed to things by the habitual sight of them, and neither wonders nor inquires about the reasons for things it sees all the time."

— **Marcus Tullius Cicero**

Table of Contents

man, swarthy and rugged, gave an indication of origin far away from this remote Roman location in the middle of Europe.

Holding out simple wooden fishing rods in both hands, each with crude hooks on their lines, Appius smiled warmly. "This is an excellent place to find our dinner, I think. Your mother waits to cook our catch, if only we are able to coax some fish into our sack."

Handing a rod to each of them, Appius bent down to meet the children's happy gazes. His piercing brown eyes, alive and amused, sparkled with love. "And we have two rods today, so perhaps both of you will hook a substantial one. They say the big fishes wait to be caught by only the best fishermen."

Appius held out his hands to mimic the size of their hoped-for fish. The children, eyes gaping at such a prospective monster, grinned even brighter, their eagerness making their innocence even more pronounced.

Kneeling, Appius detached a leather pouch from his waist. Producing two squiggling worms from its dirt-filled interior, he began baiting the hooks for his earnest kids. Meeting his playful eyes, they returned Appius' affectionate look with open adoration, anticipating what could only be a fun day ahead.

After some time, Appius managed to properly outfit the children. Their horse-hair fishing lines, tied to the end of the poles and weighted with oddly shaped stones, drifted toward the lower edge of the expansive pool. The children focused intently into the shimmering water, waiting for a pull on their lines that would surely bring them a cherished trophy and tasty dinner.

Scanning the quiet area around, Appius breathed deep and peered contentedly down. His face, calm and reserved, beamed at the display of fishing acumen by the youngsters. His heart and mind, full of appreciation for the moment, made his attitude and worldview momentarily joyful.

Reaching down, Appius tousled the hair of Thaddeus, then patted his daughter's head with equal affection. "It is a favorable time to collect cherries in the orchard."

Looking downstream, Appius thought for a moment before pointing to a string of trees that ran along an elevated ridge to the side of the creek. "I will be within easy walking distance. Yell out when you hook into a big one, and we shall make it ready for our feast this evening."

Jumping to the muddy shore, Appius paced away from his kids. As he walked toward some shaded trees, he angled toward a crude game trail that would take him up the hill, just a short distance away from the preoccupied children.

Severina and Thaddeus, entranced with their fishing endeavor, paid Appius no attention as he moved from the immediate area. For the moment, they could think of nothing else but the tantalizing possibility of catching a stout fish, one that would make their father exceedingly proud of them.

#

The sun, not yet at its highest peak for the day, had brought the forested area into sharper focus. The mist of the morning had been burned off, making visibility excellent across an orchard of healthy cherry trees. These clusters of green-leafed trees, planted as they were in pairs to ensure they provided bountiful harvests from cross-pollination, were surrounded by the incessant chatter of playful birds providing a spirited backdrop to the calm environment.

Appius stood at the halfway point in his grove, looking up as he plucked another of the fruits from a low-hanging limb. The plump cherry, perfectly round and ripened, caused him to smile, and he slipped the morsel into his half-full bag with some degree of personal satisfaction. The time for collecting these fruits was short in duration, and this year, he had planned the harvesting event to perfection. Over the next two weeks, he and his family would eat well, and he would also be able to offer the excess to his friends in the nearby village. Maybe he would even sell some, and he could use the money to enlarge their recently completed stone home.

Appius was a man who had known trauma and tragedy in his life, like nearly everyone who made a life on the frontier. A seasoned soldier, he had been rewarded with this plot of property on the far reaches of the empire for his military exploits. Twenty-five years of service had its benefits, and men who managed to survive the brutality of the campaign life were able to live a comfortable life from Rome's generosity through land grants and a pension after they had fulfilled the terms of their military obligation.

Of course, that also meant such retired men were to be available to be called up if Rome needed them, but Appius was not a man who shied away from such commitments. His well-practiced blade had tasted blood on many occasions in service to the emperor, and the thought of being needed again was not unpleasant to his way of thinking.

Looking up into the sky, Appius' wrinkles, spider-webbed from the corners of his eyes across his dark and leathery features, revealed a person who had lived and seen more than most. Deeply loyal and committed to Rome's fortunes, he was nevertheless a man who understood that moments of joy were also to be found most acutely in the present. Fate had now given him a plot of land, a good wife, and two of the best children the Gods had offered, so for the moment, thoughts of his often-violent past were subsumed into appreciation of his current circumstance.

Over the next several minutes, Appius moved from one tree to another, carefully picking more of the fruits after making sure that they were the best from clusters hanging on each branch. Slipping them into his sarcina, a useful leather bag that he had owned since his time in the legion, his carrying capacity was soon filled, and he adjusted the bag to his back as he prepared to return to his children.

From the far end of the grove, a strange sound arose, one that caused Appius to snap his head toward the direction of the farthest trees. The staccato and throaty chirping sound, spread out over several moments and having almost a guttural, avian quality, was odd and somewhat disturbing. He hadn't really heard anything quite like it before, which was concerning for a man who had traipsed from one end of the empire to another.

Reaching under his tunic, Appius produced a long and sturdy dagger. This tool, perfectly sharp and functional, glinted in the light as he weighed its balance, and, moving it from hand to hand, he carefully considered the source of that nearby noise.

Mulling over what it could be, Appius looked up into the bright sky, then lowered his gaze to focus on the distant source of the odd sound. Moving carefully, he trudged toward the shadows of the remotest part of the grove. Scanning cautiously as he moved, he took in every bush and plant of the extended foliage, searching for an indication of man or animal that could make such a bizarre croaking noise.

As Appius moved closer to the origin of the sound, his features, formerly relaxed and joyful, sharpened into a scowl, and his face took on the severe appearance of a hunter that was approaching potentially dangerous quarry. Caution informed his expression, making his face into the image of one who was prepared for anything.

"This is my land," said Appius, and panning his head as he searched, his loud tone was rigid and uncompromising. "If you wish to gather food, it can only be with my permission."

Stepping ahead, pressing his footing carefully as he moved, Appius was confident in his gait and demeanor. As a man that had faced deadly enemies from spots as varied as Anatolia to the wilds of Britannia, his self-control and bravery were unrivaled.

Still, as he came to the shady end of his columns of trees, a chill involuntarily ran down his spine. His was a life that had experienced the worst of what was known in this brutal world, but something about his current environment told him there were things here beyond his knowledge, and he sensed there might be places where he should tread even more carefully.

Turning in a circle, Appius stayed silent as he waited for the interloper on his property to reveal himself. Over the next minute, only quietness returned his visual interrogation of the formerly pleasant surroundings. As if now working in concert with his dour demeanor, the area around him was now silent, without the gentle chirps of birds he was accustomed to hearing on his precious land.

Finally, the stoic military man, who exuded fierceness and military competency in equal degrees, grew more relaxed. Sighing deeply, he waited a final few moments, then spun to return to the creek, where he suddenly felt the need to check on his playful kids.

Shaking his head, he thought through his sudden paranoia, mentally chastising himself for the trap of thinking that every noise in the woods needed to be explained. Who was he to think the natural environment would always reveal itself to him? Men far smarter than himself, men he had served with for decades, would have laughed at him for being suddenly spooked by nothing at all.

As he passed a particularly low-limbed tree, one that had several twisted branches full of dense and shrouding leaves, a dark figure stepped from behind it and launched itself toward Appius. The unseen figure, seemingly materializing from nothing, was large and ungainly, and surged ahead with frightening speed.

With an innate sense of the oncoming danger, Appius turned to meet his assailant with little time to spare. His eyes, full of surprise at the incoming threat, opened wide just as the thick creature was upon him.

The dark pallor of the beast's thickly clawed hand was accompanied by oily skin stretched over a bulbous and grotesque arm. The misshapen appendage, looking lumpy and fiercely strong, struck forward in a vicious swipe. Ripping forward and back, the elongated arm tore through Appius' innards, half-disemboweling him in two rapid strikes.

Yet Appius was not one to go silently. As he fell back, his face astonished at the speed and shape of what assaulted him, with his guts now exposed and splashing gore to the green grass below, his own blade struck out, deeply gouging the monster. Even as he fell under the assault of the larger creature, which rained cuts and slashes from its bloody, obsidian-like claws, he was able to acquit himself well, tearing his own severe gashes into the enormous adversary with his razor-edged knife.

But in seconds it was over. With mortal wounds on his head, neck, and torso, Appius fell prey to his bizarre opponent, and he collapsed onto the fertile soil of his cherished cherry orchard. A man who had survived the clash of empires and played an integral role in the world's most climactic events was brought to an ignominious end on his modest property at the edge of the Roman frontier.

Face down on the damp ground, Appius' shocked eyes gradually clouded over, and as his blood gushed and pooled on the dark earth, his dissipating thoughts focused on his now-unprotected son and daughter at the nearby creek.

#

Along the rocky creekside, the natural environment was calm and quiet, with the relentless flush of meandering water offering a relaxing and palliative counterpoint to the recent violence in the nearby orchard.

At the place where Severina and Thaddeus had earlier been fishing, there were now two unattended fishing rods jutting over the glossy surface of the gently flowing water. The lines of each pole, now empty of bait on their hooks, drifted aimlessly into the shallows.

Like many children left to partake in something that required patience, the pair of siblings had found other things to do when their fishing efforts were not soon rewarded. Now, on a larger rock back from of the quiet stream, Severina hummed to herself and played with a crude doll, while at the shoreline on the other end of the trickling pool, Thaddeus jabbed a sword-like stick down at some minnows that darted through inch-deep water. Practicing his martial form for a future where he would be as great a soldier as his dad, Thaddeus jousted at the small fish, moving as if such practice had suddenly become more interesting than catching larger trout from the deeper water of the brook. Always a stickler for using his best fighting form, and having been coached by his father on the importance of discipline when preparing himself for battle, his splashing pokes into the water showed he was following Appius' path to eventually become a mighty warrior.

Twenty yards away, Severina stroked the hair of her doll, which only had one crude rock eye hanging from it and a bit of stitched yarn threaded across its face to make a mouth. Entranced and wholly preoccupied, she dreamily focused down, where she worked to straighten the kinks in her doll's matted wool hair by taking her time to brush it with a simple ivory comb.

From behind, a shadow detached from the tree line that ran along the ascending bank of the stream. Unnoticed by both children, the large figure hesitated as it watched the calm youngsters. Neither moving quickly nor making a sound, it observed the children for a considerable time, and its fixation on the young brother and sister suggested a very specific interest, as if nothing else currently mattered to the threatening shape.

Moving slowly, the puffy and discolored feet of the creature, with a bloated appearance and spotted pallor across its strange whitish skin, emerged and carefully paced across the muddy ground as it approached Severina.

Each step was taken with precise care, and as it moved closer to the unaware girl, there were no obvious sounds to give away its presence. The unnerving quietness of the beast was odd for such a large and hideous frame, and as it moved to peer down at the girl, she remained oblivious to its looming presence.

Over an extended time, the imposing creature stared at the back of Severina's head, and as it inched closer to where she was perched, its shadow fell across her back. At such a close distance, the unseen creature seemed to hover over the diminutive girl, blocking out both the light of day and the emotionally pleasant environment.

Unbothered for the moment and still interested in her doll, Severina noticed the encroaching shadow with childly indifference, thinking it had to be her father returning from his quest to fetch cherries from the grove. As the large form stood above her, unmoving and anticipating what came next, a slow and methodical croaking emanated from its vibrating throat.

In response, Severina turned slowly, her expression becoming curious. With the warming rays of the sun half-illuminating her wide-eyed and innocent features, a smile filled her face as she expected to witness the return of Appius.

From far above the remote area, across the peaceful woods and open fields, in a place where forbidding shapes and predatory animals were largely unknown, Severina's screams reverberated across the forested landscape. After several throaty shrieks, a THUD cut her terrified wails short. This was soon followed by the patting of small feet, undoubtedly those of Thaddeus trying to flee, which were also terminated by another jarring impact.

Thereafter, the afternoon was again quiet, and the formerly mellow surroundings reassumed a placid atmosphere in the picturesque region.

#

Deeper in the canopy of the dense forest, in a place far darker because of the impending arrival of night, branches of numerous trees shrouded the damp soil from the dimming sky.

With no noisy birds to enliven the area, little sound was present in the woods, and the region had taken on the appearance of an abandoned woodland, despite the fact that the plentiful vegetation should have held numerous scurrying animals.

A mild fog rolled over the ground, and with the game trail in this ominous environment twisting across the plant-covered area, the few rays of sunlight reaching the ground did little to improve visibility. In such stifling surroundings, directions and knowing where to proceed would have been a difficult proposition for even the best woodsmen.

Taking long strides through this stretch of woodlands was a bizarre and enormous creature. Bounding over gnarled tree roots and stepping without reservation through cloying brush and foliage, it pressed ahead, moving carefully and quickly. Its legs, puffy and fetid with ugly skin, had thick hooves on the end of its heinous limbs, and covered in the dark scruff of an unknowable fur hide, the appendages resembled the cloven limbs of some mythical demon.

On and on the beast moved, not stopping to contemplate its way forward or consider its remote surroundings. Behind it, the occasional thump of something hitting the rough forest floor was loud, and as the creature pressed onward, its arms, heavily muscled and covered with thick veins, were held behind as it strode onward.

Ahead, a brief clearing emerged to offer some illumination of the path forward. Across this bit of rocky earth, the last light of the day shone over the open ground, and as the wicked creature moved through the hazy area, the cause of the thumping sound behind it became evident.

Face down, the limp bodies of Severina and Thaddeus were being dragged by one ankle each over the twigs, stones, and raw ground of the untamed forest. In concert with the strides of the beast, their heads popped against the ground, their small skulls thumping with every strike on the hard surface.

In time, the vile march continued, and as night descended over the forbidding path, the creature and its victims were lost in vast thickets of the dreary wilderness.

Chapter Two

The afternoon was bright, and only a few shreds of clouds drifted across the intensely blue sky. Plentiful sunshine bathed the countryside below, revealing a deep echelon of ordered crops on a succession of fertile fields.

Over a hillside that descended into an attractive valley, hues of white and purple were represented in beautiful flowers laced throughout the vegetation of multiple diverse meadows. A few farmers, wearing simple rags and stooping to harvest grain, worked in a methodical manner throughout the area.

At the bottom of the valley, an attractive village, given the name of Avenio long ago, was encircled by a stone wall. Cozy and subdued, it lay next to a road running the length of a ridge, and clusters of tall trees stood to either side of a well-traveled path before it passed directly through the town's center. Set next to the sheer wall of a long-quarried hillside, the hamlet consisted of a few hundred houses, most of which were sturdy and constructed of gray material from anciently mined rock that abutted the settlement.

The tightly packed homes of the burg, solidly built and mostly painted white, were simple yet pleasant residences, and at the moment, the whole community served as a hosting place for a bustling market. On wide streets crisscrossing the village, collections of assorted citizens, dressed in flowing robes and simple tunics, haggled with vendors as they perused the varied goods on offer. Fruits, breads, and baubles such as crude jewelry and kids' toys were largely what was available for sale, but spaced throughout the stalls were also farming tools, baskets, water jugs, and other simple knickknacks.

Dressed in basic shiny armor and the red cloak of the Roman army, Marius Livonius stood patiently at a baker's stall. With an expressive and kind face, his bearing did not quite meet the seriousness that his attire and worn shortsword presented to the world.

Pointing to and receiving a fragrant loaf of flat bread from a one-eyed bald man, Marius smiled in thanks and tucked the food into a satchel at his side. After paying the vendor, he breathed deeply and panned his head to take in the wider market and the potential for spending more of his meager wages on this day of shopping.

Quintus, another soldier to his left, a man who looked more serious and weathered despite being of similar age, grunted and pointed to several booth-like places to eat near them. Wearing an immaculate uniform that barely contained his powerful frame, Quintus had mischievous eyes that were out of place with his tough physical appearance.

Shaking his head, Marius wasn't impressed with Quintus' quiet suggestion for a quick meal. Looking at a long table where several people slurped soup from pottery bowls, his lack of enthusiasm for the proffered food was clear.

"The quality of garum is poor in this hovel," Marius said, referring to the common dish of fish sauce that was an everyday staple across much of the extended empire.

"It makes me wonder why Rome ever sought to tame such a province."

Chuckling, Quintus disagreed with a sarcastic grimace. "Not having quality fish stew is a sign of intelligence. The stuff is wretched, whether in Ravenna, Athens…anywhere. How do you eat any of it?"

After flashing a knowing smile, Marius raised his voice a bit, as if pronouncing an edict from the far-away capital city. "It's one of the joys of life. As a soldier of the empire, you should be compelled to sing its praises with every meal."

"Praising anything mixed by our illustrious cook," responded Quintus, wrinkling his nose, "would be enough to make a horse retch, so it's preferable we at least have this village to pursue tastier fare."

Grinning widely, Marius acquiesced to that sentiment with a nod and firmly clapped Quintus on the shoulder. In a good mood, he moved to the next stall, which had numerous fruits on display. As he looked over rows of large melons, his eyes briefly shot to the young woman who oversaw the stand.

Julia, five years younger than Marius and pretty, with long dark hair and a button nose, met his gaze and quickly looked away. Her cheeks flushed, even as she feigned a noncommittal attitude about the soldiers' presence. As if competing to act the least interested, she and Marius took turns hiding their poorly hidden attraction for one another.

Noticing the ill-disguised exchange, a smile blossomed across Quintus' wrinkled face. "It could be that hovels such as this humble village offer up more important things to Rome than their local take on delicacies, Marius. Perhaps…their best parts are more valuable than anything to be found in the capital?"

Disconcerted, Marius peered over at his friend and subordinate. Unable to effectively refute Quintus' joking accusation, he resumed his preoccupied inspection of the fruits, letting his gaze linger on a collection of ripe plums.

As the moments passed, Marius managed to avoid engaging Julia's similar disinterest, even as Quintus leered at them both with an amused grin. As a man of the world, Quintus could really bring into the open what Marius most wanted to keep hidden. To make matters worse, because Quintus was his dearest friend and acutely perceptive, there was little Marius could do to maintain his secrets—and his attempts to do so just made the consequent humor even more pronounced on Quintus's jovial face.

From far in the busy crowd, a panicked shout arose, bringing a sudden end to the awkward interaction. As a throng of nearby shoppers arched their heads to see what was wrong, several villagers were jostled, and a short and fat man emerged from a cluster of people at the far end of the busy market square.

After scanning over and noticing Marius, the stout village mayor Ceres recognized him and made his way through the surprised onlookers. Overcome with some serious purpose, as well as his recent efforts at exercise, when the mayor came close, he put his arm on Julia's stall to steady himself.

As he tried to collect his breath, Ceres looked as if the effort to calm himself and overcome his exertions would make his jowly and sweaty face explode. Waiting with open eyes, Marius and Quintus looked at each other, then back at the overwhelmed mayor. Even Julia looked up to inspect the local leader with some alarm on her face.

"Marius…I'm glad you're…here," said Ceres, finally controlling his gasps. "There's been…a…horrible crime."

Glancing back at Quintus and to Julia, then returning his gaze to the mayor, Marius' expression, formerly lively and contented, grew cold and inquisitive. "What is it?"

#

The relaxing stream continued its mellow pace, and the flitting sounds of birds and scurrying wildlife had returned to the site of the family's former fishing expedition. On the ponderous rocks that bordered the creek, the children's rods were still suspended over the opaque current.

At the base of the pool below the lazy water, Marius, Quintus, and the mayor stared into the shallow water. While the mayor wore a look of worry and revulsion, Marius and Quintus were intrigued and curious. With eyes that had seen violence and gore on a wide scale, the soldiers were unperturbed, and they scanned the dribbling water with investigative intensity.

In the shallow stream was a detached right hand, which at some point in the recent past had been cleaved from its unfortunate owner. The pallid flesh of the limb glistened under the surface of the water, and as if to add drama of the moment, two crawdads warred for possession of it, their claws grasping at either side of the puffy digits. As they clung to sinews of meat, their struggles made the battle over the delicious meal a pitched affair, and it looked as if neither would be able to win outright and abscond with the whitish morsel.

Producing a wicked-looking dagger, Quintus bent down and speared the hand with the sharp blade. Brusquely raising it from the water, he rotated it in front of Marius for a thorough inspection. As he did so, one of the clawed combatants managed to hold on, even as the other dropped away, and suspended and twisting, the remaining scavenger clung to its prize with remarkable tenacity.

On the back of the bloodless hand was a tattoo, one that was crudely done in thick lines of some bizarre form of unknown lettering. The effect of the strange rune-like diagram, looking like a combination of odd triangles and indeterminable letters, was striking, if not particularly artistic.

"This isn't the hand of Appius," said Marius, looking fascinated and pointing at the stenciled flesh. "His skin was darker, and he didn't engage in such manipulation of his appearance."

Agreeing with a nod, Quintus moved his gaze to the mayor, who was decidedly less interested in the dangling, bloody appendage. Looking back at Marius, Quintus scowled as he ran through his memories. "Tattoos, like the barbarians use to decorate themselves?"

Crossing his arms, Marius came to his full height. Thinking carefully, he looked upstream on the bank, where he spotted Severina's abandoned doll. Her plaything was now dirty and half-buried under a mound of soggy dirt.

Walking to the toy, he picked it up and looked back at Quintus. "Yes, it looks that way. The Marcomanni do so. Their warriors employ such body art as a form of protection when they give battle. They are also the most dangerous of the tribes, which makes this scene particularly concerning."

Walking slowly back, Marius moved near the mayor, holding up the dirty doll to the shaken leader. "What of Appius' children?"

Wiping away sweat that never seemed to subside from his pudgy face, the mayor shook his head and stuttered a reply. "The...mother came to me when nobody returned from their trip to the creek. She...was fearful and desperate to see what happened. Fortunately, I came down with the blacksmith, and she did not have to see...this."

As Marius took the information in, his thoughts worked carefully through the possibilities of this worrisome development. Because of his status as the ranking soldier in this outlying province, matters of violent interaction with the northward-resident barbarian tribe were of extreme importance. With his livelihood and the safety of everyone nearby depending on his actions and planning, his face puckered in expressive concentration.

Turning to Quintus, Marius breathed slowly and spoke in a guarded tone. "She is wise to be worried. This does not bode well for her family...or...our own role here."

Flicking his hand, Marius tossed the doll to Quintus, who deftly snatched it from the air. Still maintaining his hold with his other hand on the knife and the dangling crawdad, Quintus returned his commander's grave scowl, his brows furrowing into an unspoken question.

"Appius was able to severely injure one of the attackers, that much is clear," Marius finally said, his face becoming ever more contemplative. "But now we have three citizens missing...and a severe problem for our future."

Quintus, continuing his fascinated look, merely nodded at the statement, while the mayor, clearly out of his element and plumbing new depths of disgust with each passing second, appeared ready to flee from the disturbing scene.

Still deep in thought, Marius reached out and grasped the crawdad. Pulling if free from the severed hand, he tightened his grip and crushed the poor creature, its shell and claws cracking under his tightening grip. For a considerable time, he kept his hand closed, and as his mental considerations roamed elsewhere, his knuckles turned white from the effort.

Coming out of his deliberations, Marius' face sharpened, and he abruptly peered between Quintus and the mayor. Not a hint of pain crossed his features, and with little sense of the dramatic, he dropped the smashed creature back into the trickling water below.

Chapter Three

The smooth water of the Danube shimmered under the glow of stars and moon. The flow of the wide expanse of river, moving in its eternal push across a hundred yards of open space between opposing lines of dark trees, produced a gentle whooshing sound as it surged through the calm, wooded environment.

Facing the water was an open embankment, where a small road led down to a simple dock. Lined with smooth stones that glistened under the faint light, the road's surface appeared off-color as it merged into the dark water.

In the water itself were two wooden barges that floated gently in the strong current. Attached by ropes to some buttresses on the shoreline, the barges were connected to ropes that stretched across the surface of the wide water toward the distant shoreline. Set as a crossing point for the substantial river, the ropes were connected to a similar docking space that could just be seen in the firelight on the opposite riverbank, where a small squad of legionaries manned the shoreline next to a dirt road that disappeared into a smudge of the forest beyond.

On this side of the river the darkness was periodically illuminated by several long poles holding oil lamps at intervals on either side of the road. The anchoring poles and lights, solid and driven deep in the earth, made the area around the road visible for several yards as it descended into the water.

Between the lamp poles, four groups of diligent Roman soldiers stood. Holding long spears and clustered in groups of three, the armored men, sharp and awake in the late night, stood warily, scanning the area around them and across the river with intense and disciplined eyes.

To the near side of the flowing water, fifty yards from the river's crossing point and on the north side of the road, was the fronting of a fort-like structure. The wooden facade of the single-story building held several entrances, most of which were dark at this late hour.

But the main entrance to the building was lit by further lamps, and a soldier stood at attention to either side of the doorway. With hands fixed on scabbarded swords at their waists, they watched the surrounding area carefully, while to their side was a large banner set on a sturdy pole, the Vexillum, which announced the headquarters as belonging to the Legion II Italica. With the words SPQR stitched above the rendering of a wolf, it served as the northern-most standard of the Roman army, signifying the protection of the empire against any prospective threat of invasion from across the Danube River.

Inside the entrance was a wide office. Clean, orderly, and well-lit by numerous candles, it held several tables, most of which were stacked with precisely arranged rolled parchments. At the far point of the room, near a basic window that would allow light in during the day, a bust of Emperor Marcus Aurelius Antoninus was perched on a small desk. With curly hair and a wavy, well-tended beard, the sculpture of the respected leader seemed almost to smile into the room's officious interior.

On the largest table in the center of the room was an extensive map of the northern Roman border and the area beyond it. On the south of the map were several place names, with Roman cities such as Aquincum and Savaria, while across the squiggly line of the Danube to the northern side were designations of barbarian tribes, from the Quadi to the Sarmatian Lazyges, and finally, the Marcomanni. These groups, known to all on the frontier as dangerous and often blood-thirsty enemies, were circled with red ink, as if to accentuate their threatening existence.

Marius stood over the map, his hands pressed on the table as he concentrated. Across from him stood Quintus, who also had a glum look as he studied the map. Both peered down with hard and reflective expressions, as if they were working through some particularly vexing and unsolvable problem.

After an extended silence, Marius spoke evenly. "Appius was a formidable soldier and good friend. Twenty-five years of dedicated service."

Raising his eyes, Quintus nodded. "He will be mourned by one and all. He deserved better. Those vile animals will pay for this."

Marius met Quintus' earnest gaze but didn't immediately respond. In deep thought, he turned and walked to the window, where he peered out into the night. Taking in the calm, moonlit area outside and glancing up at the cloudless, partially luminescent sky, he considered the grave circumstances the soldiers faced.

Finally speaking, Marius sounded noncommittal. "He may yet live, though I hold no great hope for his survival."

Turning back to Quintus, Marius kept his voice low and parsed his words cautiously. "I assume you have heard of the disaster that occurred under Emperor Augustus?"

Taken aback, Quintus tilted his head, almost like a curious dog caught unaware from a new subject of interest. "I...have heard of many old battles, including that which you refer to. Are you suggesting that we again are living in such trying times?"

Continuing on, Marius avoided the question. "General Varus, more than a century and a half ago, sought to tame the tribes to our north with a punishing offensive. Taking three legions deep into Germania, his intent was to wipe away all threats to Rome—to make them pay for the insolence of resisting our empire."

Waiting a moment, Marius' eyes grew dark and serious. "All three legions—and their auxiliaries—were annihilated in an ambush in the Teutoburg Forest, in a crushing defeat by these 'animals.' Few escaped the slaughter. Perhaps twenty thousand died."

"Yes, Marius, because they were betrayed by that Germanic dog, Arminius. Treachery is a way of life for those who inhabit the untamed lands."

Marius smiled and shook his head, but he showed no humor in his expression. "No, because they underestimated an enemy...which is a mistake we should be wary of repeating."

Breathing deep, Quintus shook his head. Clearly, he disagreed, but for the moment he held his thoughts to himself. Returning his gaze to the map, Quintus brooded.

Moving back to the table, Marius pointed to an area to the unnamed north, where the tribes and their methods were in control up to this day. "More than forty years after the battle, at another place entirely, our army destroyed one of their tribes. While sacking their camp, we liberated soldiers who had been made slaves from that original fight. Their decades-long wait for freedom from the barbarians had been long and torturous."

Emerging from his emotional funk, Quintus cheered up a bit. "A testament to Rome's power and perseverance. It will always be so. We bring civilization to the masses and justice to the wicked."

"Perhaps, Quintus, perhaps. But…I do not intend that Appius and his children will have so long to wait."

Moving quickly to another of the tables, Marius unrolled a parchment. Grabbing a quill, he dipped it in ink and scrawled several sentences in meticulous writing, taking his time to convey recent events in a factual manner. Rolling it back up, he reached to the side and took a candle. After using it to let wax dribble on the document's rolled edge, he sealed it by pressing his commander's ring into the melted wax and blowing it until cool.

Sighing, Marius raised the paper, holding it out to Quintus. "After a period of peace, war again returns to the empire. We must prepare ourselves. Send Vitus with this message to the cohort in Salvio. Immediately."

Suddenly appearing happier, Quintus nodded and snatched the parchment. As he moved towards the door, Marius stopped him with a raised hand.

"And start regular patrols between the creek and the Danube—on horseback," said Marius, and thinking further, he made his tone more severe. "Tell the men to be cautious until we are reinforced. We are soldiers, so danger is our lot in life, but I want no lives wasted while we wait."

Agreeing with a wave, Quintus paced out through the entrance. The clack of the door behind him left the guards outside to exchange confused glances about what had just transpired. Padding into the night, Quintus angled toward a series of smaller buildings across the road, where most of the barracks were located.

Alone, Marius smiled to himself at the intensity of Quintus. As Quintus was a man who did everything he was told, and who also worked through any task with inventiveness and dedication, Marius often wondered why it was not Quintus who had been promoted to lead this remote detachment. Truth be known, Marius knew he respected his lower-ranking counterpart as much as Quintus did he himself, a fact that made for an effective working relationship between the two. In all his time in the legion, he had never had a better arrangement—or a better friend.

But now something new and dangerous was upon them, and Marius needed to ensure his men and the town of Avenio were ready for what came next. His people's time of laziness and well-deserved rest was coming to an end, and it was solely his responsibility to plan for eventualities and protect his people—as well as the empire.

Losing his smile, Marius returned his stare to the map, and as he peered at the untamed region of the tribes on the crude drawing, his thoughts wandered to the disturbing possibility of wide-scale death in their very near future.

#

It was always this way with Quintus, Vitus thought, irritation filling his face. Not only could nothing ever please the man, but he also had a way of springing new tasks on him with little warning, like this sudden ride to Salvio in the middle of the night.

Stepping into the darkness from the small building that served as his barracks, Vitus tucked the message from Marius into his pouch, which was bound tight to his front armor by several leather straps. After a steady breath, he strode towards the distant outline of the stables, which were located off the road, away from any cart or trade traffic that might spook the horses.

It wasn't that Vitus didn't respect Quintus, because anyone with a brain knew Quintus looked after his men with knowledge and care. Nor was it the case that as optio, or sergeant, Quintus didn't have the authority to do as he pleased. He had earned his place as the right-hand of Marius and had killed more enemies than were countable in a score of diverse battles. The infantry of the detachment was to a man awed by Quintus' prowess on the battlefield and in his knowledge of soldierly tactics.

No, the infuriating thing to Vitus was that Quintus was always right. The sergeant seemed to be right about everything, and even though they had similar time in the army, Quintus was bound for a much higher position, one that everyone knew would be at least a centurion, if not higher. Rome had a way of ensuring its military was formed on the basis of merit, where those that knew their business and performed well were rewarded with prestige and rank.

Unfortunately, with Vitus that meant the best he could hope for would be jobs like this, where he would carry important messages when the task called for someone who made sure to complete their duties.

Vitus wasn't the smartest soldier in the legion, but he knew enough to get the message where it needed to be, and at all times, he would sacrifice himself for that goal. At this point in his life, where he had now moved into early middle age, with thinning hair and little coin to his name, that was at least something to be proud of. Of course, that meant Vitus sometimes had to upset people in his work, such as the time he carried an important communication to the praefectus castrorum in Aquincum, only to be told the officer was away from the area with his mistress. Instead of settling down for a few days of fun in the provincial city while he awaited the official's return, Vitus told a host of local officials that to miss the message would mean the legion commander himself would be disappointed due to the untimely communication.

The result was his message quickly found its way to the prefect, and Vitus was able to get back on the road to Avenio before they found out the legion commander had nothing whatsoever to do with the delivery.

Chuckling to himself, Vitus recalled Marius' approving look when he found out about the deception, and in a rare bit of humor for Marius, he had stated, "If the prefect would like to discuss how his love for women was more important than the needs of Rome, I would be happy to bring it up with the legion commander himself."

That was the beauty of being a centurion, as Marius had now been for some time. Even the emperor had respect for the rank, a position that was the backbone of the entire army. Centurions were paid to be smart and skilled in battle, as well as provide unvarnished truth to their leaders, and in this manner of conducting himself, Marius had a very clear talent. Marius openly told the truth as he saw it, and after decades in the army, he was rarely questioned, either by superiors or subordinates. Competency made your word into a sort of priceless currency in the Roman world.

Grimacing, the smile drained from Vitus' face, and he canted his steps to the side as he tried to adjust his ass in his britches. One bad thing about being the go-to messenger for this remote military unit was all this riding inflamed his hemorrhoids. It wasn't a big deal when camp duties and proper food were on his daily menu, but being perched on his uncomfortable saddle for days at a time, he would eventually need to find a hot spa where he could soak his backside. Pannonia was full of natural hot springs for people with such conditions, but the trick for him was actually getting the time off to go to one. *What I go through for the empire*, mused Vitus.

Coming near the stables, Vitus refocused himself and quickened his pace. After moving inside the musty and dark building, which was full of horses, equipment, and had that lazy guard Crispus lounging in some hay against the wall to the side of the open entrance, he lit a torch and placed it in a sconce at the back of the stalls, near his favorite animal, a white stallion of admirable grace and musculature.

Outside, crickets began to chirp, and he began to mentally prepare himself for the upcoming ride and the dusty road awaiting him. His whole life as an adult had held the smells and sights of such preparations, of working through his duties as he readied himself, but just now, on the tip of his thoughts, something else was making itself known, like an emotional itch that was for the moment unscratched. Abruptly, as he worked through his mundane preparations, a feeling of dread seemed to intrude on his mind, making him stop for a moment, forcing him to review his duties for something that was out of place. Something…missing.

Shaking his head, Vitus tried to push away such feelings. He was not a man who thought in terms of the supernatural—he left that for the priests at the various temples—but he also couldn't help but sense something was amiss, like all was not quite right in the normal world around him. In the fog of his deep subconscious mind, it was as if something craved his attention. Something…was *calling* to him.

Finally, after pushing away the weird sensation, he took a minute, concentrating and making deliberate movements to saddle the beast for the long ride ahead. After some moments passed, he was at last able to make sure the horse was healthy and prepared for the exertions of a long trip.

Gently stroking its snout, Vitus looked lovingly into the horse's eyes and was relieved to see, in turn, something like affection from the animal's unsure gaze. He knew displays of caring for animals were often frowned upon in the service, but to his way of thinking, he cared as much for his horse as he did for his fellow soldiers, which was to say, quite a lot.

As he started feeling more like his normal self, Vitus released the intrusions of angst that had just taken hold of him, and in little time, he was able to push them away, just as if they never existed.

After pulling himself up on the saddle, Vitus assumed a relaxed position, then spurred the horse toward the exit. Emerging from the stables, he burst into a gallop towards the south of the village and the far-away, more-populated regions of the province.

Making a commotion as he departed, he even managed to awaken a blurry-eyed Crispus, who, as the paid local whose job it was to oversee the stables, was surprised to see he had missed yet another visitor when he stumbled to his feet.

Chapter Four

Sunlight poured through loose gaps of the wooden building's exterior, forcing illumination into the corners of the wide and gloomy room. Deeply grained pillars of various logs, roughly hewn and running in two rows across the center of the hall-like structure, provided support for the thick-planked roof above.

Scattered within the interior, amongst dark walls painted a browner color than the already-darkish slabs of wood, were the remains of several forest animals. Wolves and bears, their matted hair still holding portions of embedded flesh within their drying skins, were nailed to the timbered walls in a display of crude ornamentation. With maws full of sharp and bloody teeth, their extended mouths seemed to cry out at the indignity of their trophy status.

Against the back wall, facing directly toward the room's front entrance, was a large wooden chair. Laced with carved, head-like structures of various forest deities, the enormous throne held sufficient space for several men to sit along its wide bench.

But now there was only one man sitting under the painted faces of pagan idols mounted above him. Ballomar, a grizzled, muscular, and bulky man draped in animal skins, was perched on the throne's place of honor. With a thick beard covering an aggressive-looking face, one that held a deep and poorly mended scar over his right eye that bisected his forehead and hairline, his was not an appearance that evoked feelings of kindness or subtlety; instead, his cold expression indicated a tendency towards wanton savagery.

The front door abruptly opened, and Ballomar, looking unbothered, glanced up to see his incoming visitors.

Two guards, heavyset and severe-looking men, trudged into the room, soon followed by a skinny fellow dressed in a simple bluish tunic. The guards took their silent place to either side of Ballomar, while the third man stepped carefully in front of Ballomar's unpretentious throne.

Speaking in a cautious tone, with the voice of a person who wished not to offend, Alwin kept his eyes from meeting his chieftain's. "He has arrived, my king. He is not…in a mood that befits meeting you. Perhaps we…should wait until his temper has calmed from the long trip here?"

The room was silent for a time. Ballomar, leader of his people and with the patience of a starving coyote, collected his thoughts and glanced around his personal residence. Puckering his lips, he rubbed his beard several times with dirty hands, showing some eagerness to get on with matters at hand. After several deep breaths, he huffed and spoke with annoyance. "No, I'll see him now…show him in. Tell the others they'll have to wait. Make sure they know my expectations…in advance."

Nodding, Alwin lowered his eyes and backed towards the door. Showing a subservient stance, he continued nodding as he backed out of the front entrance. After moving over the door's threshold and out through the flooding remains of daylight, he was soon out of view.

In a moment, a new hulking presence took up the doorway. Stepping into the room, Ulrich was even larger than Ballomar, if older by a few years, and as the room's open flames lit up his dour features, he didn't appear any friendlier than his host. With a mane of reddish hair and darkish eye circles above a lengthy and unkempt beard, the man's rough lineage and difficult manner of living were on open display.

Striding in front of the seated Ballomar, Ulrich's leather boots scraped across the hardened dirt floor, and looking up, he flashed an unrestrained scowl. "Ballomar, I'm here, as you requested. What is it that couldn't be relayed by rider?"

Staring carefully at Ulrich, Ballomar stood. After taking two steps forward, his face strained, and, working through his temper, he was just able to form a rough smile, however insincere. Moving close to Ulrich, he clapped him on the shoulder. "It's good to see you, old friend. We must make for time for close allies in our…daily lives."

Frowning, Ulrich took a step back and raised an eyebrow. "We aren't friends, Ballomar, and allies only rarely. My sword has tasted more Marcomanni blood than I care to remember. Get to your point—my patience grows thin with…whatever your intentions."

Chuckling, Ballomar let his expression return to its former grim state. Not one to dwell on nuance, he motioned to the far wall, where a table piled with meats and breads stood undisturbed. "The past is behind us, Ulrich. The Quadi have been a worthy competitor for decades. You've caused many an empty seat by the campfire…and many orphans within my people."

This brought a mild smile to Ulrich's face, followed by an extended smirk as he stared at Ballomar. Shaking his head, Ulrich stepped to the table and tore free a chicken leg, taking his time as he suspiciously eyed the state of the food on offer.

Seemingly happy, Ulrich turned back to Ballomar and ripped a strip of flesh from the half-cooked poultry. As he chewed, grease dribbled into his gray-streaked red beard. For the moment, he stayed quiet and grunted contentedly as he munched on the moist meat.

Sighing, Ballomar grew stern. "Yet, you are still the less numerous of our people. You must know we could make your lives difficult—if we wished?"

Ulrich's smile waned. Continuing to chew, anger and resistance filled his features. Throughout the room, an air of expectation, one that included the possibility of violence, filled the space, and the two guards, formerly inconsequential aspects of the background, exchanged worried glances as they flexed fingers around the pommels of their swords.

Catching himself, Ballomar lightened his tone before continuing. "But that isn't the purpose of our talk. I have another reason for commanding…asking…you to come."

"Spit it out, then. You're as timid as a Parthian whore."

Feigning a smile, Ballomar took the insult with a generous nod. Stepping with heavy feet down the length of the hall, he took a deep breath and stopped near a Roman uniform hanging from a peg on a post. Next to it was a full set of Roman armor, along with a shiny sword and separate dagger suspended from leather straps in scabbards. On the next pole was a fine-silk robe, stitched with gold threads and clearly of great value.

Running his finger over the robe, Ballomar grinned to himself, then motioned to the weapons and armor with equal admiration. When he finally spoke, his voice was loud and enthusiastic. "These are just some of the items the Romans possess. Each of their soldiers wears fine armor and uses formidable weapons, and their people, even commoners, often clothe themselves in luxurious fabric—making our own products appear like those of rats. Their empire stretches for weeks in all directions, and they live charmed lives of wealth and privilege."

"But," said Ulrich, obviously unhappy with the comparison, "must I remind you, they have a well-trained army to match their lands? They've tamed tribes from one horizon to another. Their empire brings goods from the ends of the earth for their…simple enjoyment."

Nodding, Ballomar pointed vaguely to the south, towards the distant location of the Roman capital. "Yes, their army is impressive and efficient, which allows them to best either of our peoples in combat separately. Combined, however, we could…wipe them from the earth. My spies also tell me that many of their 'legions' have been recalled to the east, where they face a rebellion from some of their other subjugated people. Meaning…we face undermanned formations…who are perhaps weaker than we formerly believed."

Intrigued, the hostility lessened from Ulrich's demeanor. What had begun as an exercise in defiance turned into obvious interest with Ballomar's bold pronouncement.

Walking near the weapons, Ulrich pulled the blade from the sword's holder. Testing the sharpness of the metal with his thumb, he nodded at its condition and pushed it back into the scabbard with a SCHINK.

Looking over the robe, Ulrich wasn't much impressed with the fine clothing, but he was no longer hostile when he faced Ballomar again. His eyes, which before had been those of a competitor, now bulged with conspiracy. "You're suggesting we take the field against them? Combine our armies?"

Raising his voice another notch, Ballomar grew invigorated with pride. "I'm suggesting we obliterate them. Drive them all the way to their shiny capital. Enslave them. Steal all their wealth and populate our brothels with their women. Make their children become our children…and put anyone who opposes us to the sword or pyre."

"That's a powerful boast. And who will own their lands and rule over their people when this is done, Ballomar? Who will be the uncontested power over this new Germanic empire you propose?"

Ballomar thought carefully, but the mirthful look on his face suggested it was a question he had thought about in advance. "I've already lined up the support of most of the tribes— only a few inconsequential weaklings remain. It is you whom I value most in this proposed action. Your support and soldiers are essential, which of course…you already know."

Ballomar stepped closer to Ulrich, and meeting his eyes with false warmth, clapped him on the shoulder again. This time, Ulrich didn't entirely pull back from the show of camaraderie.

Dropping his voice to a whisper, Ballomar became brotherly, like they had always been the closest of confidantes. "There's room for both of us to rule over their cursed empire. There's no longer a need for us to fight each other in these damp forests while the Roman pigs lounge in their palaces."

Ulrich's face and thoughts grew receptive, even if doubts remained in his weathered features. "I…will have to hold a council with my people. But it's a prospect worth consideration."

At this, Ballomar's grin widened, making his expression enthusiastic and without doubts. Pointing down to an amulet around his neck, a crude raven's head on a black string, he sounded sure of himself, like the outcome of the prospective war and the efforts to subdue their enemies were already a certainty. "Excellent! In the meantime, I have made preparations to soften our foes. Alcis, our most vengeful and deadly God, is already preparing our march to victory."

Ulrich thought about this, and now his face became inquisitive, making his interest in Ballomar's actions obvious. Being a seasoned leader, however, he knew enough about tribal politics to be sure that Ballomar would only reveal what benefited himself. The room grew quiet, with each man taking stock of the other and his intent. As they searched one another's scraggly faces, the tension of what was and could be made both leaders oddly excited.

Ballomar smiled broadly, then motioned to the door. "Let me walk you out, old friend. I will see you on your way, and we can plot our place of power in this new world. As the strongest of our people, none can oppose us."

Pulling the door wide, Ballomar shepherded Ulrich out the entrance, and the men walked with unrefined certainty as they clomped through the mud into the early evening.

Above them, daylight receded, throwing strings of the sun's rays through canopies of substantial Beech trees. Creeping mists, always present in the confines of these forests, clung to the brush and woods all around them.

Except, as Ulrich moved toward his horse and guards, who awaited him at the end of a long wagon track near the residence, something to the side caught his eye.

On a mangled stump of one of the trees, where leaves had been torn away and open bark had been stripped from a heinous bit of a dilapidated trunk structure, several severed human limbs dangled from a thick branch. Arms and legs were attached with ropes to the tree, and while most were desiccated and old, others were relatively fresh and had streaks of black blood and moist flesh still visible. Over the twisted and sickening parts, flies buzzed around and clung to various portions of the rotting meat.

Looking back at Ballomar, Ulrich was surprised to see the leader of the Marcomanni didn't seem bothered by the display of his enemies' body parts so close to his house. Such a macabre sight, even amongst the battle-tested tribes of Germania, would generally have been viewed as unnecessary and somewhat unclean for the tastes of a normal warrior.

But Ballomar was no normal soldier, as all within and outside his domain knew well. Reaching out, Ulrich clasped hands with his host, and meeting the Ballomar's wicked smile with one of his own, the gaze of a tempered warrior meeting that of a butcher, he smiled.

His grin was diplomatic, while Ballomar's resembled that of a ravenous predator. Turning away from the dangerous man, Ulrich left Ballomar and strode to his horse. Mounting, he nodded to his seasoned retinue of cavalrymen, and kicking into a trot, rode away from the fetid scene without looking back.

As Ulrich moved into the darkening forest, Ballomar watched him go, his mouth locked in a self-confident and unrepentant grin. While his visitors' shapes disappeared into the cloying fog, his thoughts ran over a dozen possibilities for their tribes' future, and none included a straightforward outcome. His was an existence that thrived on deception and ruthlessness—whether he was dealing with allies or enemies.

With the noise of their departure receding, Ballomar spun to return to his home, where he could get on with the business of preparing for war.

Chapter Five

Moonlight played across the dark forest, casting anemic light through lines of tall trees within dense clusters of mismatched woods. Swaying mildly under the force of an eastward wind, the branches from high above, as well as the brush lining the forest floor below, moved in noisy contrast to the apparently uninhabited stretch of surrounding landscape.

Ahren, crouching near a copse of dark woods, was silent as he peered ahead. Brawny yet agile, he drew calm breaths as he assessed the surrounding foliage. With tattoos running up his arms and along his neck, every bit of his open skin was covered in a collection of badly drawn forest animals, from owls to wolves, with the substantial markings making it easier for him to blend into the dark background. His animal-skin clothing, pulled tight around his muscular frame, were tied in the firm local fashion to allow for easy combat movement.

Kellick, holding a short spear held low to the ground, kneeled nearby, and although smaller and with less tattoos than Ahren, his white eyes and intense bearing were similar in focused intent. Sweeping his gaze across opaque clusters of bushes amongst the fog, he looked for anything amiss through the rustling branches.

Neither man appeared comfortable, though both were undoubtedly at ease in such shrouded and misty surroundings. For some time, they perched there, ready for anything or anyone who might be waiting to surprise them.

But nothing happened. The twigs and branches of the undergrowth continued to sway in the dim environment, and the rolling fog spread out and back into the dark areas of the forest, continuing its ominous cycle amongst the woods' gloomy interior.

Leaning near Kellick, Ahren kept his gritty voice low. "Slow and careful. This is their domain."

Keeping cautious watch of the way forward, where a vague trail weaved between two stands of trees, Kellick nodded. Turning back, he made motions with his hands towards the darkness behind them.

Four figures detached from the cover of several trunks, and creeping forward, they made no noise as they advanced. Scampering ahead, these fellow scouts, wearing skins and light leather armor, moved past Kellick and Ahren. Quiet and efficient, their expert movements brought them past numerous trees and brush before disappearing into the night.

Stooping, Ahren and Kellick, as the most experienced and senior of the raiding party, followed in similar silence. Moving deliberately, their sandaled feet moved heel-over-heel as they avoided tangles of plants or roots that could trip them up or cause undue attention.

After several minutes of furtive movements, Ahren and Kellick emerged into a small clearing. Here their four companions waited for them, crouching carefully to either side of the open area, where there was no more than a twenty-yard break of open earthen floor. The night around them was as before—with no indication of enemies from the dark vicinity. The fog had receded a bit, allowing for easier visibility of what lay ahead.

Still, as Ahren took his place in the small area, coming to a crouch and producing an animal-skin map to peer at in the moonlight, something bothered him. Moving his head in a circle, he evaluated each portion of the forbidding area around them, where he searched for the source of his disquiet.

Ahren was not a man who was new to such an environment. He had fought throughout the domain of the Marcomanni, both against fellow tribes and with the occasional invasions of the wretched Romans, and as a warrior who had reached his fortieth summer, he was well-respected and sought after when it came to moving through such territory.

But Ahren's scowl, pronounced and grouchy even in the best of times, was positively menacing as his eyes scoured the way forward. Something seemed out of place, and his skill at listening to his gut, which at all times meant looking for that inner voice for guidance about the best manner of scouting, was telling him that their path was not without risk. Something or someone seemed just out of eyesight, waiting for them, much like a hawk might watch a field mouse from far above the rodent's perspective. And though Ahren didn't know what such a bird's-eye view would entail, he knew he wouldn't want to be the mouse in such an encounter.

Waving Kellick near him, Ahren's voice was barely audible, and Kellick needed to arch his neck and lower his ear to hear him.

"What do ye think?" asked Ahren, his eyes still probing the woods. "Do they wait for us…or hide like children?"

Kellick thought for a moment as he moved his gaze around the darkness, searching for what he knew must be close by. Shaking his head, he spoke slowly. "I think they're not cowards. We shouldn't discount their prowess, especially here."

Nodding, Ahren took a deep breath. Though continuing his mindful observation of their surroundings, he relaxed and let his muscles unwind from the day's extensive travel. Moving across fifteen miles of isolated forest through this remote area was difficult enough, but remaining hyper-aware also sapped the strength of even the most vigilant scout. Mental fatigue could be as dangerous as the physical variety.

Carefully, Ahren took a strip of jerky from a pack at his waist. Biting into it, he contemplated their direction between chews of the dried meat. "It's just a matter of time. When they're found, we'll kill the men…rape the women, and enslave the children. They'll know the wages of treachery. None will escape."

Kellick stared into the Ahren's face, as if looking to match the confidence of his words with the certainty of his expression. Unfortunately, the night's shadows hid any indication of surety in his companion.

Sighing, Kellick took a water skin and drank several swallows that had been retrieved from a stream some distance back. The cold liquid cooled his throat, and for the moment, he felt better, if not entirely confident of their proposed path into their enemy's territory.

For some time, the men crouched in and near the clearing. Disciplined and careful, they waited for the night's dangers to be revealed.

It didn't take long. From far ahead, the WHO WHO WHO of an owl broke the silence. The sound itself was not unusual, but its source was far too convenient. Ahren had lived a full life as a fighter by never believing in coincidences, either in the form of daily life or in nighttime sounds at inopportune times. Both he and any forest scout worth his salt in Germania could precisely mimic the call of that nocturnal bird.

"It's them," said Ahren, and continuing to chew, he looked behind the party, from where they had already traveled. Motioning with his head, he spoke without worry, as if he were out for a simple hunt. "Go back and fetch the rest of the men. Be quick about it—we'll hold this spot until your return."

Kellick, looking doubtful, tilted his head as he peered into Ahren's shadowed eyes. Waiting several seconds, his hesitation at the order was palpable. When on the campaign, leaving your comrades was not a decision to be taken lightly, however wise it was to do so. "You might need—."

Ahren held up a rigid finger to interrupt, but after a moment, he allowed his severe tone to lighten. "Go, now. I've never lost a fight…and won't start now. Our enemies will not dance on our corpses today."

Still reluctant, Kellick did not rush off. Licking his lips, his eyes sought out his other companions, who had moved to defensible positions around the clearing. Holding up bows and short swords, they returned his gaze with eerie calmness as they made ready for any violent eventualities.

Reaching out, Ahren firmly grasped the shoulder of the younger Kellick. His face came alive in the faint light, but his tone was calm, almost brotherly. "If I don't see ye later, Kellick, then we'll feast together in paradise. Now...go, and we'll salt the earth with the bones of these traitorous dogs."

After a final moment, Kellick nodded. Standing, he moved back into the night, dashing into the shadows toward the location of their following soldiers, who were close behind this small group, but too painfully far for his personal liking.

Quickly disappearing into the fog and darkness, Ahren watched Kellick go with a nod of approval. Turning forward, he continued his improvised meal, gulping down the last of the food.

Guardedly, Ahren stood and stretched his legs, then moved to a position between a stump and brush where he could not be easily surprised. As he fixed his eyes on the outlines of gloomy trees ahead, he quietly slid his axe from a sheath on his back.

#

Hurrying through the dim woods, Kellick ran with a carelessness that was unusual for a skilled pathfinder. The ways of the forest tribes were based on stealth as much as brutality, so it was strange to sprint this way, weaving between plants and hanging brush with little regard for silence. To run like this made his warrior's conscience scream at him, begging him to control his emotions and slow down.

But dashing through this area was not just wise, it was essential. The tribe they pursued, the Naristi, though few in number and keen to avoid enraging Kellick's far larger group, were known for their adroitness in movement and skill with weapons.

Intruding on their lands was an overt act of war, and the Naristi would respond the same as any true warriors— when pressed, they would engage in battle without mercy.

Coming to the edge of a hill, Kellick took a moment to look down the gully, where he could just see the creek they had earlier passed over and filled their carrying-skins from. Taking deep breaths, he studied the trees and low-lying foliage around the dark, trickling water, searching for any prospective dangers.

There were none visible. Seeing no evidence the enemy had gotten behind them, Kellick leapt up and rushed down the uneven grade, cutting between trees and just keeping his balance as he hopped over a dead trunk and approached the narrow stream.

Gathering himself, he bounded over two large rocks and cleared the water, then began clambering up the narrow trail that wound up the other side of the small canyon between exposed roots and clinging plants.

Steadily pumping his legs and working muscles accustomed to the labor of the campaign, the sound of his own methodical breathing quickly filled his ears, and he struggled to keep rigid focus on the gloomy and limb-shrouded trail ahead.

As he carefully ascended the earthen pathway, Kellick abruptly found his mind wandering. Working his way up the gorge over uneven rocks and matted grass, he felt doubt creep into his thoughts, forcing a sense of unease into his fervent mind.

The way forward for Kellick and his fellow warriors was to be littered with the enemies of his king, the widely feared Ballomar. As the most powerful man in Germania, it was Ballomar's iron will and unending ambition that propelled his people to widespread authority in the wide-ranging tracts of the forest clans, and the feeling amongst Kellick's personal family was that their people's ever-increasing prestige was a sign of Ballomar's rightness in pursuit of geographic domination.

But what of the other tribes? thought Kellick. Many of them spoke the same language, ate the same food, and worshiped the same forest Gods. If these other tribes did not see the inherent truth of Ballomar's quest for dominion over all he surveyed, *did it really make sense to kill them all, to wipe out anyone who did not align with the Marcomanni?*

Kellick was no leader of men, but it seemed unwise to kill and enslave other tribes who were not their direct enemies. It felt like it was possible they could be on genial terms with those various forest clans if left to their own pursuits, even if those tribes didn't send their sons and husbands to make war on behalf of Ballomar.

Of course, he would need to keep such thoughts to himself, as did any man who wished to keep his head in dangerous times such as these. The reality was, to make Kellick and his clan proud, he had to follow orders without fail, to crush all who opposed the expansion of the Marcomanni.

If he didn't agree with the methods of doing so, it was preferable for Kellick to ruminate quietly rather than be burnt alive on an impromptu funeral pyre for his lack of faith in the cause of this expanding war. He'd seen such punishment meted out on multiple occasions, and for crimes far less serious than overtly questioning the wisdom of Ballomar.

As he got closer to the top of the hill, Kellick suddenly and firmly decided to keep his intentions in the present. For the moment, that meant staying alive and accomplishing his scouting tasks, and as he crested an exposed bit of broken tree line and rocky outcroppings, he increased his pace and plunged down an embankment leading to the bottom of the next small valley. His feet, moving in a flitting fashion across clumps of dark, broken soil, fell into a controlled, hurried pace as he relaxed and pressed through sheltered stands of ancient woods.

Safety and allies were close, and Ahren was relying on Kellick's speed as a runner to bring help to them in time to crush the Naristi. It was Kellick's duty to push onward, requiring his devoted attention, so for the moment it was best not to linger on the wisdom or foolhardiness of Ballomar's violent intentions for their tribe's future.

#

Teigen, with fierce eyes and a malicious scowl, was Ahren's principal scout and strongest fighter. A man of corded muscle and explosive skill, the heavily tattooed scout peered intently at an indistinct shape across from him in the darkness.

As he considered the outline of the warrior he faced, Teigen had the presence of mind to act unimpressed. Chewing his lip, his face pinched into controlled determination, and with practiced indifference, he calmly evaluated his foe within the outlines of a patch of undergrowth.

Staying still and patient, his shadowy opponent awaited his move. In turn, Teigen nodded, as if accepting the challenge, and then lunged forward, aiming his blow in an effortless arc at the looming shape. The figure moved to evade the slash, but with the clank of his shortsword against a chain-mail shirt, followed by the rapid retreat of the opposing form, it was clear Teigen's blow was accurate, if not particularly effective, against his armor.

For the next moments, the men, one a lifelong confidant and protector of Ahren, the other a murky enemy hidden in the gloom of the failing light, faced each other across the narrow gap of the nameless forest site.

Extending his small, metal-rimmed shield, Teigen, a veteran of campaigns in all corners of the realm of the Marcomanni, lunged forward again, but he immediately absorbed a counterblow against the iron top of the wood-layered protection. The vicious clang of the hefty axe, whirling silently from the depths of the shadows, stung Teigen, and the reverberation of the attack made his arm momentarily numb within the shield, forcing him to retreat a step and alter his stance into a protective crouch.

In the broken darkness of a copse of outsized trees, where spotty moonlight played across the ground and foliage, Teigen collected himself. Considering his best plan of attack, he held a deliberate grimace, and after a moment, he let a playful smile cross his features, evincing the sort of assurance that could only come from one who had survived many such exchanges. Even against accomplished killers, he had emerged on top—his skill and reaction time were unmatched.

Around the faced-off warriors, not visible but close, came the noise of other fights in the furious battle, punctuated by grunts and the crash of weapons and armor. With a skillset and frame of mind that enjoyed this way of life, Teigen absorbed the raucous moment, and as adrenaline surged through his body, he let his confidence flow, allowing himself to alter his stance in preparation for another attack on this upstart enemy.

From the darkness behind, where Tiegen had not carefully checked before battle was joined, the long shaft of a spear, one that had a metal-tipped and viciously sharp point, thrust forward. Aimed at the unprotected area of flesh below Teigen's scapular helm, the point tore through his neck, ripping through layers of muscle and severing the carotid artery on his right side.

The tip of the weapon, emerging as a bloody surprise, burst through the front of the shocked man's neckline, tearing free from the flesh in a splash of gore. Stunned, Teigen's eyes bulged as he dropped his sword and tried to stem the flow of blood with flailing fingers.

Staggering to the side, Teigen pulled himself free of the weapon, moaning pitifully as he stumbled away. Instantly out of the fight, his mind thrashed about, trying to understand what had just happened. Like a deer that had been pierced by an arrow but did not yet know it was soon to be the object of a feast, the grizzled combatant couldn't quite understand his own sudden defeat.

Fumbling a few more steps, Teigen fell to his knees, and his fingers, vainly holding back sheets of blood pumping from his maimed neck, reached to the ground as he sought to balance himself. For a moment, he was outlined there in the night's dim light, perched on one arm and showing an image that could have served as a model to some sculptured Roman masterpiece.

As his balance faded, Teigen was not able to right himself, and he collapsed to the wet earth with an elongated groan. Rolling on his back, struggling to take in his grievous circumstance, he jerked around as if to make himself comfortable, while all the while the heat and feeling dissipated from his limbs and senses. In spasmed shock, his eyes flitted about, then moved to take in the sky and stars, which were just visible through the patches of tall trees above.

This man, experienced in death and martial combat for decades of his violent life, was just able to view the final sight of the beautiful night sky as he bled out on the cold forest floor. His last thoughts were not of a life spent in victory, but instead were focused on coming to such an inglorious end in this anonymous portion of distant woods, fighting people he never really regarded as enemies.

#

Getting nearer to his comrades was somehow having the opposite effect Kellick expected; normally he would have embraced coming back to his tribe, fully knowing that kinship and aid were close. Nothing was quite like the feeling of brotherly feelings that the campaign trail provided, especially when danger and high risk were involved.

Instead, a feeling of doom crept into his perception, forcing him to become introspective as he tried to figure the cause of this depressive feeling. As he picked his way through a shoddy tree line, toward a place where he fully anticipated seeing the first pickets of his war party, his mind reeled in worry for his friends back at the clearing.

Cresting another hill, he was disappointed to see that he had overestimated the closeness of their main camp. Where he had expected his final destination, he instead saw a gully leading to another small creek to his right, while the direct trail to the camp ascended straight ahead, up and through another patch of quiet forest.

Confused, Kellick stopped. Staring ahead, then off to his right, he calculated again in his mind the distance to his people. After a moment of indecision, he realized a shortcut through the small valley to his right would bring him to his goal faster, and without hesitation, he sprinted that direction. Picking up speed, he careened through some brush, crashing through the dry shrubbery that clustered at intervals as the ground dropped in elevation.

Coming quickly to the trickling water of an inconsequential stream, he splashed through the shallow current and bounded his way down the extended gap in the hilly terrain. Ducking under a collection of hanging limbs, his former disregard for sound became even worse, and he realized with some dismay he would soon be ridiculed for ignoring caution when he arrived.

No matter, Kellick thought, at least in a short time he would be amongst treasured companions, and together they would quickly move back to help Ahren. Time was short, but as with all matters in military tactics, fortune favored those who moved decisively.

Catching himself, his brittle confidence again moved to worry, and he struggled to believe that boastful thought almost as soon as he had it. *At least I hope so.*

#

Ahren bellowed a war cry, raising his voice to a resonant growl as he waded into his adversaries. Striking quickly at his first enemy, a tall and sinewy Naristi war scout with severe features and scars crisscrossing his face, the thud of his axe drove through the man's held-up shield and cleaved into his shoulder.

With a yelp, the scout threw himself back, clutching at the split in his leather armor where the battleax had sliced through the hardened surface. Though not mortally wounded, the seriousness of the wound was obvious, and his fingers clutched at the blood-soaked injury as he rapidly backed away in a manic bid for survival.

But other Naristi were there to take his place. In the night-shrouded forest clearing, where the fog obscured visibility beyond a few yards, several long spears held by shadowy men fended off any further advance by Ahren. Not entirely committing themselves to attack the fierce warrior, the various shafts of the looming shapes were still effective at preventing Ahren from closing the distance, and as he swung his heavy axe in wide swaths, it only clanged off their pressing spears, causing no further damage.

And Ahren was getting tired. Each labored move towards his encircling opponents, performed with heaving effort, made his subsequent efforts slower and more difficult. His boisterous shouts, refined over many years to provoke fear among his enemies, grew more exhausted, and he gasped for breath between his cries of intimidation.

Additionally, neither was Ahren unscathed in the battle up to this point. From his back stuck the shafts of two arrows, and although they were not seated too deeply, they had found their mark through his simple armor, and blood seeped from shallow wound channels in his burly flesh. His combat acumen was not disputed in the night's weak light, but Ahren was not getting stronger as time wore on—something that was obvious to both him and his indistinct opponents.

"Come on, ye curs," shouted Ahren, stressing the taunt with a hock of spit and a smile pulled back over discolored and rotting teeth. "I'll take ye to Hell with me."

Almost as if taking part of some tedious work, Ahren's demeanor, though savage and serious, was calm and accepting of the battle's development. Never in his life had he shown mercy, and with this fight in a faraway bit of forest, there would be no quarter shown. Much like a livestock animal that lives its life precisely the same way up until its day of slaughter, he would not change his ways against this band of miscreants—no matter how near he was to the end.

Raising his voice again, Ahren remained defiant and sure of himself as he mocked his cautious enemies. "There's not a man alive who can beat me. Come to yer death."

After a moment, the spears around him stopped their careful advance, almost as if they heard and believed that threat. Surprised with the success of mocking them, Ahren smiled wider, embracing the role of a cocky soldier who would never know his equal in combat and who relished the field of battle.

From the side, a long wooden pole, with its top fashioned into a dense ball of metal and spikes, was swung silently from the darkness. The mace, wielded with brutal force, clanged into Ahren's metal helm, interrupting his prideful thoughts. The jarring clunk, loud and sickening, spun Ahren around with vicious force.

His eyes rolling up, Ahren's boastful shouts melted away, and after shuffling two ponderous steps to his right, his dead weight collapsed into a scattering of bushes and dry tree limbs.

Except for some baleful moans from the now-incapacitated fighter, the woodlands thereafter became immediately quiet. In contrast to the clash that had just played out in this remote landscape, the silence of the newfound moment was complete and anticlimactic.

#

Water splashed across Ahren's haggard face. Rivulets of the liquid washed down over the wounded man, mixing with dried blood and making his beard soggy and matted.

For a brief moment there was no action, and failing a response, the fingers of a white and untattooed hand, with long and lithe fingers, snapped impatiently in front of his face, bidding the unconscious fighter to come awake.

Failing that, another container of water was shuffled into the hand, and again liquid was thrown on Ahren's face, this time with more force. Now the weathered warrior responded by forcing an eye open, and following a groggy raise of his head, he tried to take in the shadowed surroundings through his dizzy perceptions.

Burning torches, affixed to limb-hewn poles buried in the ground, were set at several points around him. In the middle of the patchy light, Ahren found himself fastened to a sturdy Beech tree, with multiple ropes crisscrossing his torso, and even as he sat with his ass on the ground, yet more bindings kept his sprawled legs secured together. His arms, held and tethered behind him with more rope, tied his limbs firmly to the tree trunk. Thoroughly incapacitated, he would not evading this circumstance anytime soon.

Leaning down, Garin, the muscular but slender man who splashed Ahren, was dressed in animal skins and simple leather armor. Seeking out Ahren's eyes, a burgeoning grin filled his bearded face, and he focused for several seconds on the captive, waiting for Ahren's return from his wound-caused slumber.

When Ahren was slow to indulge him, Garin's hand flashed out and viciously slapped the prisoner, snapping the man's face back against the hard bark of the tree. Lulling wildly, Ahren's bloody head, wrapped in a makeshift bandage by his captors, took some time to steady itself.

Ahren's eyes now shot open. Filled with hate, they immediately caught Garin's gaze, and contempt for the man washed over his injured features. Coming fully awake, Ahren's open animosity towards anyone he opposed, even when in this obviously feeble position, resumed.

Ahren took a deep breath, preparing his cloudy mind and aching lungs to shout some insult, to register his hatred for Garin, but Garin held a thin finger to his mouth, showing a need for silence.

Continuing his coy smile, Garin's eyes motioned down to his other hand, which leaned on a long mace to his side. Notably, the solid melee weapon still had Ahren's blood smeared on its black metallic end.

Rampaging anger surged through Ahren's mind, forcing up his blood pressure and making his battered face red and animated. He was not an animal to be played with, and his thoughts surged to find a way to punish this insolent whelp. Anything…

A voice from his right broke through his rage-filled considerations. "Ahren, it's been a while. What brings you to our land? Are you lost? Perhaps your poor command of geography has led you astray?"

Arching his head to the side, Ahren sought the source of the familiar voice. Peering into the lapping firelight, the face of Tarquin, the leader of the Naristi tribe and known by Ahren from diplomatic negotiations in the past, materialized.

With a knowing look on his taut, youthful features, the face of the man was not angry as he returned Ahren's gaze. Unlike most tribesmen, Tarquin wore a clean-shaven face, much like the Romans, and his piercing gray eyes lent a sense of disarming curiosity to his stare. His frame, while not overly tall, evinced strength and physical poise from under his wolf-skin cloak.

Stepping farther into the light, Tarquin kept his voice low and controlled, even as he noted the lack of a response from Ahren. Sometimes no answer at all was an answer unto itself, especially with the violent politics of the Germanic tribes. Looking over to Garin, Tarquin nodded slightly—as if to agree with some matter discussed before the current conversation.

"So, it's as Garin has suggested," said Tarquin, and he again nodded at Garin, this time with open admiration before returning his stare to Ahren. "You're moving against us. And Rome? That's not exactly wise... and because you're merely an old and rather stupid toad, I have to wonder: who would have commanded such a thing?"

Ahren's coursing anger waned a bit, and he suddenly felt the need to calm himself. In a show of keeping a secret, he dropped his gaze and looked to other parts of the clearing, in areas he hadn't yet paid attention to since returning to consciousness.

Now seeing his full surroundings, Ahren noted several other Naristi tribesmen hovering in the background, staring angrily down at him. At other varied points between the scattered trees were the strewn corpses of his fellow scouts, splayed out in death poses from their desperate fight in the recent one-sided battle. These heaps of flesh, formerly his good friends, appeared contorted and battered beyond recognition in the low light, with limbs and torsos contorted at odd angles from their last struggles on Earth.

Focusing briefly to the far left, Ahren also noted the only enemy casualty in the fight, the man he had winged with his axe. That scout's shoulder was heavily bandaged with bloody rags, and though still standing, he leaned heavily against a tree for support. The image of pain on the young man's face, while nowhere near what Ahren usually inflicted, at least gave him a small measure of happiness in this rather discouraging predicament he now found himself in.

Regarding his fellow Marcomanni scouts, Ahren felt no pity, though he knew he would miss them. Of course, to his way of thinking, they were better off at this point, as his comrades were undoubtedly feasting with the war gods most of the forest tribes worshiped.

Moving directly in front of Ahren, Tarquin leaned down and squatted near his silent captive. His voice was low, and he spoke with some empathy as his firm fingers grasped Ahren's chin to force a meeting of eyes. "I'll give you a quick and painless death, you mangy dog, but you really must tell me everything you know. Your days of rape and murder have come to an end."

Feeling emboldened, Ahren found the fortitude to meet Tarquin's gaze. Showing steely eyes to the looming chief, he kept his voice defiant and steady, spitting his words with pure conviction. "I die as a warrior, Tarquin. You'll die trying to hide under Rome's dress, just like all the cowards who've colluded with the empire."

With a wrench of his head, Ahren broke free from Tarquin's grip on his face. Almost growling, he motioned with his head into the darkness, raising his raspy voice so the others could hear. "My man is retrieving our tribe as we speak. Your pathetic people will be raped and exterminated to the last. None will survive. NONE!"

Some seconds of silence passed, and the ring of observers took in Ahren's words with surprising calmness. None of the Naristi glanced at each other with alarm. Neither did they look to Tarquin for assurance about any impending attack from the Marcomanni.

And Tarquin's response was not as Ahren expected, either. Standing slowly, Tarquin's expression softened. Reaching to his waist, where several pouches and tools were suspended on a leather belt, he withdrew a long and sharp dagger from a simple scabbard. Staring approvingly at its sharp edge, he peered over at Garin, then down to Ahren, and after a few considered moments, a broad smile replaced his stoic features.

Getting Garin's attention with a raise of his eyebrow, Tarquin again acknowledged his most loyal supporter. As longtime friends and hardened allies in a score of battles, they acknowledged the favorable moment with a period of amused silence, all the while their captive's confused gaze darted back and forth between them.

#

Later, the Naristi war party had all departed the clearing, returning to their settlements far away from the impending threat of Marcomanni invasion. The forest mist, continuing its never-ending roll through the brace of trees, kept the area obscured for the moment, with only a few of the larger trees' twisted limbs standing out from the darkened background.

But over time morning approached. Light began to shimmer through the scattered woods, burning off some of the dense fog as night gave way to the first sunshine of a new day. Birds, whose chirps had been absent throughout the darkness, began to sing again and enliven the area, forcing the dim night to move towards a pleasant daybreak. Where conflict and death had recently been, nature was once again reasserting itself.

The bodies of Ahren's men, now stripped of their possessions and weapons, were still scattered in the gloomy clearing, lying where they had fallen not long ago. Though they lived and died violent lives, their half-naked forms now appeared almost peaceful, even as a collection of insects skittered onto their dead, cooling meat and began to indulge in a bountiful meal.

At the end of the clearing, in the area that faced toward the realm of the Marcomanni and would greet any invaders from that direction, two long poles now jutted from the ground. Set in a place that would not be overlooked from the incoming trail, the rods of whittled oak, strong and firmly placed in the hard earth, awaited the illumination of more powerful light.

In time, the bright rays of early morning began to reach farther into these woods, improving visibility in the confines of the shrouded trees and irregular brush. As the hazy remnants of mist began to fade away, two objects on top of the poles became evident: Heads. Bloody heads, covered in gore and skewered deeply onto the sharpened tops of the poles.

These detached heads of two men, their eyes open and opaque, silently greeted the morning from their raised, piked position. Looking surprised at their predicament, with lulling tongues and an off-white hue to their blood-drained faces, Kellick and Ahren's decapitated remains peered sightlessly into dawn's glowing light, offering a gruesome warning to any aggressors who wished to follow into the territory of the Naristi.

Chapter Six

In the early afternoon, a small stream flowed gently, with the mild current rippling into a peaceful pool below a series of ebbing breaks in the otherwise smooth water. Above, the sky was blue and devoid of clouds, making the area clear and warm under the day's plentiful sunlight.

Around the creek were a series of ponderously hanging trees, and several of their branches jutted over the rippling water, throwing sporadic shade along its grass-covered banks. Between these trees on the south side of the water was a wide trail, which led to the nearby village, the place protected by the nearby Roman garrison.

Julia squatted with some effort, then strained to lift two water buckets hanging from a sturdy stick perched on her shoulders. The weight of the heavy wooden containers, which would have been hard for a normal-sized man to lift, forced her to readjust twice as she balanced the load and then struggled to her full height.

As she approached the stream's pebbled shoreline, her son Lucien stood up from peering into the water. Looking worried, the boy spoke with some emotion, sounding fearful as he stepped close. "Momma, I can help. It's too much for you."

Moving gingerly from the creek's shallows to the damp streamside, Julia shook her head, even while flashing an appreciative grin. "Not too much, Lucien. I just need...to get the balance right."

Frustrated, Julia pressed forward under the weight of her load, grimacing as she tried to avoid slipping. Her leather sandals, tied firmly to her dainty feet, were not easy to navigate slick surfaces, and the water-worn rocks, made slippery over a millennium of being honed by the flow of water, made simple movement precarious.

Pushing away thoughts of falling, Julia instead focused on Lucien. Showing a fatigued sigh, she appreciated her son for the miracle he was in her sometimes-strenuous life. Times on the frontier were difficult enough, with the daily exertions required to feed and house the boy, in addition to the effort needed to provide something for their future. Fortunately, in answer to her worries, his smile and gregarious nature made all her everyday stresses seem unimportant in comparison.

Waiting for Lucien to get in front of her on the way back to the village, Julia took her time and walked carefully up the path toward home. It was not a long distance, merely fifteen minutes or so, but she was careful to keep him in her view as they returned from their daily jaunt to fetch water.

From the side, Julia missed the person watching her attentively. This figure, looming in the shade of several trees, took a moment to take in the lady and son, as if enjoying the spectacle. Still and silent, eager eyes watched her pass, his breath slow and expectant.

Moving quickly, the shape launched itself from the shadows, and Julia turned just in time, eyes wide, in a moment of shock and surprise.

Reaching quickly up, Marius grabbed the thick stick and adroitly pulled it from her shoulders. In little time he managed to reverse the heft of the carrying arrangement, and with no small effort, he tilted the weight forward, keeping the buckets in front of and behind himself.

As he took over her duties, Marius smirked toward Julia, and acknowledging her gratitude, kept his supportive tone low. "I think I have this, my lady. Perhaps you should ask for assistance when collecting water?"

Returning his smile, Julia shook her head at the suggestion, but her features were playful. "Whatever would I do without you, commander? It's a long walk to the village, and you must have many duties to attend to?"

From the front, Lucien turned back to greet the new visitor. Moving close to his mom, he grinned up at Marius, who replied with a wink and a nod.

Setting down the buckets, Marius disregarded the work of hauling the water for the time being. Reaching forward, he squeezed Julia's shoulder affectionately, then tousled Lucien's hair with father-like fondness.

As he took in the sight of mother and son, good-natured and active people, the warmth of this interaction made his heart ache. A busier man than he could not be found, but Marius found himself with all the time in the world to enjoy the moment.

After a long and somewhat awkward pause, Marius bent down and lifted the buckets again. Gesturing forward, he called over his shoulder as he began the trek back to the village. "I'll lead the way. It's not often one finds a beautiful woman to stroll with in the forest. I might as well count my blessings and take my time."

Meeting her son's eyes, the kindness of Marius' words and manner struck her deeply, making her heart well up. Her thoughts drifted to the first time he met Marius, where she stared bashfully at him from across her fruit stand, trying to ignore the flutter of instant attraction she felt inside for this new rugged soldier who was recently posted to the border region.

And from that time onward, life and her personal prospects only seemed to get better due to Marius' returned affections. First came the prospect of a better life generally from the help he offered her, then came the benefits she hoped for her cherished son because of Marius's status. Prestige, as in all places in and outside the Roman world, was something of considerable importance.

Of course, that meant she had to walk a fine line due to her upbringing with the tribes of Germania. Not all, or even a majority, of the clans inhabiting the forests of the untamed tribal lands held any regard for the strangers of the Roman empire, especially their fighting men.

Working through her sometimes-cynical thoughts, Julia pondered her good fortune at having him arrive in her life, completely unexpectedly. A good and capable man was literally worth his weight in gold to a woman of humble means and limited prospects. In the tribal way of looking at men, as a protector first and as a partner a distant second, he seemed to be both at the same time. There was no end to the good fortune she felt from their relationship, and like all people dealing with the reality of life, she half-expected her good luck to collapse at any moment.

Suddenly catching her rambling thoughts, Julia exchanged a moment of shared gratitude with Lucien for their present situation. Nodding, as if to say, *he's a joy for us both, let's hope it lasts*, Julia motioned ahead and followed their unexpected visitor back toward their humble stone house in the tranquil village.

#

The tree cover grew sparser as the trio approached the village. The broad trail was flat to each side, with scattered brush and clumps of grass mixed among piles of dirt-caked rocks. Taking on a more inhabited look, simple huts in the distance stood on either side of the path, where they served as homes to outlying farmers and shepherds.

Julia walked next to Marius, who struggled somewhat with the weight of the water buckets. Feeling his ego deflated, it never ceased to surprise him how hardy and capable the locals were, even when they were half his own size and of the opposite gender.

Ahead of them, Lucien led the way to the village, jousting a stick into the air in mock combat. Like most boys without siblings, he made do with the play available, which meant improvising in order to pass the time.

Smiling hesitantly toward her son, Julia was openly discouraged, and her eyes bulged in alarm as she peered over at Marius. "Appius…and his children? That's horrible. What will his wife now do?"

Marius took a moment to respond, clenching his jaw at the depressing thought of his missing friend and innocent kids. "She will inherit his estate, I think. His holdings are substantial due to his service with the legion."

Lowering his voice, Marius sought to come across as hopeful, but the effect on his weary face, with a shadow of beard stubble and pronounced wrinkles making him appear dour, wasn't convincing. "More important is the possibility they can all be retrieved. Perhaps they will be offered in a bid for ransom."

Julia was openly doubtful, pressing her lips into a controlled frown. "If it's the Marcomanni, there's little chance of that. They're devils in everything—nobody holds them in good standing."

"You mean, because they are of a different tribe?"

Julia frowned further, realizing Marius was mixing his understanding of the tribes into one of competition for power instead of seeing the various groups as distinct entities. The tribes shared many common beliefs and methods of living, but they were not all the same.

Still, she chose not to take the bait and, keeping her voice steady, showed no indication of defensiveness. "No, because they plunder, murder, and rape without regard to honor…or allegiance. I've told you in the past, but perhaps you now understand why the Naristi allied with Rome long ago."

Her point was well made and equally well understood. Chastised, Marius nodded. He was never one to hold onto a view that was openly wrong, especially when it would mean offending an important person. And to him, nobody in the province was more important than Julia.

As they got closer to the thick walls of the village, they passed several groups of locals. Lowering his voice, Marius offered Julia a twinkling smile. "I thought the alliance with Rome was because our soldiers are so handsome."

Passing through the village's rudimentary gate, which had a bored member of the provincial guard standing near it with his spear held loosely at his side, Julia chuckled. "Well, there's that, too. It might better serve Rome's interests to export such men. It would be a more effective way to control its borders, I am certain."

Marius smiled at her candor and wit. Rounding a corner, he took the opportunity to step into a recess in the wall of a large house, in a place that was out of view— even to Lucien, who continued to play in the street.

After setting down his too-heavy load, he pulled Julia into a relaxed hug, then peered down into her dark eyes. "It's important to inform your brother of these developments. Members of your tribe will be the first threatened if the Marcomanni move south to the Danube."

Becoming reflective, Julia nodded agreement. "Tarquin won't be happy, but they must certainly be warned—if they do not yet know."

"And," said Marius, his voice becoming more serious, "Rome will want the auxiliaries promised by your people in the event of war. That will mean most of your able-bodied men."

Julia's thoughts clouded over, her demeanor becoming reserved. "Yes, but we…they are so few…."

Some seconds passed, and the moment became cumbersome, clouding over the lighthearted moment. With a sigh, Julia readjusted her frame of mind, deciding quickly she would register her displeasure with the conscription of her people by ignoring it.

Patting Marius on the chest, she raised her tone and forced a smile. "Will you stay with us tonight? Lucien misses you."

Marius shook his head, perhaps too energetically, but he hurried to correct himself and put some empathy into his words. "I…can't at the moment. There's much to do with these events. Perhaps in a few days we can meet again."

Julia dropped her head, trying to hide her disappointment. Reluctantly, she nodded, allowing her face to resume its customary impassive look. "I will hold you to that. You're a man of honor, right?"

Appearing uncomfortable, Marius nodded, then moved his gaze to the unremarkable cobblestoned street as he considered the circumstances of Julia and her fellow villagers, as well as the challenges her tribesmen faced in the forests north of here. To all these inhabitants and allies of the empire, it increasingly appeared there soon would be an acute danger to deal with—one they likely weren't prepared for.

To his way of thinking, Rome had hoped to bring civilization to this isolated area, not impending conflict, but life at times offered an opposite result to even the best of plans. The current deteriorating situation wasn't ideal, but in truth, Marius' experience had taught him that such worsening possibilities were not so unusual.

Indeed, peaceful times just made Marius more worried about what came next, instead of offering occasions for him to relax and enjoy himself. It seemed to him, from a past that included military conflict across much of the known world, that being ready for war and successfully engaging enemies meant constantly having to anticipate and plan for them. The meek and unprepared were usually the first corpses to be tossed into their freshly dug graves when the battle ended.

Growing determined, Marius scowled and spoke in an uncompromising voice as he gestured to the surrounding village. "In the meantime, only fetch water when I'm able to accompany you. And tell the other citizens to avoid going out alone. Their lives could well depend on it."

Chapter Seven

The blistering sun beat down on the parade grounds, heating the surface of the windless location and radiating hazy heat waves across the well-tended earth of the training area.

For a hundred yards in each direction, this military space, groomed for easy movement and hewn of any trees that could provide shade in the searing environment, was largely empty in the mid-afternoon.

Except there was movement near the barracks, where simple wooden tables were arranged in the drilling area near the large structure's back entrance. Here stood a large group of Roman infantrymen, each with their armor shiny and clean, which made the sunlight glare powerfully off the red-uniformed soldiers.

The soldiers were in a half circle around Quintus, their section's commander and the man directly under Marius in the chain of command for the local detachment. He was not currently in his own armor and instead wore a red tunic with a leather belt, as well as the common sandals of a normal serviceman in the legion.

Pacing impatiently, Quintus spun around and addressed his men, frustration bleeding into his voice. "No! In close battle, the unit that flights as one will always prevail over the barbarian rabble."

Showing a fighting pose, with a wooden sword held expertly at the ready, Quintus collected himself and faced Cyprian, a recent recruit to the unit. This unsure man, barely twenty and with eyes like a cornered rat, peered back with little enthusiasm. Sweat streamed down his brow, but the newcomer dared not wipe it away while waiting for Quintus' assault.

In a mad rush, Quintus burst forward, feinting and stabbing in successive thrusts, his movements so fast as to be mere blurs to both Cyprian and his fellow onlookers. So rapid and measured was his attacking lunge that the younger fighter was barely able to stumble backwards, much less preempt the aggression or put up an effective defense.

In seconds, Cyprian received one, two, and then three strikes from Quintus, with the clack of the sword blows quickly raising welts on his throat, arm, and in a final embarrassing feat, directly across his exposed face, in the area unprotected by his helmet.

Barely keeping his balance, the shame of the melee was complete, and the younger man dropped his own practice sword as he huffed for breath, swooned, and hunching over, stared pitifully down at the parade ground's dirt-packed surface. Completely bested in the mock battle, his heaving effort to draw air was his only response to the humbling fight.

Barely having broken a sweat, either from his rapid movements or the humid weather, Quintus straightened himself and nodded at his performance, letting the silence of the moment collect the surprise and awe his soldiers surely held for his undoubted skill with the sword.

Like an actor from one of the plays known to all Romans, who saw it almost as a societal duty to attend such shows in any forum within even small settlements in the empire, Quintus let the moment build, allowing his subordinates to process the ease with which Cyprian was dismantled by a superior skilled opponent.

Now speaking slower, Quintus' words were articulated carefully, much like he was a field surgeon explaining the best way to remove a bothersome arrowhead from a recent wound. "If you try to fight them man-to-man, they will cut you in half. The Marcomanni live to fight as a single brute. Ruthless and strong, they are raised to believe dominating their opponent is as important as defeating him. They do not wish to simply beat or kill you; they see combat as a challenge to increase their status as a feared warrior. The accolades they seek are individual, so they can either defeat their enemies without mercy or die trying, then bask in the afterlife with their war-loving Gods. They are barbarians in every sense of the word."

Now letting his gaze move to each of the more-than-dozen watching legionnaires, Quintus continued the slow drawl of his fighting lesson. "And this is their weakness, the best way they can be defeated. They don't fight as a unit…and can be destroyed piecemeal. Their aggression and lack of discipline can be used against them—so long as we keep to our formations and use our training."

Rubbing his stubbled face, Quintus took a moment to choose, then pointed to two other men, Antonius and Celsus, who were also young and nervous. Though stout and in superb shape, these fighters' eyes were apprehensive, no doubt due to the thrashing Cyprian had just received at the hands of their leader.

Making a triangular movement of his hand, which indicated the three-man formation they were well-drilled in following when in mixed battle, Quintus gestured to Cyprian, and the new participants nodded and slowly moved to take their place at the side of the recently defeated soldier.

With a shout, Quintus again burst forward, this time moving even faster and without restraint. His blows, blinding and vicious, moved in arcs and stabs the younger men had never witnessed. Breaking across their shields and upheld weapons, the force of his swings shook each of the men, stinging their hands and arms held behind their protective wooden defenses.

But this time the defenders could fall back on their training and numbers. Parrying his strikes, the soldiers' swords quickly blunted the surge, and in little time they were even able to push Quintus back. Gaining confidence, they covered each other's advance, and when an opening occurred in one of their attacks, the others swiftly cut off Quintus' counterstrokes.

In a few moments, the former defenders became skilled assailants, and their supporting offensive worked to perfection, driving Quintus out of the half-circle and leaving him with painful contusions across his arms, back, and face.

Holding up his weapon, Quintus signaled defeat by inverting his training sword and holding the blade area in the customary motion, a common gesture that indicated a practicing opponent was out of the fight and defeated.

As the soldiers looked on, the fact that they just witnessed a man they held in such high esteem be defeated took some time for them to absorb. Growing quiet, the transition from victim to winner was as surprising as it was complete, making the scene unnerving to the collected fighters.

Looking from Quintus to each other, the soldiers couldn't quite understand what it all meant, as well as what it could lead to in their future. Discipline in the legion meant insubordination could be met with time in the stockades or worse, so it was an open question how Quintus would deal with the sudden reversal of roles in their martial training.

In response to their open stares, Quintus again took his time to peer individually at his men. Slowly, a broad smile broke out over his damaged face. Blood, which seeped over his teeth from his swollen lip, highlighted the grin on his ecstatic features.

"Yes," Quintus shouted, his eyes alive and proud. "Much better. At all times, fight TOGETHER. Ego has no place in battle. Determination and training will always mean victory, and hopefully…your lives."

Walking to one of the tables, Quintus tossed his sword down, where it thudded next to an assortment of other blunted spears, wooden maces, and dull swords. The arranged weapons, made to mimic what would be fought against on the real field of battle, appeared dangerous, even in their less-lethal state.

Grabbing two water skins from a secondary table, Quintus took a swig from one, then moved back to his soldiers, where he passed the refreshing liquid around, and smiling, he kept his expression happy, like life had never been better.

"Rome reigns supreme," said Quintus, looking at the men much like a mother hen might her chicks, "in a sea of enemies by virtue of its legions. We are the backbone of the empire, and our enemies rightfully fear us when we take the field. We pacify, and when needed, crush all that oppose peace and civilization. Pax Romana."

Using the Latin term for "Roman Peace," a widely uttered term because Rome was considered the center of both the literal and figurative world, evoked a strong response from the men, and cheers and repeats of "PAX ROMANA" broke out in response to Quintus' speech.

The feeling in the air, formerly reserved and careful, evolved into an intense moment of camaraderie, bonding the soldiers into a shared experience of their place in the army, and more importantly, to this individual unit. They were to be as one, with fate making their futures indistinguishable from one another.

Returning to one of the tables, Quintus grabbed a rag, and motioning carefully by lowering his arms, silenced all the soldiers' overt display of emotion. Removing his tunic, he remained only in his triangular tied loincloth, and he began to wipe down his muscular frame, carefully patting at the welts inflicted by the soldiers.

Now speaking slower, Quintus grew contemplative. "It will always be so, so long as we remain steady. You are to practice here for four more hours. Switch opponents, weapons, and formations. But just as you will for real in the near future, fight as one."

Internalizing the moment, Quintus' mind drifted to a time in his own past, specifically to a period when he himself had learned this same brutal lesson about teamwork.

Quintus hesitated, then focused on recalling the face of his long-forgotten trainer, who, like himself, had seen much suffering and violence in his life. That grizzled warrior must have long since either retired or been killed in the service, but Quintus was just able to grasp the man's words from deep in his memory.

Thinking hard, Quintus could almost hear that man's distant voice. As he turned to face his soldiers with iron eyes and a firm jaw, he finished his lecture in a deadpan voice, staying true to that long-ago training. "KILL as one."

Chapter Eight

The perception over the world was strange. Across the foggy forest, where the evening had created a dark pall over endless brush and clusters of broken tree trunks, there was further darkening, like the colors of nature itself had disappeared and been replaced by monotoned, grayish tones.

Further, the precise outlines of the background were off. Unlike with normal visibility, the sharp silhouettes of reality were now fuzzy, and the unnatural edges of the landscape now seemed to hover, as if the normal environment were replaced by a dream that blurred everything in view.

The focus of this strange perception shifted downward, moving towards a specific trail in the vast expanse of forest below. Zooming across the bizarre woodlands, the attention moved to two horsemen who rode in the encroaching darkness.

Second in line, Albrecht was a brawny man, even in a place where such men were routinely imposing. Almost as if he himself was carved from the oak forests he routinely traveled through, his shaggy beard, pasted on his broad and firm face, made his appearance as much a part of this world as the stags and bears that occasionally dwelled here.

His father Ulrich, the leader of the Quadi, Germania's second-largest tribe, clopped over clods of dirt and uneven stones as he set a relaxing pace. The pathway into the failing light was wide and relatively passable, something unusual for such a densely treed area. Strangely, the riders did not seem to notice or care about the abnormal hue and inexplicable appearance of the background around them.

Older and wise, Ulrich shook his head as he plodded ahead, unhappy as he considered his son. Jutting his jaw out, his appearance had the look of one who was unlikely to change his mind in the near future—the unmistakable image of a stubborn brute.

After a faltering hesitation, then catching himself, Albrecht raised his voice to his father, clearly unhappy with the direction of their conversation. "So…you're going to risk war with Ballomar? You sure that's smart?"

Keeping his view forward, Ulrich continued shaking his head. His voice, gruff and direct, still managed a bit of patience. "Nothing we do for our people is without risk, Albrecht. You need to keep that in my mind for our present, as well as the future, because I won't always be with you."

Albrecht didn't appear worried about that prospect, and he kept his tone displeased, ignoring Ulrich's cryptic comment. "It looks…cowardly…that's all I'm saying."

Pulling his horse up, Ulrich stopped. Silent for a moment, he nimbly turned the animal around, and peering at his son with a dour expression, his patience vanished. "Careful, Albrecht. Words like that can get a man killed, even within family."

Breathing deep, Albrecht fought back the urge to raise his voice. By nature, he was not a man to quibble or hold his tongue, but neither was he stupid. When he finally spoke, his tone was calmer. "I didn't mean disrespect, but the rest of our people won't be so honest with you. You…we…have enemies."

Gazing at his son, the skeptical and intense focus of his eyes was Ulrich's only response. After a moment, he nodded, then turned his horse to continue their journey. Albrecht followed slowly behind, his horse slogging carefully across the damp forest floor.

Ulrich resumed his fatherly tone, calling back over his shoulder. "We carve our place of glory from this land. We're feared by all within Germania, even Ballomar. Nobody owns the Quadi, and nobody orders us to battle against our interests."

Albrecht remained unconvinced. Leaning forward, as if it might make his words more convincing, he muttered a rough question. "Why not join them? There's enough Roman blood to go around. We can take our portion from the Mediterranean swine on our own terms…no permission needed…or asked for."

Slowing his horse, Ulrich grimaced, but he didn't immediately respond. He was proud of his son's eagerness for conquest, but in leadership, there was always more than just battle to consider. His eyes growing distant, he raised his voice. "In the time of our forefathers, the tribes all allied against Rome. We lured their soldiers into our lands and destroyed them all— almost none escaped."

Stopping his animal, Ulrich continued his speech, though he didn't turn to face Albrecht. "And we sent their general's head back to their emperor in their sunny capital, spiked like all devious dogs should be."

At this, Albrecht grinned, his lips pulling back to reveal, even in the faint light, his crooked and broken teeth. Much like he was personally there in that distant time, the younger man could almost feel the joy of such a victorious moment.

Ulrich continued, his tone reserved. "But even with such a great victory, the price was great. Their endless legions invaded and punished us for DECADES after. Their efforts divided and destroyed us. Many of the smaller tribes disappeared entirely. We became weak, even in our homeland."

Albrecht was unimpressed. "That was long ago. Our warriors are fierce. Think of the treasures and women available for plunder. We could decorate our lands with their bones…and raise their children as our own. To the victors goes glory. To the weak…death."

Ulrich sighed, then shook his head. "Even if we defeat all their forces here, they'll spend a generation attacking us. Rome has an empire twenty times our size."

Finally, Ulrich glanced back. His features were now deadly serious, his scowl intimidating. "When you're a leader, you must learn to understand. Know what you want from battle— for you and our people. Choose your own time to vanquish your enemy…and only if it's in your interest."

Looking around the quiet forest, which still seemed to shimmer in the fuzzy light, Ulrich gestured to the west, where Ballomar and the Marcomanni held sway. "And Ballomar also cannot be trusted. He consorts with witches and black magic to support his efforts. To cast our lot with him would mean certain death…or worse, subjugation."

"Father, avoiding this fight," responded Albrecht, his tone imploring, "will make us weaker. We'll lose respect with the other tribes."

Ulrich shook his head determinedly, his voice assuming a coldness, one that showed his word and decision were final. "I won't spend our people's lives just to destroy our future. The Romans leave us at peace in our realm now. They won't if we cross the Danube; it's a line we won't be able to return from."

Staring at his father and leader of the tribe, Albrecht remained unsure. Even as he lightly nodded at Ulrich's words, his cool demeanor, like that of a briefly submissive wolf who would later reassert itself to reclaim a missed meal, showed this wouldn't be the last discussion they would have on the matter.

#

Alia rasped and collapsed, falling back into fluffy animal skins laid over the crude chair. Her fatigued face, pale and drawn in, was lightly streaked with wispy fingers of black and red paint. Oval in shape, her unusual complexion, mixed with her oddly emaciated features, accentuated the bizarre look of a sun-deprived woman living in vast forests beneath the usually overcast skies of Germania.

Exhausted, she drew scratchy breaths, struggling to control herself and comprehend precisely what she had just witnessed. The downside of her ability to view distant events, which was just one facet of her unique gifts, was it overwhelmed her physically, making the experience feel the same as several days' exercise condensed into a few minutes.

As Alia's blood pressure spiked, then gradually receded, sweat continued seeping from her pallid face and forehead, dripping to her bosom and soaking into her vest-like frock. Having been under duress for some time, her loose woolen outer-garments, held loosely around her thin shoulders, had become engorged with perspiration from her viewing experience. Alia was not an ugly woman, but her bizarre hazel eyes, holding an accumulation of reddish streaks within irises set within her starkly white face, made her openly difficult to look at. Much like a traveler might glance away from the burning sun's intense glare off smooth water, this was also the effect of her deeply unusual appearance; to stare directly into her face was an endeavor few could manage, and even fewer would want.

In front of her, perched on an equally crude oak table that still held bits of bark on its crooked legs, was a large bowl. Made of a black rock-like substance, the bowl's off-white color made it appear valuable, priceless even, and was certainly not of local manufacture.

Inside the bowl, contrasting strongly with its pasty hue, was a small pool of darkish blood. In the blood was a collection of black jewels, half-submerged and at least ten in number, which were stacked haphazardly in the gory display, glistening under the firelight of several torches suspended from poles near the table.

Around Alia, a spacious tent encompassed her. The rough-leather fabric of the simple construct was not opulent, but for her purposes, it made for a comfortable place of repose. Past the small table to the extended side of the large tent, several places to sleep were arranged, and piles of cozy mismatched skins marked it as an appropriate place for Alia to entertain any prospective partners.

It took time for her to collect herself, to bring herself back from the place where she went to see that specific trail of the remote woods, many miles from where she now sat. Her feeling was precisely the same as when a person has stood too quickly and gets a rush of blood that dizzies the senses, except on Alia that effect was many times worse. She took time to recover, blinking repeatedly as she waited for her perceptions to return to normal.

And finally, her local awareness resumed. At last able to keep her eyes open, to readjust to the spotty light and quietness around her, she came fully awake. Her frantic breathing dying down, she peered into the soft light, and now she was able to take in the moment, understanding that she was back in her element, back in her home. By herself in this space, nothing from the outside world would now absorb her attention.

Gazing over to several chests in the back of the tent, ones that held jewelry together with bindings of ancient papyrus scrolls, as well as the more modern type of book-like codex volumes, she spent some time considering where she was. Taking in the solitude of her inner sanctum and the items she'd collected over a lifetime of bizarre happenings, a sense of contentedness washed over her.

Moving her gaze back to the bowl, where the blood was thickening around the dark jewels, Alia at last reached a point of perfect clarity, a moment when she was completely in tune with both her current environment and the wider, more mystical one.

Pulling her lips back over her straight-white teeth, lips that seemed entirely too large for her waifish face, Alia smiled. That serene smile, full of expectant attention, was firm and untroubled as she peered down. Absorbed in the moment, it was as if she was waiting for something very specific to occur.

Chapter Nine

The tall building was cavernous, offering a supply of weaponry that could outfit a large detachment of soldiers. As an armory, it had many racks of weapons, from braces of spears to shorter javelins, swords, and collections of bows with their attendant arrows.

The width of the building was substantial, allowing for two separate rows of meticulously arranged battle implements stretching for thirty yards under decreasing torchlight toward the back of the crowded building.

Marius walked near Quintus, perusing the weapons with a practiced eye. Feeling the edges of several swords, he nodded silently before moving farther down the room and pulling a javelin from its rack to check its sharp point and heft. Apparently happy with the result, he nodded further and replaced the missile weapon.

Turning carefully, he met eyes with Quintus and gestured with a wave to the wider world outside their current location. "See to it that the guard is doubled. Have our men coordinate with the men in the village. I want them all protected."

Quintus cocked his head, doubt creeping into his features. "The auxiliaries aren't prepared to fight—at least in a rigorous manner. They'll just be in the way—they're mostly old men."

Remaining serious, Marius kept his tone flat, but the firmness in his eyes showed an inclination towards empathy for the locals. "Perhaps, but many of them served in the legion, at least long ago, and Rome gave them property here in return for their efforts. It won't do for our purposes or their egos to have them cower in their homes."

Suddenly noticing something, Marius reached toward a collection of shortswords, where he plucked one out, and holding it up to the torchlight, tested its blade by running its edge along the back of his hand. "And have Longinus sharpen every edge in the armory. Again. I want every blade checked and rechecked for battle worthiness."

Nodding, Quintus took a moment to stare at several of the blades in their respective slots. Appearing meek, he spoke in a low voice as he pretended to inspect the weapons. "But…what about Julia?"

"What do you mean?"

"Won't you move them to your quarters? As commander, it's in your power to—."

"—We would have to be married, as you well know. Under regulations, I cannot marry until discharged."

First frowning, then chuckling, Quintus took a while to contemplate the explanation. Plainly he was not convinced by Marius, whatever the rules his commander claimed he was forced to follow. Moving to the door, he held it open for Marius, who eyed him suspiciously as he exited the armory.

Outside, it was much noisier, as the clanking of metal filled the air, which emanated from a metal workshop across the broad parade grounds lit by lamps suspended from poles. Separately, sounds from weapons training drifted through the early night, with both the clack of weapons being used in mock combat and matching shouts of fighters struggling to win their melee practice resounding through the encampment.

Drawing himself upright, Marius gestured towards an armored guard to the side of the armory entrance, clearly not wanting the soldier to hear them talking. Motioning to a tree line near the edge of the base, which lay near a tower overlooking the surrounding open country, Marius walked away with some purpose.

Quintus took a few steps to catch up, talking with some annoyance as he hurried to draw abreast of Marius. "I've served in many theaters, Marius, and it was always accepted practice for the commander to take a wife."

Shaking his head, Marius increased his pace, as if his efforts to move faster might well outrun the conversation. "We can't marry until my time of release from the legion. The rules governing our lives are clear and unavoidable."

Flashing a dubious frown, Quintus grew more assertive. "Those rules are ignored everywhere. You would be exactly the first commander I've known who bothered to abide by them."

Marius came to a stop. Turning to Quintus, who had caught up and flashed a mischievous smile, Marius breathed patiently before talking. "My hope is to be assigned to Rome at the end of my service. I...won't have that chance if I take a wife in the provinces. It's one of the matters that are most frowned upon—."

"Aha, I understand," replied Quintus, interrupting, even while his features maintained a bit of respect. "So...you will continue your current situation, even as Julia needs a husband...and the boy, a father? Where will they fit into your plans?"

A dark frown clouded Marius' face. Dropping his voice, a tinge of regret, almost shame, filled his expression. "He is not mine, Quintus. His father abandoned them long ago."

"There you are wrong, my obstinate friend. You are his father in fact, if not by birth. I've seen how you interact, and most families of their own lineage do not communicate with such affection."

Quintus was not wrong, at least if the following look on Marius' face was to be believed. Shaking his head, Marius pointed to some nearby woods and changed the subject. "Have the men cut down several of those trees. Use the logs to barricade the road from the ferry crossing at the river."

Looking into Quintus' eyes, Marius flashed his own smile, one that acknowledged his reluctance to talk further about Julia or Lucien. "We are overly exposed here, and the situation will not resolve itself by waiting. And…I hope you can show as much intuition with our defense as you do with my personal life."

With that, Marius clapped Quintus on the shoulder, and, not looking back, paced rapidly across the hard ground of the practice area towards the front of the fort, where a thousand other duties awaited him.

As he moved away, Quintus frowned, and turning inward toward his own thoughts and tasks, he considered the stubbornness of his otherwise considerate and very capable commander.

#

Mist churned slowly over the dark trail, largely blocking the view of the path forward during the gloomy night's predawn hours. In the sky above, there loomed blotted gray shapes of swirling fog that hovered above the forest and mingled with rays from the large and luminescent moon.

Throughout this faintly lighted landscape, lying to either side of the shadowy path, was a forest of muck, which consisted of stunted trees and swampy ground extending into the farthest corners of the forbidding wilderness. Plants and trunks that grew here were misshapen and ugly, looking oddly unnatural in their contorted expressions, much like the foliage itself was complaining at the fact of having to grow in such a cursed environment.

Three men stepped gingerly along the trail, leaning carefully into each step as they avoided tripping over roots or making much noise. Dressed in dark armor, they each held a long sword in their strong hands, and their careful eyes, wide and investigative, flitted over the dark trees in rapt anticipation of what could lie ahead.

To the back of these three men was a taller, more powerful, and by the way he strode without regard to noise, less cautious individual. Ballomar's pace matched that of his men ahead, but his mind and bearing were confident, not filled with any hesitation as his steps cracked through light brush and bunched sticks on the soft ground.

In Ballomar's hand was a leash of sorts. Made of abrasive rope, he clutched it tightly and pulled hard, yanking along three shapes from behind him who were roughly tied together at the hands and waists. The figures he tugged onward were much smaller than he, and swathed in dirty linens covering their diminutive heads, they moved in starts, trying to find their footing with every forced step ahead. Obviously children, they stayed quiet, even as they shook under the fear of an environment they couldn't readily see.

The air around the group was filled with buzzing insects. The warriors and Ballomar constantly swatted at the invasive pests, while the children, unable to keep the bugs away, merely mewled in discomfort and shook under the onslaught of mosquitoes and gnats.

Grunting, Ballomar called the impromptu expedition to a halt. Panning his head, his eyes sought out something in the dismal surroundings, as if his intuition had told him their destination was near. For several minutes he stood there, waiting and becoming impatient with each successive moment, while also swiveling his head in order to identify some expected visitor.

"Witch," shouted Ballomar, his brusque voice seeming strangely alone in the quiet forest. "Where are ye? You're trying my patience."

Detaching from a mist-shrouded copse ahead, a dark shape greeted this expectation. Covered in a dark cloak and hood, the person was not immediately identifiable. For some time, the unknown figure stood and evaluated the group, while Ballomar and his retinue returned the curiosity from a distance of twenty yards. The breaths of the Ballomar's warriors, spewing condensation from their mouths, increased in the late-night standoff, as even the hardened men felt uneasy in this unappealing environment,

Finally moving, the unknown guest stepped nearer, and with a flourish, Alia threw aside her hood to greet Ballomar. Even in the mild light, where specific features were difficult to discern, it was obvious she was unafraid of the developing encounter with her powerful visitor.

Striding past his guards, Alia got close to Ballomar, and within an arm's length, she smiled up, her dark eyes focusing curiously on the imposing man. "I'm here, King Ballomar. I was beginning to think...you would disappoint me."

Ballomar fixed his stout gaze on Alia. Clearly unnerved by her presence and closeness, he nevertheless was not given to showing fear. First looking down on her, he shuffled closer, moving his head within inches and breathing his foul breath over her dainty face.

Alia accepted the stench, knowing that outward signs of aggression and ego were part of any dealings with such brutish men. For some time they stood, mismatched and stern, peering at one another with equal measures of revulsion and antipathy.

But it was Ballomar who looked away first. Sighing, he looked back at the children, who stood quietly in the night's chill air. "Hard to find the right ones...for your payment. Took them from another tribe. It wouldn't do to use children from my own people—or allies."

Alia moved her gaze to the children, and they seemed to wilt under her stare, even as their covered faces prevented them from seeing her. As if sensing that a predator now had them in its acute interest, they each leaned back and began pulling on Ballomar's tether.

It took a hard wrench of the rope, a harsh force from Ballomar's powerful arms, for them to calm themselves and accept their current circumstance. As if they were now sheep to be led to slaughter, their bearings became docile when confronted by Ballomar's strength.

Moving past Ballomar, Alia snatched the leash from his hand. Gently tugging the rope, she moved the children forward, where they clearly were intended to accompany her into the night.

As she led them back past the brawny leader, one of the children abruptly began to cry, his irate sobs growing louder by the second. All children, even in this harsh land where innocence was usually lost at a very young age, had their breaking point, and it appeared this child was well on his way to a mental breakdown.

Rearing back, Ballomar prepared to smack the child, ending his foray into uncontrolled fear and letting him know only pain awaited any complaints about his treatment. Holding her hand up, it was Alia that stopped the impending discipline, her eyes flashing in warning at the surprised king.

Instead, Alia began whispering words, words that became bizarrely harsh and full of indescribably strange tones, almost like they were uttered from an abused and corroded larynx, not from the delicate outline of her fragile throat. Though in an unknown language, it took little time for the child to calm himself, and the youngster grew quiet as he resumed his normal stance under the cloth hood.

Surprised, Ballomar lowered his hand, and something like respect for Alia filled his face as he looked back at her. Her own features, however, did not hide her own feelings of repulsiveness for the Marcomanni leader.

Shrugging, Ballomar readjusted his thoughts and motioned back into the darkness from where he had come. "My men are almost ready. How much longer before they attack my enemies?"

Looking first at the forms of the children, then towards the trees where she had just emerged, Alia's tone was quiet. "The Verisi have already begun. It won't be long before they've sown chaos before your march to victory."

Stepping closer to Ballomar, her voice grew inquisitive, but her eyes, dark and self-assured, gave a hint of knowledge of other things. "That is, if you have everything in order? If all your allies are ready? Perhaps you need help with that, as well?"

Ballomar began chewing on his lip, his stare becoming thoughtful as he peered down. For a long time, he weighed her words before finally agreeing with a vigorous nod. "It might be necessary, witch. Not everyone has my vision for our future. Some need to be convinced of my right to conquer...and rule."

Considering his thoughts and intentions, Alia took some time to work through the tyrant's request. Moving quickly to a decision, she sighed and turned away from Ballomar.

She soon began leading the children away from the men and into the trees and brush of the fetid swamp. While gently pulling them towards the darkness, she called forcefully back, speaking with a plain voice that evidenced no emotion. "Continue your payments, King Ballomar, and none can oppose you, either inside or outside of Germania. Your future—and glory—are certain."

As the witch and her new charges disappeared into the murky swamp, Ballomar focused on Alia with a certain intensity, mulling over the arrangement he had come to with this worker of sorcery. All things considered, her price for aiding his cause was reasonable and rather easy to fulfill. The world was full of children, and if a few were required to ensure his destiny, then it was a payment he was happy to make.

His was not a cause that would be without cost, both in lives lost and from alliances formed. The potential of great men required great ambition and ruthlessness, and these were qualities he possessed in abundance. To make history and assume his place in the world, nothing would stand in his path—not even the hesitation most warriors had with harming children.

When their forms melted into the night towards whatever place Alia called home, Ballomar briefly faced his men. Gesturing back to their camp, he turned and walked with a lightness in his step, a sudden buoyancy caused by the bountiful confidence he had in his personal prospects.

And as he plodded on his way, briefly stooping to avoid a hanging limb, a wicked smile, one filled with cunning malice and unrelenting certainty, filled Ballomar's scarred face.

Chapter Ten

S everal bonfires burned intensely in the darkness, their flames casting blotchy light across the village's building-lined main streets. The collection of rock-encased circles, where stacked wood was abundantly engulfed in flames within the hearths, made most of the settlement's public areas somewhat visible under the scant illumination of the moonless night.

Septimus, in his late thirties and donning the shiny armor of the legion, stood near one of the vigorous fires. Holding a long spear braced smartly on the cobblestoned ground, he looked grouchy, and, fighting off fatigue, he adjusted his helmet and cast a disdainful glare across the crackling flames. His face indicated a man unhappy with his duty, especially for this late period of night.

Across the fire stood Florus, who was equally unhappy with their current guard assignment. This man's spear was a bit crooked, and its point was less sharp, while his physical bearing, with a bent spine and scrawny arms, did not exactly invoke fear as a warrior.

Unlike Septimus, Florus was several decades removed from his peak physical condition, and his armor, which was cracked leather layered over a simple tunic and topped with a bulky red cloak, did not present an intimidating military demeanor. On the exterior of his cloak was a simple metal ornament of the provincial guard, which identified him as a man who would provide basic security tasks to the village and province for a few dinars each month.

Chewing on a bitter root, a practice that long ago made his already-poor teeth become streaked in various shades of yellow and black, Florus thought carefully as he peered at Septimus. His bountiful wrinkles, which conspired to make him appear ancient under the dancing firelight, formed into an unrepentant scowl.

Spitting to the side, Florus raised his voice above the noise of the licking fire. "What's your commander thinking? It's not like we got gladiators to help with this."

Surprised by the open negativity, Septimus shook his head and offered a matter-of-fact shrug. "I think he wants you to help with protecting yourselves. It doesn't take the poetic intellect of Ovid to figure that out. Is that expecting too much, or must you shelter like a woman and wait for your end?"

"No," replied Florus, seemingly unfazed and unoffended by the insult. Holding up his hands, he stared at his fingers, showing swollen, arthritic knuckles. "It's just that my joints are cracking louder than the fire."

Septimus smiled, his bad mood briefly interrupted by the witty response. One thing about living around old legionnaires in the provinces, even ones who needed the money from a steady peripheral duty, was they didn't always give a donkey's ass about rank or the mission. Getting close to the end of life, particularly among those who faced danger for decades, often made a man insolent to the point of being a crusty bastard. And

Septimus found he tended to like crusty bastards, perhaps because he too aspired to have such an irreverent personality when he retired from active duty. Glancing across the village square, he peered at two more fires, each of which held a soldier and a local guard standing near them. The mismatched men were similar to himself and Florus, which was kind of the point of the joint defensive endeavor—to put experienced fighters with those that would be easily defeated if fighting by themselves.

Catching the notice of one of the other soldiers, Gaius, an affable young fellow from the Frankish province, the man waved back at the sudden attention. Septimus returned the gesture with some sincerity, even if he didn't feel particularly steeped in military protocol at the moment.

Collecting himself, Septimus leaned closer to the fire, where he rubbed his hands in a bid to keep warm from the constant chill that plagued this area of the empire. In his experience in Pannonia, he liked the never-ending forests, as well as the abundant rivers and lakes, but getting used to the constant wintriness of the nights, even in otherwise-warm seasons, made him long for a return to the much hotter area of the main Roman peninsula.

Looking up, Septimus suddenly caught a flash of something, as if a figure had suddenly run by in one of the alleyways that riddled the village. It was just fast enough that he questioned himself for a moment, thinking he had imagined the movement as a function of the flickering firelight.

But pondering the solidness of the flitting figure, which seemed black, large and oddly formed, made him rethink his first impression. Gone as quickly as it had come, Septimus calculated exactly who or what it could be, and trying to assuage his doubts about the size of the shape, he hoped it must have been a figment of his imagination.

For several seconds he contemplated precisely what he had seen, but before Septimus was to act on it, he had to work his way through a bit of interior reluctance. To raise the alarm over nothing would be embarrassing, but to do nothing, particularly when an enemy could be close, would be a far worse option.

With an unsure sigh, Septimus leaned his spear to the side, then drew his short sword in an adroit motion. Grabbing a torch from the ground, he dipped it into the bonfire to bring its head into a bright flame, then held it out to gauge its ability to light the way. Staring at the far alley, he breathed deep and stepped that way, moving hesitantly.

Florus was quick to follow, though his face was confused as he held his spear at the ready. "What is it?"

"I saw…something…over there. Perhaps a citizen out to use the latrine."

Pointing to where the movement occurred, Septimus motioned back to the fire. "Stay here. Raise the alarm if you see anything, and don't get yourself killed."

Gesturing to the another of the fires, Septimus got the attention of Gaius, who quickly responded by detaching himself from the light and rushing to Septimus' side.

With a whispered word of "there," Septimus pointed toward the now-empty spot, and with cautious steps, the two soldiers crept carefully toward the alleyway. Gauis, staring into the shadows, leveled his spear as he approached the darkness, while Septimus walked next to him, arm and torch extended.

In little time they managed to reach the corner, where the rough edge of the building led to a path behind it that was eight feet wide. Looking ahead, moving slowly as they watched for a foe from any direction, Septimus noticed the ground had several recently made scratching marks. The disturbed surface of the uneven dirt, where dust and soil had been scraped aside, also had something else, which looked to be very recent splotches of a dark liquid...*blood?*

Looking over to Gaius, who was painfully nervous and peered back with a gulp, Septimus frowned and pointed ahead. Moving even more carefully, the duo tread with a maniacal degree of precision, stopping and listening every few steps as they followed the indentations and marks of apparent blood.

After thirty more yards, taking their time and sweeping the torch around them, the pair came to the exterior wall of the village. The wall was thick and high, built sturdily to keep people from coming into the town without knowledge of its inhabitants, but here the marks stopped and dark-liquid stains ascended the wall, almost as if someone had simply walked up its sheer face.

As they gazed at each other, each not knowing precisely what it could mean, Septimus and Gaius abruptly looked to the side, where they spied two more torch-carrying men coming their direction from the main gate. These men, village guards who appeared scared and halting as they walked, soon came within easy distance of the soldiers.

Septimus recognized the men as the best of the provincial auxiliaries, men who cared for and tried to ensure the safety of their local citizens and villagers. Though obviously not of an elite status within the military establishment, they nevertheless had realized something was amiss and in turn sought the source of trouble at this late time of night.

Motioning them over, Septimus spoke loudly and with clarity, ensuring he would not be misunderstood as he met their gazes with insistent eyes. "Awaken every man who can fight. Surround the village so that nothing can escape. Nobody is to leave their homes unless they are to join us under arms."

Tapping his blade with several clinks against the wall, Septimus looked into the scared eyes of the guards, then into the equally fearful ones of Gaius, before accentuating his point with a raised voice. "Quickly."

Nodding, the two protective villagers hurried off into the night, breaking into an awkward scamper as they went. Trudging into the darkness, their movements were jittery and hurried, appearing almost childish in their ill-suited armor and jerky motions.

As they rushed away, Septimus faced Gaius, and his expression became more severe as the moments passed. Their boring guard duty had just become something else, but it remained to be seen what exactly that was. And whatever had just happened, it was clear that matters at hand didn't bode well for their near future.

His focus growing grim, Septimus spoke to the younger soldier without restraint about their impending troubles. "Now get back to the barracks. Tell Quintus and the commander we have…someone else here. Make haste, and don't stop until you've found help."

#

The room was quaint, and only a few rays of firelight careened through the basic wood-shuttered windows of the small building. Throughout the room there was some simple furniture, which consisted of a small desk and chair sitting near the door, while a straw-stuffed mattress lay over the concrete space used for sleeping in the opposite corner.

Marius lay deep in slumber on that mattress, his face arched to the side and with one arm pinned below his sprawled form. His inelegant pose was made more ungraceful by a calamitous snore erupting from his drooling mouth, with the echoes from his slumbering depths forcefully disturbing the peace in the otherwise-calm room.

Sandaled feet walked carefully across the well-swept floor, stopping just short of the bed. For several moments the figure stood above him, and holding a gently burning clay lamp, was completely silent.

Finally kicking at the straw-filled linen, it took Quintus several tries to raise Marius from his contented sleep. In time, the commander was finally able to pry open an eye, and as his blurry perception formed into awareness, he peered up to see his trusted subordinate standing above him. Quintus, looking something like a curious researcher of long-forgotten historical texts, fixed the commander with fascinated eyes.

"Marius, how does Julia tolerate your sleeping roar?" asked Quintus, a grin widening on his fully-awake features. "A lion makes less noise. Even a horribly wounded beast, growling and near death, would be less noisy in its sufferings."

As he came into something like normal perception, Marius suddenly sat up. After blinking several times, he adjusted his vision across the room, and pulling himself up, he stumbled across the open space to a bowl of water on a wooden box in the place he used for shaving.

Grumbling, Marius splashed several handfuls of water on his face, and after rubbing his eyes with a simple rag, turned to face Quintus. "What…brings you here at such an early hour? What time is it…three?"

"More like two, I should think," retorted Quintus, his face losing some of its playfulness.

With that, Marius nodded, then held up a polished copper mirror to check his appearance. Not many of his features were identifiable in the deficient light, but what he could see, from his deep age lines to his puffy eyes, didn't seem to make him happy.

Sighing, Marius set aside the mirror, then let his weight fall onto a squeaking stool near the desk. Taking several deep breaths, he rubbed his face with fumbling hands, struggling to overcome his fatigue.

"Vitus has returned from Salvio," continued Quintus, referring to the rider Marius had earlier sent to warn the Roman cohort of the developing violence in the region, "and…we've had an intruder in the village."

Marius' eyes flashed with anxiety, but Quintus held his hand out to calm him, while also keeping a tone that implied something more serious had happened. "Julia and Lucien are unharmed—I have a man watching over them."

Some moments passed, and a look of haunted confusion passed over Quintus' face, even as Marius waited expectantly for what clearly was to be the next bit of unwelcome news.

"But," Quintus said, his expression dropping all pretense of good humor, "there's something dreadful you're going to want to see. And…it's not like anything I've ever witnessed in this strange life."

#

Trudging in the relative darkness through the narrow alleyways of the village, the two soldiers ahead of Marius and Quintus marched in perfect lockstep. Their legs, almost as if tied together in absolute harmony, clacked so hard against the ground that the leather soles of their slapping sandals appeared designed for the sole purpose of creating a loud and distinct marching rhythm.

In fact, drilling in the Roman legions was first and foremost an aspect of fanatical attention to discipline and focus. Men coming into this way of life might be ignorant or educated, poor or of relative prosperity, but the essential aspect of their developed character was always primarily to do what they were told—and to do it well.

In this way, the legions spread across the known world on cleverly engineered and impressively constructed roads that encircled the Mediterranean, always carrying with them the knowledge they were the best, the feared vanguard of an ever-expanding civilization. The empire relied on them, and they embraced their role with knowledge of their own uniqueness and irreplaceability in that cause.

These legionnaires marched thirty or more miles a day, then stopped and dug defensible trenches around their nighttime camps in order to ensure the security of the unit, as well as the civilian followers who usually tagged along behind them as they moved about the provinces. Much in the way that a wild animal trained its muscles to run without regard to its endurance, the legion trained to march and fight without hesitation, not stopping until their goal was achieved. The individual man was without personal cause as he partook in the duties of fighting and extending the power of Rome.

Fatigue was not only ignored, but it was also ridiculed and quickly drilled out of the sore muscles of the army. Men such as the simple soldiers leading them through the village were part of something that was far stronger than the sum of its parts. And they each knew it.

Marius smiled with some pride as he paced behind the soldiers. He remembered his youth well, at a time when he took part in the Parthian wars in Anatolia, with the mind of a novice fighter who had become one to take his orders efficiently and without regard for his own safety.

Marius' first time facing death was under a shield wall in that distant land, during one of many border wars with that vicious and merciless Parthian enemy, when thousands of arrows peppered the shields held in a line over the heads of the first ranks of the legion. When the occasional missile got through the slots and maimed or killed a fellow soldier, it became one of his most frightful experiences in life.

Even worse, looking through the spaces in the protective shields, seeing thousands of enemy infantry marching towards him with shields and wicked spears raised, pressing toward his lines under the cover of that shower of arrows, Marius saw these men who wanted to kill him, to bash his head in or run a pike through his guts. Under those conditions, terror flooded into his inexperienced heart.

Yet it also did something else. It made him feel alive, in the way that facing brutal and sudden death in the heat of battle could often do to a soldier. When you closed with a fearsome foe, sweat covering your face, hacking with blades and hearing screams, death, and the crunch of splintering armor all around you, it evoked something that could only be explained and understood by men who had similar experiences.

The truth was, the trauma of war could be an addictive experience, especially once a soldier got over the initial revulsion to blood, pain, and physical misery. Men who lived through the brutality of up-close battle were forever changed by it, and it was usually not in a way that non-military people would consider civilized. It somehow made many soldiers long for a return to that riveting terror, even if they wouldn't admit it to themselves. The cost of glory in battle was usually a warped perception of the world, but it was often a price a soldier was willing to pay—so long as he survived the jarring violence of the clash of arms.

Turning left, the group passed the sole brothel of the village, one that was owned by one of the former legion members. Claudius, now an elderly fellow of sixty-five, had parlayed his place on the frontier into ownership of the house, and through the process of making his business appealing to locals and travelers alike, had attained a handsome income from the sweat of his whores. He even managed to put some of his profit aside for his girls, which, to his way of thinking, made him a true humanitarian by helping women who had no other means to make a living.

Putting aside thoughts of that business—he had never been comfortable with such endeavors—Marius focused on the throngs of people who lined the avenue they now approached.

Turning left, they now marched past houses with women and children peeking from open windows and shadowed doorways. Men with rusty swords and disused spears also met their eyes from the sides of the street, and by the way that hushed tones and quivering voices followed them, it was obvious a feeling of open gloom had overtaken the village inhabitants. They were scared and anxious, looking to Marius and his men to make things safe again.

Approaching a modest brick building, which was made to house people cheaply with uneven leaning walls and cheap mortar, the escorting guards turned to either side of the humble entryway, and affecting a smart facing movement, placed their hands on their swords and stood at outward attention.

Pointing at the door, Quintus didn't break stride, and pushing inward, the thick exterior door creaked open. Stopping, Marius first stared at his men, then back towards the street, before taking a strong breath and pressing after him.

The inside of the place was well lit by several torches, full of cheap ceramic bowls in a simple kitchen and crude furniture in the area used for communal interaction. Behind a simple wooden divider, one of Quintus' best men, a sturdy fellow of broad shoulders and too-big ears named Lotharius, stood in the back of the large room, idly waiting in the place usually reserved for sleeping in a typical domestic arrangement.

Striding into that area, Quintus wriggled his nose in open disgust, then snatched a torch from the hand of Lotharius. Bending down, he lowered the torch to spread its light over a couple of unmoving shapes on the dark brick floor.

And Marius immediately saw the bizarre nature of what Quintus had alluded to before. Catching his breath, Marius scrunched his face in confusion, and moving closer, he leaned down to investigate what his eyes couldn't yet understand.

Two peasant-clothed corpses lay on the ground, face up and with arms partially extended to the roof, like they were trying to ward off what was coming for them.

Their skin was almost midnight black, pulled tight around knotted bones that stuck out from beneath the grotesque exterior of their bodies. Their faces, sunken and without eyeballs within their shriveled eye sockets, gave the impression of a long-dead corpse that had been soaked in black oil.

"By Mithras," exclaimed Marius, his skin growing pale. "What...could have done such a thing?"

Bending down to the bodies, Quintus produced a dagger, and grabbing one of the dead by the hair, he moved the head to the side, revealing the back hairline of the unfortunate villager. Pointing to the base of the skull with his knife, where two large holes were evident in the black flesh, he tapped them with the point of his weapon.

Speaking calmly, Quintus poked at the thick, leather-like skin. "Two holes just below the skull line. Almost like they've been shot by conical arrows."

Marius took a moment to absorb that observation. Taking out his own knife, he bent down and also probed the skin and holes before looking to the side to meet Quintus' severe gaze. "Yet there exists no shaft inside the wound. It is like they've been punctured and drained of blood. Like a mosquito?"

Pulling himself erect, Marius sheathed his dagger and grasped the leather straps of his armor with his hands, striking a contemplative pose. "Who are they?"

"It's the home of Felix and Alba Romilius. It's not certain this is them, with the difficulty to discern who...."

"I know them...both. He's a cobbler of some skill," said Marius, who then shook his head as he pointed down to the bodies. "But he's rather young, unlike the age this body would indicate."

Nodding, Quintus stood from the corpses. Absorbed in his thoughts, he passed the torch back to Lotharius, who stood silent and stared at the dead villagers.

"These bodies appear to be ancient," Quintus said, slowly shaking his head. "It's as if they've been buried for centuries and...preserved somehow."

Perplexed, Marius looked across the room, and walking carefully towards the corner, he pointed to a bedroll fit for a child. Turning towards Quintus, he then gestured to a doll that lay near the blankets. "And their child?"

"A girl. She is missing, precisely like the children of Appius. Not far from here, the intruder scaled the exterior wall. Smears of blood went up the wall and over it. It would appear the killer has fled back into the forest."

The shock of the moment, punctuating Marius's already sleep-deprived mood, made Marius remain silent for some time. Rage and...fear, an emotion he was unaccustomed to, filled his thoughts. To kill someone in battle was one thing, but this type of death was not easily understood. Precisely like Quintus, he had never seen anything like it.

"So," Marius said, his voice now thicker with emotion, "we now have two dead and four missing, three of them children—all without a cause or motivation."

"What now?" asked Quintus, cutting to the practical matter of what they were facing.

Pacing over to the simple table, Marius rubbed his finger over the lip of one of the bowls, lifting his digit to see a bit of soup residue that remained from the doomed family's supper. "We change our plans.

What...of Vitus? When can we expect reinforcement from Salvio?

Quintus shook his head, obviously unhappy with the information he was about to pass on. "Two weeks, no less. The cohort commander prepares for an invasion. He directs you to scout for incursions and to keep him informed of anything that might be to our advantage in the meantime."

Turning, Marius looked quizzically at Quintus. "That seems a long wait. They...must be preparing for extensive operations. The logistics of the upcoming campaign will be considerable."

Quintus, working through possibilities, offered a suggestion. "We could pull everyone out and fall back. Civilians included. Assuming we are to be overwhelmed, we could save what is possible."

"Not wise, I fear," replied Marius. "The Centurion commander won't be amenable to retreat, principally because our presence here is meant to screen the area in anticipation of an invasion. Whatever difficulties we face, we are here for a reason, not to run away due to poor military prospects."

"But we only have fifty men, Marius—and five of those are currently on bed rest. What are our options?"

Pondering a moment, Marius rummaged through his thoughts, looking for the path forward that would most assure their survival. Coming to a quick decision, he gestured out the door. "We pull back from our fort near the river. We fortify the village, dig trenches, and control our surroundings. We create a defensive posture and protect our citizens. We patrol only in force, not allowing any easy victims for our foes."

Walking near the door, Marius rubbed his hands over his face, still trying to awaken his sleep-encumbered senses. Turning back, he raised his tone, making sure his intent and orders were understood. "We will still man the checkpoint at the river in shifts, but the buildings will all be abandoned. All weapons and usable gear are to be moved here."

Catching himself, he peered again over at the corpses, a scowl forming on his determined features. "Nobody goes anywhere alone...we do our duty, and we make do with what we have—until help arrives."

Chapter Eleven

S tanding at the edge of the village's perimeter, Marius stared into the darkness of the nearby woods. On the outline of the tree line were open spots of sparse vegetation, which offered some visibility into the dim interior of the forest. Forever vigilant, his eyes sought out potential foes amongst the backdrop of low-lying limbs and sturdy undergrowth.

Marius peered for some time into the patchwork of shadowy foliage, his mind working through the possibilities of an incoming siege for their small settlement.

The impending conflict with the barbarian peoples of Germania made the hostile tribes' arrival indisputable, but at the same time, his adversaries would not be able to invade without scouting beforehand. The activities of battle, requiring extensive planning and mobilization by both sides, meant the Legionaries would have ample occasion to get ready for them. Marius had become acquainted with this logistical certainty from a lifetime of military experience.

Glimpsing down, Marius sighed and let the tension drain from his sinewy frame. Kitted out in fully polished armor and Roman helm with cheek guards and *Crista*, or red plume, along with a freshly oiled shortsword in a scabbard at his waist, he presented an imposing silhouette in the flickering torchlight on the exterior of the village.

Below him were the outlines of the deep and wide ditch, which had been carefully shoveled and implanted with rows of upward-facing wooden spikes. Now fully stretching along the outside of the town walls and in front of the few entry points into the village, the earthen channel was an impressive barrier, especially considering how quickly it had been carved from the rocky earth.

No enemies would easily pass such an obstacle, and if they tried, one of his soldiers or the provincial guard standing at intervals along the interior trench line would greet such intruders with the sharp point of a deadly spear.

Nodding, Marius chewed on his lip, a nervous habit that had long ago left thick scarring on the interior of his cheek. Glancing behind, he looked at Quintus, who stood quietly, squinting down at a scroll in his hands.

"Excellent," said Marius, his demeanor firm yet contented. "See to it that the guards are changed every twelve hours. To be effective, the villagers must feel like they are a trusted component of our defenses."

Glancing up from his notes, Quintus chuckled. "With so few men, they're exactly that. No need to pretend that we rely on them. Their help is essential."

Crinkling his parchment, Quintus focused back down on flowing script of fastidiously scrawled notes arranged in columns on the scroll. When he spoke, his tone was bored, as if he were idly discussing the composition of everyday dirt. "We have sufficient stores for a protracted wait…that is, at least until the cohort arrives."

"Then it is as we discussed. And what of the men at the forward post, by the river? Are they properly briefed and prepared?"

Quintus responded with a frown, apparently annoyed with the niggling question of what he considered a basic aspect of his duty. "No traffic has passed them, and they have horses if a need for a hurried withdrawal is required."

Marius nodded, and his gaze grew unfocused as his thoughts drifted to other details of the village's defense. Moving his head to the side, his clouded expression became inquisitive as he subsequently studied the exterior of the town wall, as he visually evaluated its solidness in the splotchy light of the torches.

Liking what he saw, Marius again turned and faced outward, falling into the tough pose of a man who watched and worried about everything. Command made him into a creature of fanatical devotion to his duty and men, requiring him to focus his efforts on any small detail that could endanger civilians, his soldiers, or even Rome itself.

Marius had long in the past understood that expecting the worst in war was the wisest method of preparing for it, and now, in this volatile situation where they faced wretched adversaries, his military sense, that innate part of his mind that had protected him throughout his lengthy career, was telling him that planning for the worst was this village's only chance to survive what was coming their way.

#

On the next day, the village center was not too busy. Few people were out and about on the largely empty streets, with only an occasional resident moving hurriedly between the squat stone structures in the bright rays of early afternoon.

From the stalls that normally held raucous crowds of people buying bread, fruits, and basic wares, only a single dispirited merchant peered from behind an overpriced collection of mismatched personal goods.

In the town's central square, at the place where cheap meals were usually taken from communal pots of boiling soups in a large open kitchen behind a line of stalls, there was currently only one such pot in operation. Smoke drifted from this lone cooking location, and only a few quiet villagers sipped from ceramic bowls, taking their time to enjoy each bite of a basic meal.

Julia was the operator of this single food business, taking a chance to supplement her scant earnings by offering an option for locals to partake in a hearty meal, even in such dour and worrisome times. Moving with some haste, she peered into her bubbling cauldron, threw some vegetables into the steaming broth, then hurriedly used a metal spatula to extract several flat bread loaves from a wood-heated oven to the right of the boiling pot.

Turning around, her eyes lit up as she spied Lucien, who, being a bored boy, just arrived at the cooking station to look for some interesting fare to quench the hunger in his empty belly. With sleepy-looking eyes, his face became openly eager when Julia motioned for him to have a seat at the kitchen's little-attended counter. Placing his arms on the rough-cut feeding area, he awaited his food with an expressive grin of youthful impatience.

After Julia had ladled a hefty serving into his bowl and added a steaming bit of crust to the side of the simmering lunch, she stopped and smiled, enjoying the view of a boy doing what they always did best: eating earnestly, slurping down his food like it was the last in the whole world.

So enmeshed was Julia in enjoying the feeding spectacle that she missed the incoming shadow of another visitor to her humble eating establishment. Moving carefully, Marius dropped onto the stone seat next to Lucien with a squeak of his armor and a fatigued sigh.

Flashing a mischievous grin, first at Julia, then to the boy, Marius set a cloth bag in front of Lucien. Perplexed, Lucien stared at the rumpled sack, not sure of what it could be or why it was offered to him. Leaning close to it, he stared with a considerable amount of expectation.

After getting an approving nod from his mom, Lucien carefully moved aside the top of the bag to reveal three hand-carved wooden soldiers; the first was a legate, or overall legion commander, who pointed ahead, much like he was directing the entire legion into battle; the next was of a simple infantryman clutching a well-fashioned spear; while the third was a lower-level commander, much like Marius, who wielded a small sword in a fighting pose. The figures were remarkable for their similarity to real life, and they clearly took some skill to sculpt and sand into their realistic condition.

"W...wow," exclaimed Lucien, plucking the soldiers up and examining each with fascinated eyes, his tasty meal now forgotten. "Are they...mine?"

Looking much like a boy himself, Marius leaned close and touched the sharp sword edge of the toy commander. "That they are, young man. They are some presents from the wagon-maker. He happened to owe me a favor, and I could think of no better idea than providing you with some top-level legionnaires. He is skilled with a carving knife."

Eyes growing wider still, Lucien continued to marvel at the toys, and stopping for a second, he reached up to give Marius a hug. Draping himself on Marius' shoulder, he kept the embrace for several seconds, and Marius' surprised eyes beamed as he met Julia's gaze from her place in the kitchen.

His appreciation soon forgotten, Lucien stood and ran to the far side of the square, where he went about setting the soldiers up for a protracted battle in some clumps of grass next to a deserted shop. Uttering commands such as "ahhh, that way, you evil man" and "destroy them now, I say," he was soon lost in an approximation of fighting that soon might take place in their very real world.

Staring at her son and his newly acquired toy soldiers, Julia suddenly felt overwhelmed. As she processed the charity and kindness of Marius, in a current time when brutality and indifference were often the normal ways of daily relations, her eyes teared up.

Unable to immediately look at Marius, she shook with surge of emotions, and only by raising her hand to wipe away an errant tear was she able to tame the moment and control herself.

The issue was simple: in her way of viewing the world, raised in a tribe and environment where showing weakness was the same as pleading for one's own death, she simply had no prior understanding to grasp how such a good man could be in her life.

Who was this person, so strong and gentle, who would work to make her and her son happy, against all the communal conventions she had ever known? For her, it was the same as suddenly understanding the purpose and cause of the stars in the sky, which was to say, not understandable at all.

Like a pet that, through some amazing transformation was suddenly made aware of its place in the world, Julia was bewildered and simply unable to catch her mental breath from the poignant moment. With her eyes now open to the possibility of her and her son being an essential part of another's life, it left her grasping at what was supposed to come next.

Marius seemed to understand her emotional incomprehension, and he offered her a moment to work through her sentiments. When she finally looked up, forcing herself to overcome the momentary weakness of mind, Marius acted like nothing at all had happened.

In his circles, Marius had always seen men struggle with their feelings, and he often found that giving people space allowed them to come to terms with shifts in their moods. It wasn't the manly thing to do in the traditional sense, but it was simply what worked to improve the prospects for his mission. And, to Marius, the mission always came first, whether in his personal life now or with his dutiful responsibilities in everyday life.

When Julia's face reached an almost-normal expression, Marius finally took the moment to step closer and gently tug her into his grasp. Julia returned the hug and peered up at him with open relief and some degree of desire.

"That's deserving of a healthy meal, commander," said Julia, her eyes glowing with appreciation. "Thank you. He'll keep me awake with those for weeks."

Marius grinned in response. "There's not a better lad in the province. I wish I could do more for him, and with your delicious stew, the debt is more than paid."

Motioning to his chair, Julia indicated for him to sit. As he did so, Julia fetched another bowl of her soup and a large hunk of bread, plopping both in front of Marius with a decisive thud and a broad smile.

Taking his time, Marius slowly brought a wooden spoonful of the concoction to his lips, and blowing gently, took a tentative sip. His expression immediately grew delighted, and as he hungrily gulped each successive bite, his eyes rolled back at its simple, delicious taste.

Leaning towards Marius from the other side of the counter, Julia pointed in the general direction of the rest of the village as he ate. "I wish the rest of your men could also have some. They need good and solid food for energy. For that matter, a good woman would also do them well."

Marius frowned in response, looking a bit guilty as he dipped a piece of bread and swallowed it down with a contented grunt. "Yes, but they would then go soft and...forget how to fight."

Shaking her head, Julia didn't hide her disagreement. "Have you forgotten how to do battle? Am I such a bad influence on your soldiering?"

Marius took some time to respond because, truthfully, she wasn't wrong. The Roman Army forbade men, especially youthful soldiers, from marrying, but he couldn't deny the logic of them needing someone to fight for when the enemy was close. When far away on campaign, that was a different matter, but glory in distant battle could only take a man so far. Up close and near home, the motivation to fight like a demon to protect your own loved ones was undeniable and could perhaps be decisive.

As with all the logic, however, when it didn't meet his preconceptions of the world or his duty in it, Marius simply pushed it from his mind. Setting aside his partially eaten meal, he reached forward and gently took Julia's hands in his.

"You and Lucien are my influence, Julia, and indeed one of the few things worth having. What talents I have are only enhanced by your presence."

Smiling, Julia responded with a playful pat on his arm. "With words like that, you could act in the greatest amphitheaters of Rome."

For a few moments, they exchanged happy expressions, the looks of people who shared a growing bond and more than a bit of mutual attraction. Whatever the problems in the world, they at least had this short moment in time to themselves.

But Marius' mind moved to other subjects, and after a moment of consideration, he spoke softly, as if to dampen the effect of his next words. "We must discuss something…we are going to have to send you and Lucien away from this area. War is coming, which is hardly a secret at this point."

Julia's smile wilted. "Is it so bad? This is our home; we have nowhere else to go…and nobody else to go to."

"The Germanic tribes are moving this way as we speak. They're not gentle enemies. You know this."

Pulling her hands back, Julia cocked an eyebrow. It was a beautiful eyebrow, but the tone that matched her attractive face was losing its open affection for Marius. "I also know that my brother stands in the way, along with you. How could I leave you both? Who will shelter us? Who cares enough to take in a woman and her bastard son?"

The acidic words she spoke made Marius flinch. Dropping his eyes, he nodded his understanding, because not for the first time, he confronted her defensiveness at not having a legal father for her son. But, breathing deep, he pressed beyond the matter of her societal status. Survival of the both of them was far more important than emotional issues. "There will be shelter in Salvio. Other civilians will also seek safety there. The empire does not abandon its citizens."

Leaning farther back, Julia now assumed an even more stubborn pose. Her arms crossed, she raised her voice to a point of unhidden irritation. "The empire will not replace my brother…or the man I love. I won't go anywhere without him—or you."

Clenching his hands together, Marius sought to tame his frustration. Giving up on his inclination to decrease the anxiety of the moment, he instead forged ahead into an increasingly hostile conversation. "Speaking of your brother, I am sure you know he intends to avoid joining with Rome. Even a first-year recruit can see that. I am not so stupid that I would not see his intentions."

"He's trying to keep a dying tribe together. Would you expect him to throw away his people?"

Marius' own tone grew colder. "You mean your people?"

Surprised by the comment, Julia stood, and moving backwards, turned to fix Marius with a direct stare—not exactly a cold stare, but far from adoring. "No, I mean this: the Naristi matter nothing to me, but to Tarquin they mean everything. He would die for them in a moment, without hesitation."

The kitchen and eating area became quiet. As if on cue, the remaining customer, an older man with feathery white hair, took the occasion to stand and walk away, not looking back on his way out.

Frustrated, Marius also stood. Planting his hands on the gnarled top of the chair, which was carved stone depicting some sort of smiling lion-beast, he spoke in a controlled manner. "Julia, if I could be so bold, I want to tell you a story. It's a true story, a matter of distant history. It's about Rome…specifically about a time of military upheaval from another era, though not so distant in essence from our current period of conflict."

Julia frowned at the proposed story, smacking her lips in open annoyance. But she still waited quietly for it.

Running his hand through his graying hair, Marius assumed the voice of a lecturer, with his words flat and pointed. "More than two centuries ago, a large revolt coursed through the empire. Gladiators, led by a skilled warrior named Spartacus, threw off their masters, and over several months they proceeded to engage and destroy several legions, all the while freeing slaves from the Roman peninsula in huge numbers."

"Everything about the empire was in peril," continued Marius, and walking to the side, he collected his memories to describe what he had long ago been taught by his superiors in the legion. "The world as the empire knew it teetered on the verge of annihilation. Nobody was safe from this revolution from below, and many loyal estates' workers and their wealthy owners were viciously murdered in a most heinous invocation of revenge for past deeds, whether real or imagined. And…unfortunately, facing this scourge of lawlessness, military men feared this rebel army and ran away from it by the thousands. Cowardice was like a virulent infection, and as it spread, the number of men who would fight decreased sharply. Too few would stand for Rome or what was just. The land suffered, and the people became lost due to the ascendancy of wicked rebels in the countryside between the cities."

Stepping around the counter, Marius moved closer to Julia. She met his incoming gaze with clear eyes, curiosity filling her demeanor.

"On the edge of losing everything, a general by the name of Crassus called his remaining legions and their leaders together," Marius said, his mood growing severe. "Because of their shame and cowardice before the rebels, he had every tenth man in the army executed. They were slain by their own comrades, beaten to death with clubs…and the victims were drawn by lottery, not by anything they had done individually."

Gulping, Julia turned her head to the side, as if avoiding her man's stare might make such hideous possibilities go away. Her voice became less confrontational and was full of dread. "Are you saying you will kill my brother and part of his people? Is this Rome's justice that you speak so fondly of?"

Marius shook his head, holding up his arms to mollify her. "No, dear Julia, I'm saying this: if Rome will do such things to its own soldiers, what do you think they will do to allies who evade their duties?"

Reaching out, he brushed aside a lock of her dark brown hair, then rubbed his thumb over her pale cheek, tracing where the tear had earlier been wiped away.

"He's…my brother," Julia responded, her face filling with fear but also retaining a vestige of her rebellious nature.

"I know," Marius said, trying to sound caring. "But you must tell him the consequences if he chooses badly. I won't be able to save him—if it comes to that. I am a soldier of the empire and will do what I must."

With that pronouncement, the fear left Julia's face, and it was soon replaced by open defiance. Turning her fierce eyes to Marius, she raised her hand to his. With a firm shove, she pushed it away.

Spinning around, Julia moved near the cooking pot and gathered some food, quickly stuffing it into a personal sack. Keeping her head down, she strode across the road, where she soon got Lucien's attention. Crouching to speak with the boy, she gestured to his new toy soldiers, and for them to get moving from this place to their home.

Walking on the main road from the town square, Julia moved well in front of Lucien, who looked puzzled as he glanced back several times at Marius. Around them, the day remained quiet, with no spectators to witness the unhappy exchange and abrupt departure of mother and son.

And while they were leaving, Julia didn't make eye contact with Marius, as for the moment it appeared she had nothing more to say to him. Lost between love for Marius and her own brother, her current mindset battled with itself over loyalties and affections that couldn't easily coexist.

Left alone, Marius could only frown at the unpleasant interaction. Glancing around, like he was hoping someone nearby could tell him what to do next, he contemplated his next actions. In his mind, he hoped the situation would not deteriorate further—but he also knew it certainly might become much worse.

Downcast, Marius grimaced at the complexity of it all. Life as a commander of men was difficult enough, but the idea of involving a cadre of loving civilians in his decision-making made his leadership calculations far more problematic.

Grabbing the hunk of bread remaining from his incomplete meal, he shook his head and paced back toward the command post near the front entrance of the village. Despite his individual adversity, there was a separate deadly build-up of troubles awaiting his immediate attention.

Chapter Twelve

The overcast sky shed a pale light over the Quadi camp. Smudgy rays of midday sun leaked through the cover of dark clouds overhead, illuminating a vast tribal encampment across the green valley floor.

At the largest of the tents spread across the lightly treed area, where a fire burned in a pit in front of the leather flaps of its broad entrance, there stood several bored guards. Standing in groups of three near the fire, the two collections of men, dressed in loose-fitting animal skins and heavy chain-mail armor, braced immense spears on the ground while appearing unworried about their surroundings.

Chatting with measured voices and casually sweeping the surrounding forest with impassive eyes, their presence near the large main tent of the Quadi tribe was not an accident. The lives of the forest clans had been dangerous throughout their history, and any leader who sought to continue his hold on power amongst antagonistic political factions was wise to keep proficient soldiers close at hand.

Around the Quadi leader's enormous tent, across the reach of the extensive location, there were hundreds of other members of the tribe taking part in daily life, from soldiers sauntering near their communal sleeping arrangements, to workers cleaning clothing and cooking, to slaves going through the effort of providing for a host of resident needs. The living conditions appeared tranquil, and smells and sounds of unhurried everyday living were evident across the camp.

Inside the tent, Ulrich stood near a dark wooden table, one that was polished to a high sheen and had a vast map of the surrounding forests on it. Peering down at what he held in his hand, his eyes fixed on an odd-looking figurine beast that was expertly carved from wood into the image of a bear. The burning torches around him, placed in metal sconces on wooden poles of the tent's supports, threw light across the artifact.

But the figure was more than a bear. Its head, where the growling maw of the forest animal would have been expected to be, was instead that of a wolf. The mix of the animals' features was odd, with the pagan amulet evoking a sense of dark religious symbols that so characterized the endless superstitions of the tribe.

Rubbing his fingers over the object, Ulrich was contemplative, and his stern eyes focused searchingly over the amulet, almost as if he expected it to respond in some overt way to his interior thoughts. For a considerable time, he massaged the ancient figure, taking his time to consider what the inanimate object might offer in the way of wisdom for his personal circumstance. The God-beast it represented was clearly of great interest to the Quadi leader, making the quiet interaction particularly meaningful for his deliberations.

Outside, from a distant trail, a horse detached from a patch of particularly dark woods. Moving at a deliberate pace, the rider on it angled toward the main tent, its steed clumping across the pine needles and over patches of damp earth on its way to the leader's residence.

This movement caught the eyes of the guards, and assuming the bearing of protective men who knew their way around and into a fight, they spread out to physically prepare for the arrival of the new visitor. Leaning their shafts towards the incoming guest, their readiness for anything out of the ordinary was unconcealed and bold.

They needn't have worried, for when the rider came close, his identity was clear: Albrecht, son of Ulrich and presumptive heir to the leadership of the Quadi. As he came near the guards, Albrecht nodded down at them, and pulling his legs over the back of the horse, he dismounted somewhat clumsily near the flaming pit.

Emerging from the tent, from where he had heard the noise of his son's arrival, Ulrich paced rapidly up to him. Stopping short, Ulrich gazed into Albrecht's eyes, his face curious and somewhat surprised at the sudden arrival.

The awkward moment lasted for some time, and the guards, long accustomed to the up-and-down interactions of father and son, looked away and found other interests to occupy their attention.

Ulrich, his expression still curious, leaned in close, as if to evaluate in detail something he was having trouble understanding. His serious voice was low and inquisitive. "Where have you been? Not the best of times to be out of our area. Our potential enemies are not without reach here."

"I was…scouting the region—our region—to the north," replied Albrecht, his unsure eyes seeming to search for something in his father. "I…wanted to make sure we would have no unwanted guests."

To this, Ulrich tilted his head, his face filling with an acute interest at the strange explanation. "We have scouts to do that, and you're needed here. What's wrong with you? You drunk?"

Blinking several times, Albrecht's eyes swam for a minute, much like they were trying to bring the current moment into reality. As if awakening, his features began to clear up, and something like normalcy returned to his expression. "No...father, just a little tired. All of these negotiations are wearing me down."

Ulrich didn't appear contented with that answer, and a scowl formed across his gruff face. The unhappiness of a father with his offspring, where the son was caught doing something unwise or dangerous, was as timeless as the eternal trees that surrounded this forested redoubt.

After another disapproving moment, Ulrich finally shook his head and sighed. Biting back a sarcastic remark, he instead motioned toward the tent. "Follow me. With what's going on, we must seize our course of action. That evil bastard Ballomar isn't taking 'no' for an answer."

Turning, Ulrich retraced his steps to the tent. With Albrecht in tow, two of the guards followed them to the threshold of the entrance, then faced outwards to block the way from any interruptions to their pending discussions of strategy.

Inside, Ulrich lumbered to the table, where his hurried movements suddenly showed an inclination to act quickly. Stopping across the table from his father, Albrecht peered down with some interest, his eyes playing across the sketched geography of the wider region.

On the table were several wooden carvings denoting the disposition of Quadi forces in their realm, as well as other figurines indicating the location of the Marcomanni and other tribes across the expansive woodlands. Two heavy daggers acted as paperweights to hold down either end of the cluttered map.

All told, the reputation that Germania had shifting alliances and competing political leanings was valid, as the rash of competing clans on display showed many different allegiances.

Though the Quadi were powerful in their own right, when surrounded by potential rivals, it was often wise to use diplomacy when dealing with neighbors. Violent confrontation was all well and good with the fierce clans, but getting along within certain boundaries was the better course of action most of the time.

Pointing down to the map, towards a location where the forests changed to a lowland area that held soil more suited to raising crops, Ulrich spoke with calculated frustration. "Ballomar has convinced the Warini to join his invasion. That leaves us and the Alemanni as the last major tribes to hold out from the invasion...and unfortunately, I'm not sure they haven't already decided to throw in their lot with him."

Ulrich took a moment to control himself, and inhaling a long breath, he reached to the side, where he picked up a scroll with several markings on it, marks that appeared to indicate attempts at counting next to various scrawled names of Quadi tribal elders.

Raising the paper in front of his eyes, his words were severe. "The Quadi Council is split, but if we get to Hathgul, we can sway him and stop this suicide Ballomar is forcing upon us. I've known him most of my life, and he—."

The THUNK of the impact abruptly interrupted his determined considerations on the matter of their plans.

Piercing through the paper, the dagger thrust through and pinned the parchment to Ulrich's unarmored chest. The knife, long and wickedly sharp, was stabbed three inches deep into his torso, making agonizing headway into his breast and easily slicing through organs as it pushed inward.

Eyes wide and in shock, Ulrich looked up from his grievous wound to see his son. Albrecht stood there, his expression unemotional and unworried. Still holding the hilt of the dagger, Albrecht leaned harder on it, plunging the blade to the hilt and cutting farther into his father's mortally maimed innards.

Blood gushed from the wound, already announcing Ulrich's impending death through the sheets of it pumping down over his dark-linen undershirt. Stumbling backwards, Ulrich was able to pull free, but the blade, buried completely, stayed with him as he retreated two ponderous steps from the table and his looming attacker.

Something new came over Albrecht's physical features as his father struggled to stay on his feet and looked at his son with bulging eyes. Over a short time, the skin of Albrecht's face, formerly bearded and lined with wrinkles, began to alter and change, as if the confines of his features could not decide what image to form.

The structure of Albrecht's visage and head appeared to melt through several iterations, forcibly moving to that of an older Oriental person, then to the darker-skinned features of a man from Egypt, and finally, to a young white female with broad and freckled cheekbones. Bones in his face and skull popped as they formed and reformed at bizarre angles, growing hair and losing it again in rapid succession. At last, while Ulrich somehow managed to stay on his feet, the face reassumed its form to the familiar image of Albrecht.

And that was the final thing Ulrich was to witness in his brutal and contentious life. With a gurgle and a despondent sigh, he collapsed back into the side of the tent. Sliding to the ground, he landed on his rump, and with unseeing eyes, he slumped to the side, finally coming to rest in a strange contortion on the earthen floor of the tent.

Hearing the commotion, the two guards rushed in from outside, holding their spears up in anticipation of some unexpected moment, perhaps to confront an assassin or someone else who had sneaked into the living quarters.

Instead, the shocked sentries quickly met the gaze of Albrecht, who smiled back at them with undisguised glee. It seemed to the men, and soon to all their extended tribe of tens of thousands of members, that the sudden ascendancy of an heir to his father's throne had progressed rather unexpectedly in this otherwise peaceful day.

Such a manner of changing leadership wasn't uncommon in Germania, and even though it hadn't been anticipated by anyone near Ulrich or his son, the fact of its happening would make the tribe's subsequent decision to join Ballomar's proposed invasion of Rome completely valid in the eyes of the Quadi.

Chapter Thirteen

The long ditch extended under the night's hazy starlight. Curving into the darkness, the ditch circled around the edge of the town. Carved from both the hard dirt and rock, as well as the softer areas of earth which held few obstructions to shovels, the trench stretched around the approach to the village, as well as around the substantial wall ringing most of the town's exterior.

Every few feet a pole was elevated above the ditch, and workers, toiling hurriedly and continually glancing out toward the encircling forest, worked feverishly under the pale light of torches suspended from those poles. Flinging soil with each swing of their crude shovels, it appeared almost the entire village was involved in the rigorous construction of the new barrier.

Soldiers stood at intervals along the expanse of the trench, looking warily over the villagers as they toiled. Holding long polearms, whose sharpened and curved edges were held at the ready above the working civilians, the men of the legion peered carefully around, ready for any encroachment towards the settlement from any enemies. Despite the late hour, the eyes and attention of the armed guardians were not dulled by fatigue.

At various points in the burgeoning trench there had already been sharp stakes driven into the soil. Pointing upwards, the intent was to impale any attackers who would jump into the ditch on their way to attack the town. Moreover, the stacks of yet more stakes lying next to the trench showed that many more such obstacles were planned in the near future. The defensive obstacle being created may have been crude and of quick construction, but its deadliness for any unwelcome visitor was unmistakable.

There was little talk exchanged amongst the workers or the protective sentries above them, showing the extreme importance of their labors for the future safety of the village. Idle chatter was the refuge of those who had time to spare, and in this case, neither of the groups of men were eager to engage in pointless banter.

Clearly there seemed to be a time element of the work, in which each passing moment, each hasty shovel of earth, was considered essential for the people involved in it. Equal parts of fright and anxiousness filled the workers' eyes as they frantically cut deeper into the soil, and their jerky movements indicated speed was more important than the trench's precise shape.

From the interior of the village, a slight figure moved free of the outlines of an exterior building. Wrapped in a warm cloak and fur-lined hat, Julia was careful as she stopped to make sure she was unseen. Leaning against an unguarded opening in the wall, she took measure of the work around her and tried to remain still. Breathing deeply, she looked for her chance as she sought to avoid the gazes of the posted soldiers.

Scurrying ahead, she moved forward and hopped over the line of a recently marked area, a place that had not yet been chiseled into a ditch. Moving as quietly as she could, she quickly made her way across the open ground to the tree line, toward a place well shielded from observation in the village.

In thirty seconds, Julia was able to make it to the protection of the darkness. Sheltered from view, her slim shape was now lost from into the interior of the surrounding forest, into a place that was formerly thought to be safe and well known—but now seemed neither.

Behind her, in a shadowed place near an open water well, Quintus stepped under the light of a torch. Moving to the edge of a ditch, he stared carefully into the spot where Julia had just disappeared. Perplexed, a worried frown creased his face, and rubbing a hand over his face, he pondered where and what she was doing.

Thinking carefully, it did not take Quintus long to come to a decision, and motioning to a nearby sentry to let the man know his intentions, he quietly set out after her.

Bundled in armor and his dark cloak, Quintus' approach to the forest was less careful, though no less quiet, as he picked his way over the rocks and through brush in the diminished light. In little time, his cautious form melded into the gloom of the dark woods after her.

#

As Julia moved rapidly through the woods, the crisp night air lost its cold bite on her skin, and she instead began to sweat from the exercise. Stepping in and out of bushes, moving across trails she had known since being a young girl, and stopping at regular intervals to gauge her precise location, she traveled for forty minutes in the lonely darkness.

And finally, she came to a clearing she knew well, a place that was wide and bereft of trees. This area only had scrub brush and grass, and limited starlight provided ample visibility across its consistently flat terrain.

Padding carefully across the open ground, Julia arrived at the middle of the meadow, stopping exactly at a prearranged break in the vegetation near a circle of worn rocks. This part of the meadow was ideal for having a rest and perhaps a meal, and she had done so many times in the past.

After looking around, she took stock of her location, then got to work. Knowing her body's exercise-driven heat would soon dissipate, she began collecting kindling from the ground and soon arranged it inside the makeshift hearth of the stones.

Moving her hands with some skill, Julia produced a chunk of flint and quickly began striking it against an oblong piece of metal to create sparks. In no time the sparks ignited an expanding fire from the moisture-free branches she had collected.

It didn't take Julia long to coax the flames into a comfortable temperature to shield her from the chilly night. After stocking the fire with more scattered wood, she found a comfortable rock to sit on, and leaning towards its warmth, she rubbed her hands and waited.

For some time nothing happened, but to Julia, the expectant moment was merely a formality. She knew the time and this location to perfection, and if it were possible for him to meet, even under the scant light of the moon and in these increasingly dangerous times, he would be here. That was as certain as the sun was to rise the following day.

In another half hour, after shifting her weight on her perch and occasionally standing to stretch her legs, a dark silhouette stepped free from the opposite side of the clearing.

The figure, obviously a male from his bearing and size, walked with some authority as he moved, angling toward her with a saunter that indicated a sense of familiarity. Dressed in the customary fashion of the forest people, except in this case wearing thick leather under his long cloak that covered his bulky metal armor, the lanky individual appeared ready for anything as he paced toward her.

Smiling, Tarquin strode into the light of the fire. His thin but handsome face, appearing peaceful and without undue stress, focused down on Julia as he stepped close.

"Tarquin," exclaimed Julia, rushing up to meet him with ecstatic eyes. "I was afraid you'd miss our meeting. Again. I know that times for the tribe are…difficult."

Clutching her close, Tarquin held her in his embrace for a considerable time, his face filled with appreciation of the treasured moment. "I was worried I would miss it as well, sister. In these present times, we cannot always be sure of our commitments."

Stepping back, some of the happiness drained from his face, and even in the inadequate firelight, Tarquin's worry became evident. "The situation with our people is dire, and it will only get worse."

To these discouraging words, Julia's face tilted sadly in acknowledgment. Glancing down, an acceptance of the moment, along with a bit of grief, filled her otherwise positive features. Looking up, she nodded at her brother, then motioned to the fire behind her. "Let us sit down and talk openly. There's much to tell you."

#

Some time later, Tarquin hunched near the fire. Brooding, he chewed on a steaming piece of recently cooked rabbit. Taking his time, he gnawed on the last stringy bits of the tasty meat, then picked a bit of gristle from his teeth. When he finished, in a show of casual manners, he carefully wiped grease away from his shiny chin with a simple rag.

Staring toward his sister, Tarquin's voice rose as his inquisitive eyes found Julia's depressed gaze. "Marius already knew? And the village...has already been violated by the tribes? This is strange news. How did Ballomar's men get past us, and why would he want children before he has even invaded?"

The questions Tarquin just breathed out were filled with curiosity and more than a little dread. His features, usually controlled and considerate, drifted between consternation and open confusion.

Standing, Tarquin turned away, almost as if looking at the distant outlines of the surrounding woods might offer some respite from the baffling news he had just received. Peering at a collection of sturdy trees, he maintained his calm by deep and slow pulls of oxygen into his lungs, allowing the clean forest air to force anxiety from his tightened torso.

Turning back, he stepped closer to Julia, hoping that some knowledgeable answer might be forthcoming from his sister. With some measure of expectancy, he waited for her to speak.

But, unsure of herself, Julia was just as confused as he. "I was hoping you would know. Stealing kids to serve their tribal interest—to expand their numbers in the long run—is nothing new, but it's always after they obliterate the male population of their enemies. Something is wrong, and from your puzzled face...it would seem you have no answers either, despite your normal grasp of common sense?"

The upturned question, offering Tarquin a compliment in the middle of this vexing discussion, chased away his dour mood, at least for the moment, and he smiled down on Julia. "Agreed, sister. It doesn't sound right…and it also does not make what we must do any easier."

Now it was Julia who showed a bewildered expression. "We?"

"The Naristi are also your people, Julia. Ballomar gathers a host that is big enough to challenge Rome itself. We'll be wiped from the Earth if we stay as we are. We shall have to flee."

"My people?" asked Julia, her tone and face filling with annoyance. "Surely, you're joking? You lead a few hundred men and women of a small tribe. You still think I'm part of…them?"

"You're my sister—."

"—and always will be," Julia exclaimed, her face growing as hard as stone. "But the rest are not—and never will be—my people."

Lowering himself to a crouch, where his lanky frame allowed his face to hover at a similar height to hers, Tarquin spoke softly. "I know that it seems—."

"You know nothing, Tarquin. When I had Lucien, one of those 'forest men' left me to fend for myself. The rest of the tribe would do nothing to help, and only your presence allowed us to survive at all. Even when…that pathetic man…was killed in a raid, I was still treated as an outsider. I had to come to the Romans to make a life for us and be treated like an actual person."

Nodding, Tarquin dropped his gaze. Reaching out, his strong hand gently grasped her shoulder. "We can't change the ways of our people, at least right away.

Someday they'll accept everything…as they should have, before."

Julia's eyes welled with tears, but as her face reddened, none escaped. "I'll say it again, to be clear. You are my brother, and I love you. I will do anything for you. Until the end, I am here, without hesitation. But…you are all that matters."

Raising her tone, anger pulsed through her, forcing a sharp finality into her next words. "The rest can burn in Hell."

Some awkward moments passed. Appearing increasingly sad, the flash of outrage gently ebbed from Julia's pretty features. Slowly, a single tear ran from the corner of her left eye. In contrast to an expression that was normally soft and considerate, her countenance turned to pure sadness, and she suddenly appeared like a young girl, alone and without options for an uncertain future.

"Am I interrupting?" came a loud voice, far away to carry for a good distance, but close enough to be easily understood.

From the direction to the south where Julia had earlier arrived, the shadowed form of Marius walked towards the siblings. Moving without hesitation, in the manner reserved for men who were accustomed to going wherever they must, he was halfway from the line of trees where he recently emerged.

Behind Marius, standing as just a dark blurb near the backdrop of gloomy woods, was Quintus. With his arms crossed and a scowl on his face, he alertly watched Marius pace towards the campfire.

Surprised, Tarquin did a double-take, for the moment unsure how he could have missed the arrival of Julia's long-term lover mere moments ago. For a man like Tarquin, who spent most of his life trying to move unnoticed in the forest, being surprised in this way was a robust compliment to Marius' scouting skills.

As he came closer to the fire, both Tarquin and Julia stood to greet Marius. Julia, who usually was ecstatic to see her erstwhile man, seemed reserved, while Tarquin struck a more diplomatic pose as Marius drew closer. Expectantly, each was nervous for their own reasons, and the quiet atmosphere could only be described as worrying for the surprised hosts.

Slowing his walk, Marius came into the light of fire with a bit of hesitation to his expression, like he wasn't happy with what he had to do next. Still, the firmness of his frown also made clear that he would do what he must, whatever the consequences. The life of a responsible leader meant performing the mission without fail, even when the mission was not of a military nature.

Stopping in front of the duo, who stood protectively close to one another, Marius kept his outward appearance cool and calm, but something else, almost a fierce expectation of conflict, coursed under the surface of his demeanor. Letting his hand fall to his scabbard, he thumbed the worn leather of his sword's scabbard with idle energy.

"Marius," said Tarquin, and finally breaking free from the tense moment, he jutted out his hand, "it's good to see you."

Without hesitation, Marius returned the gesture of greeting, grasping Tarquin's hand in a firm grip. His face locked in a calculated and almost officious manner as he spoke. "And you, Tarquin. It has been a long time since we last met. Too long, perhaps."

Silence took over the moment as each man jockeyed for a proper understanding of what was going on, with the awkward pause only interrupted by Julia moving to Marius' side, where she put her arm around his waist and faced her brother.

Speaking haltingly, Julia nevertheless sounded pleasant, even while the subject of her words was anything but enjoyable. "Tarquin says...the tribe is under attack from Ballomar's scouts...he also says that the tyrant gathers a large army to invade Roman territory."

Marius, unsurprised, nodded at the information. Sighing, he wetted his dry lips by puckering his mouth, then motioned down to Julia and into the darkness towards Quintus. "Julia, please wait for me over there. I wish to speak with your brother, privately."

Hesitating, Julia looked at Tarquin, who showed no worry about the request as he nodded agreement. Detaching herself from Marius, she stepped into the darkness, moving many yards away and out of easy earshot.

Leaning closer to Tarquin, Marius' words were firm and cold. "I'm disappointed you didn't come see me first, Tarquin. I'm your contact with Rome—and your only hope for safety from the Marcomanni."

Marius obviously expected a reply, but for the moment, none came. After another pause, he continued. "And your men are subject to my command. Entirely at my disposal for...Rome's interests and defense."

Still there was no response. After more silence, Marius sighed, then gestured to the darkness behind the tribal leader. "Let me be frank, Tarquin: I don't like you, or your people for that matter. You have all left your sister, whom I hold in very high esteem, to her own fate.

This is cowardly, by any estimation, and shows me your people are a collection of whelps who would throw away honor at a moment's notice."

"Marius, I—."

"And I suspect," continued Marius, talking over Tarquin, "that you're trying to avoid serving as auxiliaries for Rome in the upcoming invasion, which is…overtly, more cowardice. Unforgivable, really."

Tarquin stiffened at the accusation, particularly because of its truth. "We…will honor our commitments."

Marius nodded, but he didn't hide his skepticism. The disrespect inherent in such an accusation wasn't lost on either side of the conversation.

Stepping toward the crackling flames, Marius glanced down and then back towards Julia, who stood some distance away in the darkness, watching both of them attentively.

Dropping his contempt for Tarquin, Marius' voice suddenly changed to a matter-of-fact tone, revealing the military manner of one who now wanted to get things done. "There is something more going on with Ballomar, I fear. Something that is neither normal nor expected, even in matters of battle. I…need a favor of you, one that must be done promptly."

Surprised, Tarquin tilted his head. "What is it?"

"Send your scouts into the area directly north of the river and the village. There is a camp there—there must be a camp there—where children are being kept. Find it for me, soon. I must discover where these children are. Only then can we affect a rescue of them."

Leaning even closer, Marius' tone became sincere, and the cold professionalism in his bearing melted away. "Inform me of how well it is defended and gather any information you can. Something dreadful is happening, and I worry it is more than Ballomar alone we are confronting."

Tarquin focused his eyes on Marius, trying to figure out what the commander was talking about. Something in Marius' expression made Tarquin hesitate, as if there might indeed be something unusual to investigate with the kidnappings of children. As he thought through the logistics of the request, he considered where and how an enemy's camp might have been established so close to the village.

Nodding, Tarquin motioned to his sister that he was soon to depart and, quickly returning to the campfire, began packing his scant belongings. Momentarily, as he arranged his thoughts into what planning was required to seek out this new prospective adversary, his considerations for the present drifted away.

"And…Tarquin?" asked Marius, interrupting the woodsman's planning with an inflexible tone.

Looking up, Tarquin responded with a questioning stare. It was the stare of a man who didn't like this soldier or desire to interact with him in any way, but who still had to go through the motions of being compliant. At least for now.

Tarquin's silence, and the contemptuous frown he shared with the imposing Marius, were the only answers he was willing to offer for the moment. For several seconds they shared the icy bond of men who held little regard for one another—except for the kind woman they both so adored.

"When we next meet," said Marius, and with firm eyes, he finally made his closing point with the experienced Naristi leader, "see to it that you have your men with you—armed…and prepared to serve."

Chapter Fourteen

Tilting his head back, Ballomar drank deeply from the thick metal cup. Gasping for breath between each extended gulp, dark liquid leaked from the sides of the tankard, drenching his raggedy beard as he quaffed the last of the aromatic brew.

Lowering his somewhat malformed mug, Ballomar belched loudly, then smacked his lips in appreciation of the satisfying experience. Running a hand over his glistening mop of matted whiskers, his face glowed with appreciation of the moment, showing a man who never wavered from enhancing his mood with a bit of strong drink.

Around the extended clearing, daylight illuminated a wide, dusty camp positioned between thickets of dense trees. Close behind him was Ballomar's large personal tent, while farther away stood various huts with sewn goat-skin walls used by his bodyguards and personal advisers for quarters while on campaign.

Holding the cup out, Ballomar motioned to Alwin with an impatient jerk of his arm. Obediently, the servant approached and held up an empty wooden tray.

Farther to his right, a lonely campfire burned inside an arrangement of fire-singed rocks. In the middle of the circled stones, suspended on a spit over the flames, were the charred remains of some kind of large fowl, while nearby, several of Ballomar's personal guards gnawed on the remains of the unfortunate bird.

Peering around with dreamy eyes, Ballomar dropped his empty mug on the tray. With an effort to control his wavering mind, he spoke with an imprecise drawl, indicating the drink was having a dulling effect on his perceptions. "Get me another, but no more of our rancid piss. Break out the stuff we traded with the Gauls for. Now…they know how to brew spirits—good and proper!"

Nodding, Alwin scurried away, while Ballomar, after hacking up phlegm from a throat made hoarse by bellowing too often at his subordinates, pulled himself to his full height and plodded towards the campfire.

With a gruff push past his detachment of burly guards, Ballomar grabbed the bird carcass and tore the last wing off the overdone creature. Sinking his teeth into the smoky meat, he ripped off a large strip of flesh in one ravenous bite.

Eating with a frown, Ballomar wasn't happy with the flavor, but overcoming his distaste, he shrugged and continued his midday snack. With grease from the meal running over his bright-red lips, he chewed on the burnt meat, while also casting a disapproving glare at his men for their poor cooking skills.

Always wary of their king's tendency for disappointment, as well as occasional violence he wielded to express displeasure with his inferiors, the guards nodded at the unspoken criticism and avoided direct eye contact.

Pleased with himself, as Ballomar often felt the need to denigrate his most trusted soldiers, he then raised his eyes to his tent, and tossing aside the now-meatless wing, paced toward it. Moving with a jaunt in his step, his guards fell behind him in quick order, clearly relieved at not having to further explain their weak culinary abilities.

Pushing the large tent flap out of the way, Ballomar's features grew ecstatic as he stopped inside the threshold of his temporary residence. Panning his head around, his blurry eyes took in the cavernous inside and all its contents.

Oil lamps were posted on several shelves affixed to tent poles scattered around the high-ceilinged interior. Throughout the inside was an extensive collection of furniture, with dissimilar tables, desks, and chairs—all plundered from Roman settlements at some point in the past—arranged at several points among the open space.

Farthest away from the entrance was Ballomar's extravagant down bed, which was plenty large to hold several people at once. Inundated with several heavy furs and colorful blankets, two of his skinny concubines slumbered amongst the covers, currently unaware of his arrival.

Weapon racks to the left of the entrance held a variety of implements, most of them strange-looking. The spiked metal heads of mace-like instruments and bent blades on long, dagger-like handles looked similar to normal weapons, but due to their unmaintained condition and being covered with a dried, dark substance, the tools appeared more ominous than common types of weaponry.

Grunting contentedly, Ballomar moved to the nearest rack, and showing a triumphant grin, peered down at an extended form on a long table to its side. Garin, Tarquin's right-hand man and a scout of considerable repute within the Naristi tribe, was stretched out and pulled tight on the wooden tabletop.

Naked except for a loin cloth, heavy bindings held Garin fast and were knotted around his wrists and ankles. Such was the roughness of the constricting ropes that most of his skin was worn down to open sores under the knots, and the rest of his exposed body was crisscrossed in welts, obscene cuts, and various discolored bruises.

Garin's face was pummeled and abused, and while one of his eyes was completely swollen shut, the other was wide open and filled with unrestrained terror. A vague whine escaped his misshapen and cracked lips, sounding almost like a pathetic creature struggling to free itself from a common game trap.

Feeling energized, Ballomar leaned his face within inches of the miserable man. "I bet you wish you'd allied with us now, you inbred whelp. Now…tell me, where's your pitiful tribe? Have all your warriors hidden themselves from the real men of Germania?"

Only the sound of a guttural sob came in reply, and Garin's lone working eye, already exploring a new level of fear with each passing moment, shot around the area, as if seeking a savior who would free him from the wicked hell he found himself in.

From the end of the table, an ugly man, a torturer as evidenced by spurts of blood and other unrecognizable substances on his leather apron, stepped near to Ballomar. This man, fat and jowly with buggy eyes and a pockmarked face, also had the unique composition of having almost no muscle mass on his skinny arms.

Bringing himself near Ballomar, the awkward man whispered into his leader's ear, apparently not wanting the prisoner to eavesdrop on the conversation. "He revealed that already, King Ballomar. I already got from him the location of his people, as well as who is their contact with the Romans."

Impressed, Ballomar tilted his head at the news, staring at this vile-looking man with a measure of newfound respect. Speaking forcefully, he met the torturer's eyes. "Who is it?"

"A soldier named Marius. Apparently, he's a warrior of considerable reputation and has a history of…good relations with the tribes he has contact with."

Frowning, Ballomar didn't respond, not at all liking the sound of an opposing commander, however insignificant, who could fight effectively and also deal respectably with Germania's tribes.

Much of Ballomar's allure to his army, the reason they were allowing him to confront the vast empire south of them, was because of a generalized belief the Romans were cruel and unacceptable rulers of the varied clans. Having warred with the Latins for more than two centuries, it was not overly difficult to persuade his fellow tribes to go on the offensive against them.

Still, it could become a significant problem if Marius managed to convince some of the free-willed forest people that their interests could be better served by living under Roman governance, or worse, to coexist in relative peace, even if they weren't beholden to Rome's direct control. Ballomar's rampant brutality could only go so far to keep the tribes in line, and he really needed the outside irritant of a hated enemy to make his rule over Germania indisputable.

With a quick look around, Ballomar saw Alwin had arrived from retrieving another drink and pitcher, and motioning him over, snatched his now-full mug from the tray.

Raising the cup, he drained it in several protracted gulps. After finishing, he licked his lips and looked down into the empty mug, flashing an intrigued smile as he nodded. "That's much better. Next time we meet them for trade, we need to get more of this. Problem is, those Gaulish bastards are always so cheap. They want half our meat for a few barrels of the stuff."

The room grew quiet, with nobody, not Alwin, the torturer, nor his brawny guards taking the initiative to reply to Ballomar's feelings about trade with the far-western tribes of Gaul. Glaring at each of them, the Marcomanni leader scowled at the lack of interaction.

Suddenly growing interested in his cup, Ballomar lifted it to look at the base of the weathered tankard. Focusing on its underside, his eyes grew hazy, as if momentarily his mind had drifted to some other place.

With a sharp swing of his hand, he brought the sturdy vessel down on Garin's shocked face. With a CRACK, the bones of the restrained tribesman's jaw splintered, and a spray of blood erupted from the grotesque wound.

Raising the cup, Ballomar again swung it down, bringing all his weight and considerable strength to bear on the next blow. The resulting smash into his nose caved in much of Garin's upper face, and the man's pitiable gurgles resounded through the tent. More blood spouted from the horrific injury and was flung across the interior tent wall.

Again and again, Ballomar brought down his improvised weapon, each blow causing ever-more-horrible wounds to the gasping, floundering prisoner. The garbled screams of the man rose higher with the intensity of the strikes, like a demonic chorus of suffering had matched the hideous assaults on his helpless victim.

In time, after a dozen more impacts on the undefended Garin, his shrieks and pain died away. His arms ceased struggling against his bindings, and his body went limp under the incessant strikes of his looming assailant. Blood was cast everywhere, especially on Ballomar himself, soaking his beard in the doomed man's gore.

With two final crashes of the mug, which now caused only a mushy sound when they struck the man's shattered face, Ballomar finally ended the assault.

Not bothered in the least by his violent binge, Ballomar held up the cup to examine its shape, nodding with approval that it had managed to retain almost all its prior form. Such was his affection for this particular mug, as it had been in his possession for at least a decade, that he would have been heartbroken if it were permanently damaged from the impromptu killing. He was a man of nostalgia, after all.

Breathing hard, Ballomar had actually broken into a sweat due to the intense and rather odd execution of his hapless opponent. A wide grin broke out on his face, and with some excitement, he motioned down to Garin's still-bleeding corpse, which intermittently flopped in convulsive death throes. "That…was much harder than I thought. You never know how strong the skull is. It's…not a simple way to dispatch an enemy."

His men merely nodded at their king, faces somewhat pale but utterly emotionless under his inquisitive gaze. From the back of the tent, his now-awakened mistresses crouched behind the bed, staring in fearful disgust at what had just occurred.

Quiet now dominated the area, and except for the sounds of Ballomar's labored breathing, nobody seemed eager to break the silence.

Ignoring them all, Ballomar reached towards Alwin, nodding towards the pitcher of ale the servant had brought from his personal stock of goods. "Fill it up, again."

In response, and with remarkably stable hands, Alwin poured a stream of golden ale into the durable mug. Keeping his smile, Ballomar took another pull of the tasty liquid, his eyes and demeanor growing happier by the moment due to its invigorating taste.

As Ballomar stood and sipped his brew, a bit of the blood from the attack managed to drip from his whiskers to mingle with the refreshment in the cup. Obviously not bothered by it, perhaps even showing some pride from drinking his enemy's blood, the tent remained quiet while he peered smugly around at the gathering of his most trusted followers.

Carefully, each of his underlings made eye contact with one another, appearing as if they really didn't know what to think. They wisely weren't prepared to comment on what had just transpired, but their silence seemed to reveal some worry over the means and timing of Garin's ruthless murder. With Ballomar's impulsive temper, they could never really know when his next bout of violence would break out—and on whom it might be focused.

And, all the while, Ballomar continued his unrepentant smile, holding the appearance of a man who was completely in his element. A man who would soon move to conquer all that lay before him.

Chapter Fifteen

T he sun's glare made the village mayor Ceres squint in frustration. Peering up into the day's intense light, his puffy gray eyebrows, so full they seemed to sprout from his forehead into an overgrown nest, did not quite hide the disappointment in his dejected features.

"But, you indicated otherwise, Marius," exclaimed the mayor, and trying to shield his eyes with a flabby arm, his whine became unrestrained and rather pathetic. "You said you'd help keep them in line."

Marius, sitting on his horse, took a deep breath. Keeping a diplomatic posture, he let his eyes move to the surrounding area.

The village was rather busy in the late morning. People were trying to engage in normal business today, taking in the sunshine and trying to interact with their neighbors. Many of the town's residents, having been encouraged by Marius to leave their homes and meet those around them in a social setting, seemed to have actually listened to his advice.

That anybody really followed his suggestion offered a hope of sorts for their future, or at least for Marius to feel like he was doing some good with the village's communal prospects.

He was a military man first, but his feeling of responsibility for the civilians under his protection was very real, and that duty included encouraging the common people to try to have a somewhat normal life—not just to survive, but to actually live.

The town center was busy with people doing some simple shopping and otherwise acting like life was ordinary. Even a few children played in the streets, with shouts and shrill laughs filling out the background noise of neighing animals and loud haggling from the few merchants' stalls.

Lowering his gaze, Marius spoke in a tone that struggled to remain respectful. "It is you who is the civil authority, mayor. The villagers must abide by your wishes regarding the defense of...your town."

Letting his words draw out the mention of the mayor's town did not seem to make him self-conscious about not properly using his authority. Instead, the sweaty leader's expression grew more pronounced, with anxiousness causing his ruddy cheeks to grow even redder in the bright light. "But, they won't listen to me, commander. The blacksmith called me a 'greasy swine.' He also said I'm dumber than an 'inbred sheep.'"

Sitting on his own horse behind Marius, Quintus coughed, barely covering up an urge to laugh openly at the mayor. Glancing back, Marius' stern gaze focused on his sergeant, but when they met eyes, the moment merely became more humorous between them. Both soldiers, normally severe and stoic, barely contained the urge to cackle like young men at a comedic play.

It took some time, but their efforts to subdue the amusement tugging on their lips were eventually successful. Keeping their expressions guarded, each regained his professional composure.

At last, Marius sighed, and leaning down towards the rotund mayor, controlled the exasperation that had threatened to overcome his calm exterior. "As you will it, mayor. After our patrol, I shall see what I can do to accommodate their desires for more...food. But, for the near future, we shall have to continue with rationing. If the time should come when the people are starving, they would be sorry for indulging their appetites too much in the present."

Sitting back up, Marius lightened his tone, wishing to sound more charitable. "And...please don't antagonize any of the citizens...the situation is fraught enough. Simply tell them the rationing is necessary to maintain our food stocks—under my orders."

Taking a moment to absorb the advice, the mayor nodded, then smiled at the support he had just gained, however grudgingly it was offered. Waving a quick goodbye, the man turned and waddled away, mission accomplished.

Canting his horse to the side, Marius was relieved, having briefly avoided the conflict inherent in a remote village that was in a state of siege. Twisting around, his gaze met that of Vitus, one of his most able cavalrymen and messengers, who sat calmly on his horse, observing the town square and all its people.

Vitus seemed preoccupied, his eyes darting confusedly around, as if he were looking for something specific among the surrounding crowd. This surprised Marius, due to the man's normally solid commitment to the task at hand.

After Marius gestured towards the main gate, Vitus came to his senses, and acknowledging Marius' silent order with a nod, he kicked his horse to lead them on their daily patrol. Gingerly picking their way between stragglers in the narrow street, Vitus went first, followed by Quintus, and finally, Marius.

Riding slowly ahead, the armored riders proceeded through the lone opening out of the village, towards the settlement's surrounding ditch, which also only had a single exit over it—a wooden crossing bridge. Guarded by a movable gate that was currently set to the side, they filed outside the village's perimeter towards the hostile-looking wilds of the formerly peaceful countryside.

As they exited, two soldiers saluted from the side, while four other local men-at-arms, holding spears and looking tired, nodded respectfully. Feeling somewhat positive, Marius returned their nods with an optimistic smile.

However, as they moved to leave, Marius caught sight of Julia in the distance, as she and a group of other villagers, flanked by guards, carried bags of flour towards the gate from a soon-to-be-abandoned storage building located outside the village.

When Marius raised a hesitant hand to offer a greeting, she ignored his effort, keeping her eyes focused in front as her party paced quietly towards the entrance.

Ahead of him, Quintus noticed the failed interaction, and glancing back, shook his head at his commander's relationship troubles.

Frustrated, Marius grimaced at Julia ignoring him.

With their horses moving towards the tree line, the three legionnaires fell into the demeanors of warriors, their eyes searching each inch of the woods around them.

Prepared for an intensive patrol of the surrounding forest, Marius refocused and pushed away his personal distractions; he had lived a long time as a fighter in dangerous lands, and now it was necessary to filter out matters that detracted from his readiness for strategy and combat.

Behind them, Julia walked quietly towards the front gate, where she stubbornly avoided turning to watch them depart.

#

Unfortunately, after half an hour, Marius' worries about Julia and Lucien had returned to reoccupy his mind. Instead of carefully inspecting the surrounding undergrowth and watching for signs of trespass in the gloomy forest environment, his thoughts drifted again to the problems of his cherished woman and her son, as well as their precarious place in the evolving conflict with the tribes of Germania.

Quintus must have sensed Marius' inner difficulties, and as the group's horses clumped over loose rocks and clusters of plants on the narrow trail, he slowed his animal to fall back alongside him.

Panning his gaze to peer into thickets of the shadowed forest, which appeared quiet and lifeless in the faint sunlight of midday, Quintus spoke quietly from the side of his mouth. "Tell me, Marius…when am I to hear about what ails you…and Julia?"

Frowning, Marius stared straight ahead, his eyes focused on Vitus' back. "Do you ever have your own relations to discuss?"

Quintus chuckled, looking at Marius and raising an eyebrow. Patiently he waited for his longtime partner-in-arms to look at him. "Not really, commander. Women are usually too intelligent to entertain thoughts of relations with me."

With a deep breath, a brief grin crossed Marius' face. Finally gazing over, he spoke truthfully. "Julia is concerned I will flay her brother alive, as he will undoubtedly avoid the upcoming war."

Nodding, Quintus' voice retained a bit of humor. "Killing her brother will certainly dampen the air of romance. Will Tarquin and his men make a difference in the impending fight?"

"Not really. They really only have value to Rome as scouts, particularly once our own reinforcements arrive. Otherwise, the enemy will sweep them aside when they move into Pannonia. Their numbers are too few to make a significant difference."

With a grimace, Quintus pointed to the North, where the far-off Naristi tribe lay directly in the way of the incoming invasion. "Then…I propose you find a way to use them in that capacity, at least until Rome marshals its forces to meet the Marcomanni and its client tribes."

Assuming a humorless voice, Marius didn't sound enthusiastic. "If only it were that simple."

A wide grin broke out over Quintus' weathered face. "Make it simple, Marius. Life is best when it's simple. The path to misery is filled with wasting time on elaborate anxieties, and that has been the case in all times and places. An old classmate of mine, who now lives in Rome and tutors wealthy children in Oratory, once taught me that."

Shaking his head, a smirk replaced Marius' serious expression, for the moment melting away his frustration. "I am glad it is he who performs that job, Quintus. It is likely you would be without work if such an occupation were yours. You are a much better soldier than philosopher."

For several moments, the friends both held their smiles, each thinking over the matter of their duty, as well as the broader consequences the impending war would leave on their lives.

Marius realized their prospects were not good for long-term survival, no matter the course they were soon to take. Luck might play a part in their personal destinies, or it might be of no importance whatsoever. War often made the proficient fighter a dead man, while a man with few skills could soldier on for decades without injury. It was better to be good and experienced in battle, but that did not always secure the hoped-for outcome.

The point Marius understood best was that, like an inveterate gambler who waited for the best moment in a game of chance to make a large single bet, it was Marius alone who would have to decide when and where such a wager was to be made. And the lives of everyone, from loved ones to his own men, were the stakes in that critical bet.

Keeping his playful grin, Quintus kicked his horse into a trot. Riding past Vitus, who seemed surprised at his sudden surge past him, Quintus' bearing suddenly became quite intense, with his eyes sharp and his movements cautious.

Scanning the forest as he rode farther ahead, Quintus had returned to his capacity as a competent soldier over that of a wise advice-giver for his conflicted commander.

Marius watched him go, and with an appreciative nod, he understood for the hundredth time in their service together how fortunate he was to have Quintus in both roles.

#

The daytime was overcast, and only limited light streamed through the canopy of limbs shrouding the wagon trail. Mist, that ever-present aspect of mornings in this heavily forested region, churned gently over the path, offering little visibility beyond a few yards.

An occasional chatter of birds filled the woods, making the early day somewhat pleasant. In the distance, other sounds of a random scurrying animal or the energetic rustle of wind through trees helped to fill out the serene environment.

The wagon trundled ahead, its squeaky wheels moving ponderously slow as they mounted bumps in the dirt and bits of clumped grass on the faded trail. The pace of the Roman-made vehicle, held together with iron fittings and covered with a robust cloth cover, was tedious, almost like it was left to wander under the gentle urgings of the two scraggly horses pulling it. Controlling the wagon, the apathetic form of a single morose driver, sitting atop the splinter-filled riding bench, coaxed the animals forward.

Following the wagon were six men, all walking confidently as they scanned the forest around the slow-moving party. These individuals, bearded and with heavy swords, wore rugged armor and sour demeanors. Looking the part of tough warriors, they were unbothered as they plodded onward, walking smooth and undaunted through the peaceful forest. Being experienced tribesmen, they were the type raised to impose their will on all around them, and despite their cautious eyes, not a hint of worry filled their steely expressions.

Behind them, Ballomar also walked, glancing around the forest with distinctive nonchalance. His unique form of obnoxious indifference, forged through a lifetime of brutality and assertive dominance over those he interacted with, was displayed in each step of his slow saunter, such that even a passing forest animal might have wished to avoid meeting his intimidating gaze.

Another sound became evident as the group of men moved ahead. The crying of despairing children erupted from the unseen inside of the covered wagon, and the sorrowful whimpers were often heightened by a particularly rough bump of a wagon wheel over the uneven ground. Over several minutes, the emitted sounds were uneven, and the sobbing ebbed and flowed, making it seem at intervals like it was either packed full of frightened kids or entirely empty.

Rounding a gentle turn of the path, a wide clearing opened up ahead of the group. Here the fog was less solid, and the open area held sufficient space for the wagon to stop and its escort to arrange themselves close to it.

Near the middle of the clearing was a large campfire, its flames crackling under an enormous cauldron. Unattended, the bountiful container was filled with dark liquid, which bubbled loudly with the frequency of some long-simmering concoction.

The weirdness of a boiling vessel without a cook to oversee it was not lost on Ballomar, and the group of men spread out to surround the wagon, keeping their hands comfortably on the cold pommels of their swords as they peered into the calm forest.

Glancing around, the impatient Ballomar did not take long before raising his voice to a shout. "Witch? We're here. Show yourself and be quick about it. I've got no mood for your schemes today."

Some time passed before, as if on delayed command, Alia stepped from mist shrouding the distant part of the forest, from the area opposite where they had just arrived. Because the wagon trail had ended at the clearing, it appeared as if she emerged from a seemingly impassable location that was overgrown with bushes and tightly packed trees.

The stealth with which Alia emerged from the surrounding foliage surprised the guards, causing more than a few to exchange bewildered glances. Even Ballomar, never one to shower praise on others, nodded with admiration at her silent approach.

"King Ballomar," said Alia, disregarding her own impressive entrance. "Again, it's good to see you keep your promises."

Walking directly to the back of the wagon, Alia wrenched back the cart's cover. Exposed in the pale light were six huddled figures with hoods, and when she pulled back the cowl of one, a sickly boy was revealed. Alia took her time to look over the boy, touching the skin on his emaciated face as she evaluated the thin child's physical condition. The youth was in a silent stupor, seemingly unbothered as his empty gaze returned Alia's examining stare.

From a few of the others, however, sobs and frightened mewls emerged.

"I had the children dulled with some roots," said Ballomar, interrupting her inspection with clear apathy and pointing to the whimpering kids. "But apparently, some of the…herbs didn't work as promised. I think I'll have to lash our shaman."

Alia took a moment to finish her inspection of the child before dropping the hood back over his head. Turning her gaze to Ballomar, a hint of a smile crossed her face. "I'm sure keeping them quiet made bringing them to me easier, King Ballomar."

With that simple remark, Alia now let her eyes remain on Ballomar, in a way that few in Germania would dare. The grin that stayed on her face, focused and predatory, implied through its openness that there was something else on her mind waiting to be revealed. Ballomar noticed this, and not knowing what to say, frowned back before turning away.

"I …uhh…brought the men, witch, the ones you requested…the ones to protect your camp," Ballomar said, motioning to the hard warriors facing outward from the wagon. "They're some of my best…I'll rotate them out with the next shipment."

Alia's grin widened, and she spun to each of Ballomar's protectors, observing their massive height, broad shoulders, and calm bearings. They seemed less enamored with her, however, and returned her visual examination with open suspicion.

"That is appreciated, King Ballomar," replied Alia, and speaking carefully, her face flushed with an odd certainty. "I'm afraid for the moment…such considerations are necessary."

Walking a few steps towards the edge of the clearing, Alia gestured to Ballomar with a tilt of her head, indicating the need for privacy in their ongoing conversation. Annoyed, Ballomar glowered and followed her away from the others, where they could speak without risk of being overheard.

Huffing, the imposing Ballomar came close and peered down at the fragile woman. "What is it now, witch? What game are you playing?"

"No game. The Verisi are doing your work, as promised. They are a fierce ally—and capable. You are lucky to have them to implement your designs on your enemies."

Not getting her point, Ballomar tilted his head. "What more do you need? Spit it out, my patience grows thin."

Alia took some time to ruminate over her next words. Dealing with men such as Ballomar meant knowing when to be honest and direct, either of which could get her dead in short order. But, he was also a man of force and boldness, which usually meant he respected those who spoke up to achieve their own ends. That was, at least, if he allowed you to live until the process when you made your needs known.

Finally, she spoke, keeping her tone calculated and respectful. "King Ballomar, the Romans have a powerful empire. It matches the size of any other in history, from the Persians to the Egyptians. These Romans are proud and well-organized, with huge reserves of men and incalculable wealth. Destroying them won't be easy…sacrifices are required."

Nodding, Ballomar motioned to the wagon. "I'll continue with the young ones."

Chuckling with just a hint of nervousness, Alia crossed her arms and faced back toward the wagon. "Yes, but the 'young ones' as you say, are only needed to keep the Verisi from aging."

Turning back to Ballomar and peering up into his cold but expressive face, she spoke quieter. "For strength and power, they need something more. They need…strong and able men."

Trying to get her meaning, Ballomar glanced around, first looking at the wagon, then into the forest, then at his men. Confused, his mind wandered until…peering back at Alia, for the first occasion in an exceptionally long time, he was shocked.

"My men?" asked Ballomar, his tone incredulous. "You would have me offer my loyal soldiers for your purposes? Never! They commit themselves to me absolutely...."

Moving her hand up to his face, Alia took the chance to place her index finger to his lips, silencing him in a show of voluptuous female influence. Locking eyes with a man who could order the deaths of hundreds without a thought, she slowly shook her head.

"The Quadi are now in alliance with you, King Ballomar. You know this was no easy task to accomplish, correct? All of Germania has fallen in line with your plans. Whenever a problem has developed that could endanger your right to rule, the Verisi have dealt with it."

Pulling her hand back, Alia laced her fingers together in a show of humbleness and spoke lower still. "All great men MUST pay a price for their destiny. The higher the price, the greater the reward. You must know this the only way to obtain what you seek."

Turning towards the circle of his men surrounding the cart, a smile crossed her lips, revealing an expression that was contented and full of self-assurance. "Will you pay what is required to take your place in the family of great leaders, King Ballomar? Or will you return to the forest to...become a petty chieftain?"

Ballomar's stern face locked in thought. His mind, suspended between equal considerations of inner disgust and rampant lust for subjugation of his enemies, mulled over his personal options. While it was true the idea of sacrificing loyal soldiers to undoubtedly tortuous ends made him uncomfortable, not least of which because he knew these same men were so effective and unrelenting in battle, the notion of conquering much of the known world was a far more attractive idea.

In fact, to Ballomar, a man who lived for the thrill and pursuit of raw power, there wasn't much of a comparison when it came to deciding which path to follow. Looking down and to the side, he met Alia's gaze, and, although flashing her a distasteful scowl, he slowly nodded his agreement to…whatever was next to happen.

Alia's face beamed. Returning the nod, her smile grew wide, and moving methodically, she spun in a circle. Holding her hands up, she made a circular motion with her fingers, like she was invoking some arcane spell from one of the obscure temple cults that so plagued the Roman Empire.

Stopping, Alia waited with expectant eyes, but her movements had attracted the attention of Ballomar's guards, who looked her way and scrunched their faces in confusion. For some time nothing happened, with no apparent result forthcoming from the bizarre hand movements.

Suddenly, the fog surrounding the clearing began to swirl, growing denser as it seemed to creep closer to the wagon and its defenders. The effect was minimal at first, but over time, the thicker mist came first a few steps closer and then inched even nearer still, with encroaching swirls of its impenetrable depths appearing almost alive.

Next came the sound. The clicking, guttural chirp of something emanated from the fog. First it came from one direction, then it expanded to several locations, sounding as if there was an unearthly, indescribable language surrounding the party members.

Ballomar's men had lived long fighting lives by knowing danger and acting accordingly, and on this occasion the potential for an as-yet unseen threat was obvious and imminent. With a collective SCHIIK, they drew their weapons, and as each man moved to a defensive crouch, they also shuffled to cover one another's flanks. Acutely prepared, they waited with martial intensity for what came next.

Ballomar was intrigued by the development of something he'd never seen, and stepping closer, he moved to the side of Alia, who also had closed the distance to more easily witness the unfolding event.

Abruptly, a cascade of enemies charged from the gloomy mist. Grunting with those same odd clicking sounds, ten devilish figures surged forward, crossing the distance towards the tribesmen in mere seconds, lunging ahead without fear or reservation.

And the incoming adversaries were not human, running in looping movements on bulbous frames as they burst toward the shocked warriors. Their large heads were grotesque, having no discernible features or identifiable outlines beyond their odd, long-toothed mouths and circular black eyes. Rags of some kind of robes covered much of their bodies, but underneath the clothing, the flesh appeared to flow and reform as they reached out to engage the warriors.

On the tips of hands they extended were elongated claws, viciously sharp and blindingly fast as they snapped and clacked together. The men they faced were professionals and fast in their own right, but they barely managed to slash out before being overwhelmed in the rush.

As quickly as they'd come, the blindingly fast digits flashed under the guard of the warriors, and in moments the creatures ripped through their leather armor, eviscerating and swarming over them. In only the briefest of time, the rush of monsters held most of the frantically struggling combatants down, and the meadow was quickly alive with the despondent shrieks of tortured men who knew their end must be near.

Except there was one who had survived the initial onslaught. Malorix, a beefy and skilled fighter, struck out with lethal slashes, fighting off the initial attack and wounding two of the beasts with long cuts into their pasty arms as he backed towards Ballomar.

Glancing behind, he yelled at his leader. "Ballomar, retreat towards the forest. I'll cover your escape. Go, now."

Ballomar merely stared at Malorix's back in response. Impressed with his man's gumption and skill, as well as his intention to save his king, Ballomar focused on the creatures that now encircled him. With the attention of a warped child who avidly watched ants battle in some existential fight for their nest, the detached leader was intrigued to see how the ongoing struggle would develop.

Looking back again, Malorix didn't take long to notice the betrayal of the Marcomanni king. While being surrounded by his circling foes, he screamed back to Ballomar. "Ballomar, what have you done? You evil dog."

As creatures closed in on his untenable defense, Malorix quickly decided to go out with a fight, and with an adept surge, he rammed his long blade into the exposed chest of one of his vile opponents. The inflicted wound was immediate and severe, causing brackish blood to pour out over the warrior's arms from the hideous, impaling gash, but in seconds, the brave fighter was swamped by his other enemies.

Over the next minutes the savage creatures took their time to properly harvest the men they had incapacitated. Inserting their claws into the necks and arteries of the warriors, they drained them alive, and the screams of their traumatic deaths lasted longer than Ballomar would have thought possible for such a peculiar manner of death.

Finally, the corpses of Ballomar's men, representing some of the best he had known in his time as reigning leader of the Marcomanni, were sucked dry, with the husks of their bodies now shriveled and black. After they had been mined of all fluids and transformed into hollow shells of their former selves, the remains of each were stripped out of their clothing and thrown into the huge cauldron over the still-burning fire. With sickening finality, each of their now-lighter bodies floated briefly in the bubbling stew before sinking into the gooey broth.

Thereafter, breathing with a contented smile, Alia slowly took the children one-by-one, leading them into the foggy forest and out of view of Ballomar. After they all had been escorted away, she reemerged from the woods and boldly smiled at the forest king. Waving carefully, she turned and calmly disappeared into the now-milder mist hanging at the edge of the clearing.

The accompanying Verisi, having fed and drunk enough to satisfy their strange biologies, also disappeared into the surrounding forest. Their huge frames, nightmarish and covered in a sheen of sickly fluid over their whitish bodies, receded into the gloom of the surrounding woods. Strangely though, these bizarre beasts had never sought to communicate with

Ballomar, almost as if they didn't care about his presence in the least.

Left with his now-empty wagon and driver, a man who now looked ready to die of fright, Ballomar had much to think about going forward. The face and intentions of his fiendish allies had been exposed, and, as with all things Ballomar did, this meant he would have to think deeply about the role of the witch and Verisi in his future empire.

Peering at the frightened driver, Ballomar felt no respect for the man. Not only was his fear open and pathetic, something inexcusable for any warrior of his tribe, but the driver had also done nothing to help his comrades in the fight, which solidified him as an abject coward. Few things made Ballomar sicker than to witness weakness of courage in a man, and with a shake of his head, he raised a nostril in revulsion.

In fact, Ballomar considered for a moment that he should just feed the man to the Verisi, even though the monsters apparently didn't want him. Ballomar's trip to see the witch and her abominable allies had been mostly secret, meaning losing another man such as this shivering wretch would have caused no problem, especially in a time of impending war.

Also, as a matter of pragmatism, the terrified man would still need to die; nobody from the Marcomanni could ever know about the bargain Ballomar had just struck with Alia, and as he knew quite well, corpses never told any tales.

Anyway, Ballomar would just have the man garroted when he returned to camp. Otherwise, he'd have to drive the wagon alone, which was obviously a monotonous task far beneath his station.

Smiling falsely, Ballomar motioned for the man to get the wagon going, and as the nervous operator snapped the reins to get the horses on their way, the lumbering leader casually climbed up next to him on the driver's bench.

#

With a scowl, Quintus stood to his full height. Putting his hands on his hips, he breathed deeply, fighting off a wave of disgust creeping up his throat.

For a moment, he peered up at the blue sky, taking in the calming sunlight and fresher air to offset the queasy feeling in his gut. Not a man to easily be made ill, he took a moment to contain the nausea gnawing at his insides.

The hunk of tissue lying in the muddy grass below him was wet and chunky, appearing like an extended slug, one that was thick and striated with an uneven hue of white and gray. The sun illuminated its uneven ridges in the full light, and except for having a non-scaly exterior, the slab of flesh looked almost like the partially molted skin of a robust snake.

After collecting himself, Quintus deftly unsheathed a sharp dagger, then bent over and poked at the glistening, fleshy glob. The stench from the detritus made his nostrils flare, and he had to hold his head back as he probed its vile outline with the point of his weapon.

Precisely as he had done with the hacked-off hand when Appius and his children disappeared, Quintus plunged the blade into the dense flesh and raised it for Marius to inspect. Holding it high, he turned it slowly, almost like it was a skewered animal being rotated for cooking, which revealed maggots and other crawling bugs throughout the inside of the putrid meat.

Marius sat transfixed on his horse, then leaned down to get a closer look. As if watching a horrific gladiator fight that he couldn't pry his eyes from, his gaze was now absorbed with the intriguing mass of tissue. It was certainly revolting, but the consistency and color of the flesh was like nothing he had seen before.

Inside the cloudy, fibrous meat, where veins would have been seen in something decaying normally, there were instead whitish swirls of a long, spirally composition. The spindly strands seemed to crawl on their own accord within the opaque flesh.

The tissue itself, though obviously dead, seemed to have a self-radiating quality to it, almost like it had its own illumination. With such a biological structure, it wasn't simple to discern from what animal it could have come—or even if it were from a normal animal at all.

Around Quintus and Marius was the extended shore of the wide Danube River. The water of the enormous waterway, which was full of eddies and deep swells within its dark-green depths, flowed to within a few feet of their current location. The sloshing of gentle waves against the pebble-filled beach provided a relaxing undertone to their exposed location on the open shoreline.

Atop a hill on their side of the river, not far from where they now stood, Vitus was perched on his horse, where he provided overwatch and possible forewarning from any possible enemies nearby. Gazing down at Marius and Quintus, he didn't appear interested in the item they were examining.

"What could this mean?" asked Quintus, still holding his face away from the bizarre flesh.

Marius didn't answer right away, instead moving his gaze up the shoreline, where the tracks of several men were still relatively fresh in the drying mud. Next to the tracks, near a shallow area that could provide a place for a small boat to beach, was the outline in the soft sand of what must have been a small craft in the recent past.

That someone had landed at this location was obvious, and more importantly, that they apparently had not bothered to cover up their presence—or had been too busy to try—was worth thinking about.

"They made landing here, that much is clear," said Marius, his eyes moving over the area, examining the specific imprints in the wet earth. Interestingly, it appeared some of the feet that made the tracks were from bare feet, which was an unusual way for Marcomanni scouts to travel. "It is an easy place to complete their crossing, and it offers a direct hike to the village from here."

Lowering the stabbed meat to his side, Quintus nodded his agreement and walked over to the footmarks in the moist soil. "Agreed. There's also an easy escape back across the river once a raid is completed. It's an ideal approach."

Bending down while still holding his macabre prize, Quintus ran his left hand over the tracks, then raised his fingers to examine the consistency of the dirt. "And it looks to be no more than a few of them, so they are not yet scouting in force. They must be limited in their numbers due to traversing Naristi territory to get here."

Marius pinched his lips into a tight frown, absorbing the information with a slight nod. Raising himself in his saddle, he peered around the calm area, scouring the nearby brush and grass for anything they might not have seen.

With nothing important having been missed, Marius raised his hand, motioning for Vitus to make his way back down to them. Acknowledging him with his own wave, Vitus nudged his horse and began picking his way through the short trees and brush toward the shoreline.

"Then…what next?" asked Quintus, sounding indecisive.

Glancing across the river, Marius scowled. Not one to accept what fate gave them when it came to warfare, his mind raced to find proactive actions to take in the face of the inevitable invasion coming their way.

After watching the opposite tree line, Marius gazed back toward Quintus. Nodding, he quickly searched through his personal supplies, and finding what he wanted, extended a cloth bag in his hand.

Quintus obliged Marius by dropping the fleshy remnant into the bag. Wrapping the sack's end over itself and tucking it away, Quintus gazed back up, waiting for the new order he knew was coming.

"I think we must change the rules of this game," said Marius, and after a slight hesitation, he gestured back toward their not-far-off village. "Get five of your best fighters together when we arrive back and be sure they get plenty of rest tonight. Soon we will go out to hunt these invaders…except now, it is our enemies who will know fear."

Chapter Sixteen

The night sky roiled, and only partial light seeped through the atmosphere to illuminate the dim valley meadow below. Radiant clouds, which gradually moved across the sky to reveal the moon and stars in brief glimpses, offered an intermittent glow across the open clearing, creating a forbidding backdrop of dull visibility in the darkness.

In this meadow was a collection of large tents, forty in number. The tents were the communal kind, expansive and made to shelter many residents at once. In the middle of the large clearing, their clustered location made their number appear as sort of a village, and open space surrounded the tents for more than a hundred yards in every direction.

Throughout the camp were large cauldrons, which were set above vigorous fires at varied intervals amongst the tents. The flames under the pots were consistent as they burned on stacked wooden fuel, providing constant heat for whatever boiled inside.

Guards, burly and with heavy swords and daggers on their belts, stood all around the camp. Mostly peering outward, these men wore severe expressions on their fully awake faces, ready for any assault or prospective interloper into the camp's activities.

Walking from the forest to the north, where the woods descended from a dark ridgeline of thick tree cover, a small figure detached itself from the gloomy background of heavy undergrowth. Padding ahead with determined steps, the form, dressed in a woolen cloak and hood that fully covered the person within, angled toward one of the guards.

Not slowing, the delicate figure nodded at the sentry, then proceeded at a hurried pace toward the interior of the encampment. Stepping around stacked supplies, wagons, and directly near several guard dogs, it moved close to the center tent, which was the largest and had yet more guards to the side of its entrance.

Pulling her hood back, Alia exposed herself in the faint light of nearby poles holding burning torches. Her pale face stood out in the fire's flames, seeming to glow as she leaned down to look into the large pot in front of her. Appearing curious, her jaw was firm and uncompromising, but under her tough appearance, some anxiety lurked in her expression.

Emerging behind her, as if her arrival had been announced in advance, a large form walked toward the fire. Stopping near her, the man, who was twice her size and appeared to hover due to his bulky outline, pulled back his own hood to show his face.

Magnir was a strange-looking...person...and he smiled down at Alia with a leering countenance. His face was truly odd, for there were no definable ridges on his milky-white skin, and his jaw and cheeks held no whiskers. In fact, his head held no hair at all, and even at the point of what should have been eyebrows, there was no blemish or facsimile of markings. Unlike nearly all the forest tribes, there were no tattoos to indicate his allegiance to a specific clan or to denote his ferocity in battle.

His eyes, entirely black and with an intrusive, predatory quality, peered eagerly toward Alia. When he spoke, his voice was raspy and whispering, and it was difficult to decipher the words, or even the gender, from the gravelly throat that spawned them. "What news do you bring, Alia?"

Not quite meeting his gaze, Alia replied quickly. "Ballomar continues to supply food for your...tribe. As I mentioned before, he has been quite accommodating."

"That's good, little Alia. We expose ourselves here...our efforts require much exertion. In turn, we require...extensive sustenance."

Alia nodded, a hint of worry pulling on her expression. "I understand, Magnir. More will be sent here soon. It has been promised and will be fulfilled— just as before."

With no immediate reply, Magnir ogled his thin guest. For some time, he peered at her, his thoughts and intentions hidden behind his utterly bizarre face. The leering from Magnir seemed to reach into her soul, and for the moment, Alia could not quite shake the feeling she was being evaluated as the principal dish in some extravagant meal.

Moving slowly, Magnir produced a bowl from his cavernous robe. Reaching to the cauldron, he used a wooden implement to ladle a large helping of steamy black goo into his container.

Standing in place, he began shoveling the concoction into his mouth, using his fingers and taking slurping bites as he gulped the hideous-smelling stew past his black teeth. The heat of the steaming contents did not seem to bother him, and it took little time to finish his meal. Leaning back, his dark eyes closed, and as if in ecstasy, he swallowed the remainder of the foul broth, licking his lips with his long, dark-red tongue.

When he lowered the bowl, Alia gazed over at him, seeing the container for what it was: a skull, sawed in half to approximate the functionality of a normal eating dish. From its small size, it had obviously been fashioned from the head of a child.

Tucking the bowl into his dark robe, Magnir sounded contented, even as his scratchy, otherworldly voice remained distant and unfathomable. "Excellent, little Alia. See to it that more are sent, and soon. We are always in need of the young ones, and with this venture, our hunger grows."

With that, the leader of the Verisi spun to return to his tent. Leaving without a goodbye, he didn't appear aware of Alia's presence, much less whether or not she was deserving of a respectful farewell.

Left to her own thoughts, Alia turned back to the pot, where she gazed into its interior with more than a bit of unease. Her plans were going roughly as expected, but it was also rather clear they involved substantial danger to her personally.

Alia was a ruthless and indiscriminate killer in her own right, but living amongst other wolves on a continual basis could well increase the odds of she herself being eaten by them. For the foreseeable future, she had to be cautious, and that was putting it mildly.

Contemplating her next moves and their attendant risks, her eyes adopted the far-away look of a person who had to plan each of her next actions carefully.

As Alia considered Ballomar, his goals, and her desire to be his controlling adviser, where she would be out of public view but with the power to control him, she was beginning to realize it might be too lofty a goal. Parsing her thoughts, she understood she might need to reconsider her place in the upcoming war. She easily grasped she was evil, whatever that word meant, but she was also not stupid, and certainly not suicidal.

Alia's life was full of danger, but like a child who had ventured too deep into the river to swim, with toes that could no longer touch the riverbed, she had the unsettling feeling her choices in controlling her own destiny might soon slip away.

Meanwhile, from the side, from a place merely thirty yards away, which was underneath a wagon and buried within supplies of wood and musty clothing, a prone figure intently watched her.

With his face smeared in a dark paste and eyes that remained half-closed to shroud his otherwise white-eyed stare, Tarquin watched and waited. Having seen everything and yet not knowing precisely what it meant to him, his sister, and his people, he breathed very quietly, not daring to make the slightest revealing movement.

And he stayed that way, keeping his bearing and controlling his muscles, making certain to avoid anything that would invite discovery and immediate death.

Chapter Seventeen

A meandering wagon rolled along the uneven road, its wheels creaking under the weight of a heavy load. The ponderous vehicle, laden with trade goods and clumping over rocks and ruts on the wagon trail, kept slow but steady progress across the open countryside.

Two haggard horses pulled the wagon, and around them, the day was bright and peaceful. In the distance, the sound of several birds, chirping as if in a competition for the loudest possible screech, accompanied the progress of the solitary cart across the dusty wagon trail.

With a huff, the driver called the horses to a stop with a "hey, hey." The animals, seemingly unbothered by the yank of their reins, stopped cold in place, and dropping their heads, looked for something tasty to nibble in the clumpy grass below.

Florin dropped to the ground with a grunt, his open-toed leather boots kicking up powdery dirt from the worn path. Deep into middle age, the nearly bald man had a temperament of a grouchy vendor, as well as a matching gut that evidenced modest success from his profession as a merchant.

He had been dragging marketable goods from one end of the province to the other for the better part of four decades, and although rumors had recently been warning of trouble stirring to the north, he was not one to miss out on profit merely due to a potential war. Reduced competition from fellow merchants during difficult times was always beneficial for those willing to seize an opportunity.

From a lifetime of looking for differences in supply and demand, Florin knew that making coin and padding his encroaching retirement meant taking chances when others were too fearful to assert themselves.

Still, he could also never be too careful, and with a prideful pat on his belt, Florin briefly massaged the hilt on his Persian dagger, a long and polished blade he had acquired many years ago. The exceedingly long knife, sharp enough to easily pierce all the way through a man's innards, had been a gift from his long-dead stepfather, who had always encouraged Florin to travel safely with a weapon. Fortunately, he had never had the need to use it, but the metallic bulge against his ample frame was nevertheless comforting.

Peering around, Florin scanned the area around the trail, first searching the tree line to his left, then the untended stocks of wheat that swayed under a gentle breeze in a field to his right. For several minutes he stood there, listening to the cries of distant birds and evaluating the peaceful environment.

Scowling, he lumbered to the rear of the wagon, and after untying a leather tarp that covered the back, looked carefully inside.

Arranged neatly within his humble cart were the chosen goods for this trip, which also; fancy dinnerware, made of metal and ceramic and recently imported from Rome itself; several large containers of wine, which had been produced in some of the best wineries on the eastern side of the Roman peninsula and were known for their smooth drinking qualities; and an assortment of toys imported from beyond the Mediterranean Sea, from a prosperous city on the African coast named Hippo Regius.

In the case of the children's items, Florin had kept the secret for most of his adult life that parents in these provincially remote areas always overpaid for dolls and toy enemies of the empire, so he found these to be his most profitable items to hawk.

Having never seen an elephant from Carthage or a chariot from the ancient Egyptians, the small hand-carved figurines, undoubtedly crafted by skilled slaves in that far-off region of Hippo, were even a prize for some of the local parents to acquire. And such a prize often meant a five hundred percent markup from the markets where Florin had acquired the items in the provincial capital of Aquincum.

Unfortunately, Florin's grin from the notion of profit disappeared when his gaze fell on another area in the back of the cart, where a dirty cloth was draped over a still figure on the wooden planks. The unmoving form of the strange body under a tawdry linen caused his heart to skip, not in mourning for the unknown dead man, but instead because Florin chose, against all common sense, to haul the corpse to the village to be investigated by the soldiers stationed there.

Frowning, Florin pulled his eyes away from the body. He had known death intimately throughout his life, but what lay under that covering was not something he was familiar with—or would want to know more about in the future. He was not a man of religions, but what he had seen provoked a sense of intense dread in his normally hard heart.

With a deep sigh, Florin shook his head at the waste of it all, and retying the tarp on the cart's top, he considered what effect the body would have on his near future. Whatever the local soldiers in the village thought about his deathly delivery, they surely wouldn't blame an old trader like himself for finding it. Maybe they'd even offer him a small reward for his discovery.

Growing more certain of himself, Florin then moved slowly around the wagon, checking the solid wooden wheels to be certain they were functional for continued travel. As a man who made his living by this conveyance, he could never be too certain about its proper maintenance. Preparation and profit always went hand in hand.

Happy with what he saw, he moved back to the front of the wagon, and patting one of his horses on its weathered coat, he looked at the horizon.

In the distance, the village of Avenio stood there, only a couple of hours away at his current pace, lying in a productive green valley. Smoke rose from the settlement, telling Florin that food and drink, and perhaps an attractive village wench, would be there to greet his arrival.

Taking a calming breath, Florin worked on finding his good mood again. It took some time, but after mentally going over the list of items he'd brought with him—minus the corpse, of course—he was finally able to put aside the unpleasant experience of the trip up to this point.

With that, a genuine smile broke out on his plump, wrinkly face, and the prospect of the village's soon-to-be customers buying his entire stock of goods changed his attitude considerably.

#

Cyprian and Antonius, two of Quintus' more capable soldiers, carefully moved into the entrance of the village's main storehouse. Stepping through the narrow doorway with full armor and bulky red cloaks, they scraped the sides as they pushed inside. Stooping low, they carried a wrapped body on a soiled blanket used as a stretcher.

Once inside, they glanced expectantly up. Making eye contact with Quintus, they nodded when he motioned for them to set their delivery to the back of the room, among several other shadowy items already laid on the hard-tiled floor of the storage area.

Built with thick walls and small windows, the storehouse was designed to keep foodstuffs for an extended time. But the single-room building wasn't constructed for material comfort, as its inner space was cluttered and difficult to move around in when too many people were present.

Stepping awkwardly away, the soldiers bumped into each other as they focused on the body, not quite understanding what they had brought with them. Uncertain of themselves, they gazed over and acknowledged Quintus and Marius, who stood on the far side of the room and returned their stares with serious expressions.

Quintus held a burning torch in his hand, while Marius nodded his thanks and moved his head to indicate the men should leave the building. Relieved, the soldiers hurried outside, not looking back as they rushed into the bright sunlight.

After they departed, Quintus crept close to the delivered remains, using his sandaled foot to move aside the blanket it was wrapped inside. Leaning down, he held out the torch to reveal the precise condition of the body.

As before, after the earlier village intruder had killed two parents and abducted the young girl, this body was dark and emaciated, having lost much of its bulk due to some undetermined process. Appropriately, this newest corpse was now arranged next to the dark, still forms of the dead husband and wife, who had been stored here after the prior unsolved attack.

The blackness and reduced weight of the new corpse appeared even more ominous under the spotty light of the torch, and moving the flame to the side, Quintus also illuminated the other bodies stretched out next to it. Now numbering three, the collected remains were of exactly the same composition, staring upward with empty black eye sockets and wide, shriveled-lipped mouths.

Next to the three bodies, laying on a tattered white cloth, was that disgusting bit of flesh that Quintus and Marius had found the day before next to the river, while along the nearby wall were stacked bags of stored grain and crates of various supplies set aside for future use by the village's inhabitants.

Looking over, Marius frowned and spoke in a low tone, acting as if the bodies might be disturbed by too loud a noise. "Can you determine who it is?"

Using the torchlight to reveal the new corpse's tall stature, even if the mass of its flesh had somehow been reduced, Quintus spoke in a careful manner. "Just another victim of…something, precisely like the others. Where was it discovered?"

Chewing on his lip, Marius shrugged. "Florin indicated the body was retrieved about ten miles toward Salvio, before the fork to Aquincum. He discovered it while relieving himself behind a tree. It had been hidden there to mask the killing, as it was hastily covered with some branches and pine needles."

Quintus chuckled, then squatted down to further examine the corpse. Hovering over the body, he inspected its dark-black features, reaching down to run his fingers over the taut, cold skin of the face. "I'm at a loss how such a condition happens with a dead body, Marius. It's impossible to determine its identity, or when the death occurred. As for that...."

Quintus pointed to the hunk of flesh next to him, which buzzed with flies. Shaking his head, he let his bafflement with the whole scene go unspoken for the moment.

Stepping nearer to the remains, Marius leaned closer, his eyes moving curiously over the dark, indecipherable flesh. "More than a decade ago, when I served as liaison to the Third Italica Legion in Carnuntum, I met...an old legionnaire who was a veteran of the campaigns in Egypt."

Crouching near Quintus, Marius met his subordinate's gaze, and moderating his breathing, his voice took on the quality of a wise teacher. When he spoke like this, he knew it irritated Quintus, which was exactly why he did it. "He told me how the Egyptians often treated their dead, at least the bodies of their ruling class. Apparently, the corpses were treated with salves and had their brains and other organs removed in a process called 'mummification.' Performed by priests of their religion, he told me their dead appeared similar to what is here. Some of the mummified corpses were thousands of years old yet may have appeared precisely as we see these citizens."

Waving off the information, Quintus shook his head. Sounding amused, he raised a disbelieving eyebrow. "So…we have dead Egyptians…in Pannonia?"

Chuckling, Marius peered skeptically down at the shrunken corpse. "No, but because we have a similar result, we at least know something like this has happened before—and over a long period."

"But these bodies are recently dead. What can both kill and preserve a cadaver in this manner? And make the corpse lose half its weight so soon after death?"

Standing back up, Marius considered the questions. Walking over to the small window, which looked out over a simple yard with chickens strutting about, he sorted through his memories, looking for some prior experience that might offer a reasonable answer for the means of death they now witnessed.

Finding none, he glanced back at Quintus, who continued his visual examination of the bodies. Marius' tone grew contemplative, but it wasn't overly hopeful. "I'm unsure of the particulars, Quintus. But tonight we…can perhaps get some indication of what is happening to this village. I fear our survival may depend on us finding an explanation soon."

Chapter Eighteen

The deep night was illuminated under the full glow of the clear, radiant sky. The soft visibility of the moon was supported by a vast arrangement of glowing stars, which combined to make the area within the wooded location visible over a substantial range of sight.

Quintus and Marius crouched behind a collection of heavy bushes, peering over a trail that originated from the Danube River, whose gentle sloshing waves could just be heard in the distance.

The forest path in front of them, flanked by shrubbery and intermittent piles of leaves, was deserted. Chirps of crickets occasionally reverberated in the night, but otherwise, the area offered little other noise to break the monotony of restrained calm within patches of thick vegetation and nearby grassy fields.

The trail that ran near their hiding place was almost visible all the way to its origin in the dim stands of trees near the river. A slight fog rolled over that distant wooded area, just preventing easy visibility into the dark foliage's dim interior.

Motioning to the thick cover of trees and bushes on the other side of the path, Marius whispered pointedly to Quintus. "Don't let them accept battle alone. Ensure you are with them when the moment comes.

Peering back at Marius, Quintus squinted curiously, as if to say, *how could it be otherwise?* His eyes were wholly unafraid, and his bearing was intense, almost eager, for whatever was coming next.

Some minutes passed, and no other sound or movement was evident in the gloom of night. Even the crickets seemed to have lost their affinity for song, and a dull silence permeated the otherwise mellow undergrowth. Only the occasional buzz of a mosquito made the moment come alive, forcing an annoyed Marius to swat them away with distracted swipes of his hand.

After more time dragged by, from the distant and foggy tree line came the slight crunch of a weighty foot pressing down on gravel. Quintus had earlier spread several handfuls of noisy rocks in that location for just this purpose, but for several moments, nothing more followed the faint noise.

Finally, the dark outlines of the woods gave up the silhouettes of one, two, and then a third and fourth figures. The four scouts, who were lanky, well-armored and warily gripping weapons in their hands, emerged cautiously from the background of dense brush and clustered trees. Spreading out, they kept a supportive distance between each other as they gently picked their way up the trail. Moving carefully and creeping ahead with practiced, fluid steps, their skills at silent movement were clearly in tune with the environment.

"Whore of Orcus," muttered Marius, keeping his tone low, even as the stark disappointment in his words was palpable. "They are professionals. I was hoping for some of their weaker warriors. Go…over and get the men ready. Wait until they've rounded the curve and take them by surprise. I'll prevent any withdrawal from behind. Remember: not even one can escape. We shall end them completely."

Without waiting, Quintus rushed silently over the trail to their south, where he couldn't be seen from the sight direction of the approaching enemy. Disappearing into the opposite undergrowth, he made no sound and was soon lost from view.

Readying himself, Marius took a deep, calming breath. Letting his mind become relaxed, he put all his focus into the present—where everything mattered. The clash of arms and the intention to inflict death was now his only goal, because to do otherwise would mean hesitation when the time came to kill his foe. Indecision meant death, and his men were far too important to risk if he ignored that simple fact.

With battle soon to be joined, victory was usually with those who were skilled and had a rehearsed plan for the engagement. Gritting his teeth, Marius hoped these facets of their training would be enough to ensure his soldiers would vanquish the approaching Marcomanni invaders.

#

Nighttime visibility was also open for a lengthy distance around the perimeter of the village. Torches burned at several points along the wall, while inside, along both the stone streets and near the open market on the main square, numerous fires provided further lighting.

In the singular entrance to the settlement, where Marius' main preparation was expended to ensure the safety of the town's inhabitants, the environment appeared too calm. Torches lit up the arch that provided access to the interior town, and even in the middle of the night, it was not difficult to see into and out of the village's gate.

Yet currently nobody was watching the lone entry-point into the town's sleepy interior. The barricade-like fence, solid and fitted with iron spikes and metal bars to ground it in place, had recently blocked off access to the village. But now it was moved out of place, allowing for easy admittance, while torchlight in the surrounding area showed neither soldiers of the legion nor the huddled outlines of the town's watchmen were there to guard it.

Instead, behind some stacked crates, which were set at the front to provide ample protection for the village's defenders against potential invaders, two bodies of uniformed legionnaires lay crumpled on the ground. Seemingly caught by surprise, their shocked hands were still caught in death grips on their spear shafts, while gaping sword wounds, inflicted by stabbing attacks into the backs of their necks, made clear the ruthless cause of their sudden demise.

Elsewhere, farther from the main entrance and near a large campfire, the corpses of three other town guards lay sprawled in distended poses. These older townsfolk-sentries, spread out and caught unaware, were collapsed around the staging area of the town's main communal point for defense. With the shocked expressions of people who were unready for their own deaths, they lay awkwardly hunched at odd angles.

But near the water well for the main square, not far from where the stalls were recently manned by a few of the village's remaining merchants, one man was still alive. This fighter, Antonius, that robust soldier who had so recently carried the cadaver of the unknown corpse into the storeroom, lay on his stomach.

Gurgling and spitting up his own blood, Antonius struggled to overcome the grievous wound that had pierced into his back and through the organs of his upper body. Over several minutes, Antonius gasped and struggled to draw air into his wrecked lungs, vainly trying to extend his last few moments of life. Unable to move his legs, he hitched as he tried scooting forward, his fingers convulsing as he grasped at nothing on the cold stones beneath his hands.

All the while, unseen shadows passed quickly by him, moving farther into the town, towards the homes of so many innocent sleeping civilians. And as the dying man finally expired, his gaze was the last living witness to their invasive presence in the village.

#

Peering with determined gazes, Quintus and his men stepped boldly from the tree line. In rigid order and with firm grips on their spears, they advanced down the partially rocky incline towards the four Marcomanni scouts on the trail below.

Moving at a brisk pace and clutching their shields at proper defensive angles, the men's bearing was solemn, but their intense eyes and the persistent shuffle of armor in their practiced march revealed a deliberate willingness to fight. To a man, each was prepared for what came next, even if some degree of worry was mixed in with their stern expressions.

Their move to attack did not go unnoticed. Spinning to their right, three of the scouts faced the legionaries, and the disciplined tribesmen, hunched under leather armor and brandishing their weapons, quickly evaluated the incoming threat.

To their back, their leader, a fierce-eyed and tall warrior, spun to face the forest behind him, as if anticipating Marius' presence amongst the dark brush.

"Ambush," grunted the scout leader, speaking over his shoulder and raising his voice into a firm, controlled shout. "Retreat to the forest. Stay together."

His hoarse words, spoken in the unknown dialect of the Germanic tribes, weren't understandable to Marius in the still night, but they really didn't need to be. Any novice tactician could see the scouting party would fall back to the safety of the forest, where it would be more difficult for the Roman soldiers to bring the weight of their numbers on the enemy.

Marius immediately understood their adversaries needed to be cut off from making it to the cover of the obscuring foliage. Escape of at least a couple of the invaders would be almost a certainty if they were allowed to pull back.

Right where the scout leader had earlier faced, Marius stepped from the shadows of the dense trees. Holding up his sword and shield, he flexed his fingers around his sword's pommel, allowing his muscles to fall into a limbered, relaxed state.

With a sharp breath, Marius began running toward the tribal warrior, raising his blade as he closed the distance. In several steps, he came nearly to a full sprint, his ferocious stare fixing on the form of the lanky fighter across the gloomy grassland.

The opposing leader's eyes went wide with acknowledgment of the incoming threat, but no apprehension filled the scout's grizzled face. Instead, he flashed an eagerness for the coming clash of arms, and snarling, the experienced man raised a large battle axe in a challenging gesture towards Marius.

Breaking into his own run, the veteran warrior rushed across the meadow, his awkward lunging gait bringing him closer to Marius beneath the faint light of the night sky. With forced breaths expelled from his lips, a sort of ecstatic glee matched the man's movement to destroy his enemy, and his pace grew quicker with each eager stride forward.

As Marius and the leader hurried to embrace in close-quarter's melee, the other scouts closed ranks, expertly covering one another's flanks as they stepped carefully backward, making for the relative safety of the woods behind them. Expecting their leader to cover their backs, the Marcomanni kept their eyes on the rank of infantry moving steadily toward them.

Motioning on his squad's pace to an ordered trot, Quintus moved to the side of his men. His face was focused and ruthless, and with a scowl, he urged them forward in a deep, gritty voice. "As we've practiced. We fight as one...and all of these dogs will die this night."

Stepping in unison, the trained men of the legion lowered their spears, moving to fight their first skirmish in what would hopefully be a long and successful campaign.

#

The village's interior streets were eerily quiet. The dense arrangement of buildings, which loosely made up the largest population of a Roman township within the nearest fifty miles, was fully retired for the night. No man or dog roamed among the damp-stone paths between the rows of houses, and no boisterous sound or idle person made themselves known throughout the village's compact districts.

Far from the main thoroughfare and near the exterior wall, mixed in with this collection of wooden and brick structures, was a squat dark-reddish home. This simple place, which held only one open room and had cheap fabric curtains over its glassless windows, was peaceful and silent for the moment. Only gentle light leaked inside from flickering street torches to illuminate the calm interior.

On the brick floor, amongst some rumpled blankets strewn over a worn cloth mattress, were the shapes of two people. Intertwined and in deep slumber, the spouses were in their forties and of good peasant stock, showing open mouths with crooked teeth as they dozed. Appearing coddled with their comfortable circumstance, they lay at odd angles, unaware of anything that could be wrong during their contented repose.

These were the strong-boned people that drove the empire and its efforts to pacify most of the known world. Short of stature, hardy, and able to endure practically any misery, they were the sort of citizens who were humble of means and contented with the place they managed to carve out in their world, whether it was in a prosperous megalopolis like the capital city of Rome or in such a provincial village like where they now lived.

Time passed in silence, and the atmosphere of the place remained without worry or obvious impending threat.

Then, a strange and sticky sound came from outside, almost like the peeling of wet plaster from a recently stuccoed wall. Though it wasn't sufficiently loud to wake the couple, there soon came more of the same noises, which finally ended with a series of strange croaks, followed by the slight thump of something hitting the ground.

Soon after, a large hand, bloated-looking and claw-tipped, emerged from the small window next to the front entrance. Backlit by the street's illumination, a puffy arm followed it into the room, where it tried reaching for the lengthy piece of metal used to bar the door from inside. But the distance was too far, and the arm, anchored to the shadowy figure of a hulking Verisi outside, struggled for a time, its whitish skin glistening in the dim light as it strained. Suspended there, its undulating muscles seemed to convulse in odd, squirming spasms.

Then, a slight crackling, and the arm itself, formerly at its maximum length, elongated more, stretching out and becoming thinner. Over the next several moments, it gained more than a foot in length, finally coming to a point where its bizarre fingers grabbed and gently lifted the iron bar from its support across the interior of the solid wooden door.

Quietly leaning the dense metal against the wall to the side, the arm carefully pulled back towards the window, its owner slowly withdrawing it outside. The room, still quiet with its slumbering occupants, stayed that way for several minutes.

In a short time, the door gently creaked open, and splotchy light from outside brightened many of the formerly dim areas within the residence. Ceramic bowls of various pasty foods and grain lay upon a short table to the side, while a wrinkly cloak and several changes of clothing hung from simple crude hooks sticking from the far wall.

And still, the forms of the home's owners slept soundly in the middle of the tranquil living area. Without a care in the world, they continued their night's rest.

Two imposing forms, thick and with enormous robes covering most of their girth, slowly made their way into the peaceful space. The Verisi, large and ungainly, moved with some caution as they shuffled near the sleeping husband and wife.

Peering down, their hooded silhouettes waited for several seconds, as if they were drinking in the luscious possibilities of what was next to come. Leaning near the slumbering duo, one of the beasts extended a clawed had, allowing its appendage to hover over the sleeping female. Facing upward, the lady was momentarily oblivious to the presence of any threat.

But that ignorance of any danger soon began to recede. The eyes of the woman began to flit underneath her eyelids, as if she were suddenly informed within her dreams that something was horribly amiss in the real world. As her conscious mind began to push up from her slumber, her features twitched, and her body wriggled as she started the unsettling process of coming awake.

With a rapid strike, the Verisi plunged three of its claws into her neckline. Reversing its hand, it ran its extended talons upwards, driving them under her skull and deep within her brain. The force of the entry was extreme, and the quick track of foreign implements squishing deep within her head caused her legs and several other muscles to spasm.

The woman's eyes shot open, her pupils wide and confused at the sudden and very lethal intrusion. As her head shook with the force of the Verisi's digits rummaging within her skull, her eyes expanded, adopting a detached consciousness that seemed to scream, *What…is…happening?*

And then the light in those eyes faded, replaced by the blank stare of the dead. Meanwhile, the Verisi's forearm surged with an inflamed swelling, like it was now engorged in a new flow of blood, one that was emerging from its helpless victim and into its own enormous physique.

Otherwise silent, the monster stood above her, its body becoming invigorated with the blood and life force of the poor woman. As the already-large beast grew in stature from the addition of so much matter to its own body, the frame of the wife shrank below it, quickly losing its color to a deep black, while her skin and muscles reduced to a wrinkled and gaunt contour. In little time, the former living and breathing women, previously a vigorous and well-known person within the community, was reduced to a dark husk.

To the side, her husband, up until now unaware and asleep, stirred quickly, as if sensing the recent departure of his spouse from the realm of the living. Jarred awake, he suddenly sat up, where he looked to the side with an awakening expression of alarm in his blurry features.

Before his eyes could adjust to the abomination around him, the other Verisi grasped his head.

"Wha...is...?" stuttered the man, even as the enormous fingers of the monster fully encompassed his head, quickly smothering his mouth and abruptly cutting off the man's growing cries.

With methodical precision, the creature likewise rammed its off-hand into his upper neck, propelling its own claws with a wet slushing sound up and into the unfortunate man's shocked brain. In seconds, the thirsty creature began absorbing the husband's bodily contents, drawing the interior elements of his corpse into its expanding body.

Continuing their ruthless assault, the wretched Verisi drank their fill from their hapless victims, taking care to extract every last bit of satisfying nourishment from the couple.

Meanwhile, from around the tragic attack, the small building and the adjacent street remained silent and entirely empty of life.

#

The squad of five soldiers pressed farther down the grass-covered grade as they steadily closed the distance towards the retreating tribesmen. With anxious eyes and hurried steps, they aimed to move fast enough to reach their enemy before the invaders would make it to the safety of the narrow trail in the woods.

To their side, Quintus kept pace. Holding a lengthy sword, he strode with purpose, his gaze fixed in a cold stare on the upcoming enemy. Always fearless, his expression was fierce and unrepentant for the damage he believed would soon be inflicted on the foreign scouts.

Yet their human quarry did not seem to mind, as the veteran scouts showed little concern while stepping carefully backwards, avoiding tripping as they retreated in good order. The imminent fight for them may not have been expected, but their brazen features did not indicate fear or worry about its outcome.

In front of the advancing wedge of spears, two of the Marcomanni fighters struck a professional fighting stance, holding out their long glistening swords as they anticipated the blows of pointed spear shafts bearing down on them.

Behind them, the third scout sheathed his sword and moved his shield to his back, instead producing a long sling he loaded with a dense lead bullet. Moving quickly, the man crouched behind one of the scouts shielding his movements, and spinning the leather launcher with considerable skill, it produced a whistling sound that reverberated across the meadow.

After grunting out a hoarse "now," his shielding comrades stepped outward, opening a lane for the man to let his missile fly. Lunging ahead, the scout cast his arm forward, and extending his twirling sling, he flung the solid ball toward their incoming attackers.

The legionaries were caught by surprise. Not easily seeing the developing missile attack, the men in the center of the formation's eyes went wide just as their enemy cast the deadly ball their way.

The scout's precise aim was accurate and uncannily effective. The ball struck the middle soldier squarely in the face, and the CRACK of the impact matched the man's orbital structure exploding into fragments of bone and blood as it passed through the eye socket and became embedded within his skull.

The stricken soldier, formerly so prepared for his moment to wade into battle, collapsed in a sprawled heap on the soft ground below. Landing face down, he vaguely grabbed at his face, but the dreadfully wounded man, racked with spasms, had lost the capacity to move his limbs with any coordinated dexterity.

Not stopping, his fellow footmen closed the newly formed gap between them as they continued their advance, leaving his flinching body behind, moving in lockstep as they pressed onward, focusing only on what lay before them.

Bellowing ecstatic war cries, the waiting scouts motioned with their weapons to the approaching soldiers. Still moving backward, the fearless tribesmen taunted their Roman enemies, shouting unintelligible exhortations at them across the rapidly closing distance. Their odd dialect stopped direct interpretation, but their intent was clear: *Come to your death.*

Farther behind the impending clash, towards the forest from where the Marcomanni had earlier emerged, Marius faced off with his taller opponent. The scout leader, snarling and vicious, hefted and swung his ax with a swift arc, aiming to decapitate Marius.

But Marius had been in such vicious struggles before, and he swiftly ducked under the powerful swing, its sharp edge swishing over his head. Leaping back, he created more space as he took a visual estimate of the formidable warrior.

Marius' own weapon, the *gladius*, was a compact and light sword that was effective for quick slashes and stabs, but what allowed it to be so lethal in close battle also meant it had limited range. He would have to be careful as he searched for the best opportunity to eviscerate his proficient enemy.

Gauging his enemy's movements and speed, Marius evaluated his prospects with detached expertise. Meeting the scout's fierce eyes, Marius didn't like what he saw, both in terms of his adversary's obvious skill as well as the confidence the man appeared to glow with.

Few older men, and this man wasn't youthful, lived to such an age in the violent Germanic society if they weren't very good at killing. Worse, the Romans' prospective battlefield advantage was based on organization and training, not on the type of armed man-to-man brawl Marius was now engaged in.

Marius' rigorous preparation in the legion had long ago disabused him of the notion of ego. Proud men did not focus on the mission, and the military culture he lived in was entirely about pursuing their goals above all else. Who won the field at the end of the day was far more important than who managed to slay the most enemies or attain the most accolades from their individual exploits.

Feinting once, the leader shocked Marius with his speed by lunging, then spinning for a back slash with the other side of his double-edged ax. Tilting his body, Marius was just able to avoid the attack, but the clang of the blade across his raised shield threw him back, producing a tingling shock in his arm muscles from the powerful impact.

The whipping strength of the warrior and his deadly weapon were even more than he expected, compelling Marius to become more cautious as he considered his next move.

Keeping his weight balanced in his fighting stance, Marius stepped farther away from his predatory enemy. Creating more distance and studying the man, he realized the commander of the scouting group was herding him towards the far side of the clearing, which would keep him away from cutting off the Marcomanni retreat. Not only was the leader confident, but he was also smart enough to think beyond his immediate combat with Marius.

Looking away from the eager features of his adversary, Marius glimpsed to his side, where his men were about to engage the other enemy scouts. Calculating the trajectory of his men, their opponents, and the fluid nature of the fight, he didn't like their chances to easily destroy all of the Marcomanni. In fact, noting the crumpled form of one of his soldiers on the ground, merely surviving the fight might be considered a success in the near term.

Returning his full attention to the scout leader, he steeled his jaw for what was a tricky and possibly extended fight. Gulping, he understood he was soon to earn the pay that Rome so lavishly provided its fighting men.

#

More bodies now lay about the entry point to the village. The communal area around the main gate, which earlier had been the location of the town's coordinated defense, was now strewn with many dead or maimed defenders.

Most of the recently slain were soldiers, and to their credit, they had gone down fighting. Their bladed weapons and spears, many of which were streaked with the blood of their assailants, were either still locked in their clenched hands or scattered where they had fought until the bitter end.

Other victims of the fighting, apparently town guards or simple residents who rushed to join the raging battle, lay crumpled and moaning at various points where the fight had occurred. Their efforts at a defensive stand were brave, but the numerous quantities of their bloody remains showed the result to be one-sided.

Yet there was some indication the village's response had yielded some success against the frightful aggressors. Amongst the hurt and deceased men, there were two large bodies, those of the Verisi, who had been overwhelmed and cut down by a surge of citizens fighting for their lives.

Lying at strange angles amidst puddles of cooling gore, the large corpses of the bulky monsters, their light skin bared in distended poses of lumpy flesh, had scores of jagged stab wounds into their bloody pallid skin. Nearby, the collection of slain village fighters who had inflicted the lethal wounds were similarly sprawled across the compacted rock of the street.

From far inside the town, emerging from a variety of tightly packed homes, a collection of more Verisi, all clad in long robes, moved down the main street towards the village's single exit. Hobbling along with their strange walk, at a pace that seemed like they were constantly out-of-step and balanced on awkward, too-large feet, they lumbered along in an almost relaxed fashion.

And most of these grotesque creatures carried something particularly despicable in their bloated arms. Ambling along the primary road through the town, they held the figures of small children within their tight grasps.

The youngsters the Verisi toted were not yet dead, as their small open eyes were glazed over, much like they were in a detached fugue state, but neither did the youthful villagers struggle against being kidnapped from the village.

As they came under the torchlight of the entrance, two of the Verisi, those who were not carrying any of the town's youth, reached down among the clustered bodies and hefted up the large forms of their fallen comrades on their backs.

First staggering under the dead weight of their enormous fellow creatures, the monsters steadied themselves and then trudged out of the village through the unmanned gate, towards the distant tree line north of Avenio.

The dark forms of twelve additional Verisi, bearing much of the town's youth in their thick arms, quietly followed them out of the village. Moving at a calm pace, they didn't appear in a hurry.

Even as the Verisi faded into the surrounding forest, disappearing among the mist and shadows of the gloomy trees, their ponderous speed did not quicken, and they displayed little concern for being followed.

Behind them, the settlement was largely silent, and only a few cries of mourning, shock, and physical agony emerged from the patchwork of humble homes. The village's remaining inhabitants, locked in their personal spaces, only had wails of anguish to accompany the exit of the fiendish attackers from the area.

#

Lunging ahead, the soldiers extended their spears in forceful, coordinated thrusts. With firm grips, they sought to impale their elusive enemy on the sharpened points of the weapons' iron ends.

With a clang off one shield, their tentative assault failed to inflict any damage, while with a long swipe and clack of their swords, two of the defending tribesmen parried away the shafts of the other spears.

And the Marcomanni scouts were not impressed with the attack. Looking up, the jeering men, faces full of open disdain and unrelenting hatred, goaded the soldiers on, all the while backing farther to the cover of forest behind them. It would not take much longer for them to get to the safety of the woods, and the men on both sides of the developing fight knew it.

Forcing several more synced thrusts ahead of them, the attacking spearmen continued to look for holes in the scouts' defense. But each time they tried to find a way to turn the retreating flanks of their enemies, their probing attacks failed. Over time, the hurried pace of the assault was faltering, and frustration was forcing their rank to sag as a result.

Creeping abreast and ahead of his line of soldiers, Quintus' expression, full of contempt and raging revulsion for the very existence of these horrid invaders, shouted at the man farthest to the right. "Come on, ye pig fuckers. Are ye men or whores?"

The insult caught the tribal man unaware, especially as it came from a foe he didn't expect could speak his forest language. Hesitating, his eyes widened, and a hateful scowl washed away his prior cockiness.

Unable to control his lust for violence, the man snarled, then struck forward with his thick sword, aiming to slash into Quintus' apparently exposed thigh, thinking Quintus had leaned too far out and exposed himself.

But the insult and feigned movement were just as Quintus wanted. While the scout took the bait, his man Cylas, a young and an enthusiastic soldier with only a year of service, struck precisely as he had been trained. The point of his long weapon, thrust exactly towards the Marcomanni's unarmored side, pierced under the leather protection and into his hip.

The scout screamed, his face growing enraged. Falling back and covering his right side, he tried to continue his pace, to cover the retreat, to fulfill his duty against these hated Romans.

But his mistake was already made, and the penance for his combat transgression, where he had given up his formation for an inopportune chance to stab his enemy, was to absorb an incoming blow from Quintus.

Swung with all his might, Quintus caught the man at the full extension of his attack, his sword ripping into the scout where his protection was weakest. Penetrating under the leather armor covering his upper body, the blade bit deep into the scout's shoulder, cleaving the man's upper arm in half and severing the brachial artery above the bicep.

Like an ornamental display fountain that spouted water in the far-way provincial capital, blood sprayed in gouts from the critical injury.

The scout's immediate scream was tortured, and his agonized bellows shook his comrades into action. As a natural consequence of battle, where all men, even those fighting for hideous ends, come to each other's aid, they shifted towards their fellow tribesman, moving to support their badly injured companion.

But that movement left them open to other attackers. The legionaries, sensing their opportunity, leveled their spears and pressed forward. The result was the Marcomanni irregular formation was broken, and the length of the Romans' weapons meant they were in a dominant tactical position.

Looking for the kill, the soldiers lunged in, ramming their spear points deep into a second man's torso. The weight of the blows, piercing into the scout's guts with heavy thuds, forced bursts of blood to spew from his wounds.

Falling to a knee, the wounded tribesman screamed in unrestrained pain. Left exposed, more stabs from the spears ripped into his cheeks and scalp, tearing out bloody veins and chunks of flesh, followed by one, two, and three more brutal thrusts to the chest and torso. With a final plunge of a vigorous jab, his throat was torn entirely out, quickly ending the scout's distressed shrieks as he crumpled to the earth.

It didn't take long for the third tribesman to see that all was lost. Turning rapidly, he sprinted for the forest behind him, plunging ahead on legs that sought every last inch of extension to take him to safety. Still clutching his sword, he pumped his arms, making for the cover of the not-too-distant brush and trees.

But Quintus was on his tail, matching the sprint with his own surging speed. Merely a few yards back, he gasped in controlled breaths as he closed the distance on his fleeing quarry, and as he came closer, the terrified scout must have sensed his looming presence behind him. Unfortunately for the Marcomanni, Quintus was more fleet of foot, and soon he would be within a sword's length to run him down.

On the other side of the clearing, Marius was in a fierce battle of his own with the remaining adversary. Facing each other, they traded blows, with the crack of an ax across Marius' shield being matched with the clang of his sword's returning blows against the scout's chain-mail armor.

For an extended time, the men feinted and circled one another, each looking for instant victory in the form of a fatal, combat-ending blow. Sweating and breathing in huffs, neither could find the upper hand, and Marius, facing away from the other melee, began to worry if he could finish his adversary off in time to help his soldiers.

Marius should have kept his thoughts on the present fight. With another feint and a spin, the leader drug his ax low and used the pole-end of the weapon to jab Marius with a smack to his face.

Falling backward, Marius' vision went blurry, his eyes watering as blood gushed from his smashed nose. Trying to create distance, he stepped away, shaking his head and seeking to clear his vision for a fight that just became much harder to win.

Forcing his eyes to focus, Marius could plainly see his sauntering opponent as the man grinned and stepped forward to finish off this upstart Roman commander.

Recognizing the difficulty of surviving the impending attack, Marius clutched his shield close and scanned for a good location to attack his skilled foe. If he hoped to save his own life and perhaps those of his men, he had to find a way to salvage victory from the real possibility of imminent death.

He needn't have worried about such a prospect. A sudden THUK came from behind the advancing enemy, and the man's eyes, which had been so odious and savage, went wide in surprise. Turning slowly, he reached toward his back, trying to extricate a short javelin that had plunged into his lower back and ran through his intestines. The wound was debilitating and deep, with the tip of the missile weapon partially emerging from the front of his torso.

Wasting no time, Marius rushed up to the wounded warrior. Wielding his weapon overhand, he rammed his shortsword into the neck of the Marcomanni leader. After the initial plunge of the blade through tendon and muscle, he forced it down with a slushing sound into the upper torso, severing organs and arteries in one brutal and decisive cut.

Shocked, the tall man's eyes went wide, having been skewered by both missile and blade. When Marius yanked his sword out, the leader gazed at him from up close, seeming to accept his fate. Like most of the Marcomanni, he saw death in battle as the proper end to life, and to his credit, when the end came, his eyes were unafraid.

For the briefest of time, as the tribesman's gaze locked with Marius, a sort of fellowship passed between them, an occurrence that sometimes transpired between violent men. The unspoken message was as if the invading warrior wanted to say, *this was a long time coming, and now it's finally my turn.*

Forcing out a last challenging growl through his quivering lips, the scout leader gurgled a death rattle and collapsed to the ground. Landing as dead weight on the clearing's surface, only a few spasms racked his body as he expired on the dirt and grass.

Glancing up, Marius saw the approach of Quintus, who smirked as he drew closer. Appearing calm and unharmed, his grin grew wider, so that even in the pale darkness, Quintus' white teeth made the moment almost comical, like they were now two smug mates who had just won a game of sport while playing with cherished friends.

Reaching down, Quintus moved to extract his javelin from the dead man's back, but it took a few pulls to fully tug it from the heavy corpse. Finally getting it free, he raised up the slim weapon, and peering at the gore stuck to the shaft, raised a nostril in a show of disgust.

After a moment, Quintus shrugged, then inserted the javelin into a thong-type quiver on the back of his pack, where it usually hung on soldiers who were kitted for battle in the legion.

This somewhat sedate moment of victory did not last long. Holding a rag to his bleeding nose, Marius grunted as he tried to stench the flow of seeping blood. Tilting his head back, he fought the urge to scream from being so stupid as to miss the attack from his now-dispatched enemy.

Catching himself, Marius kept his head in that position as his gaze shot over to his men.

Quintus' moment of contentment faded, and he nodded with some sadness. "One injured, and it's serious. He may not survive, and with the wound he received, he may wish he had not."

Frowning, Marius stripped bits from his cloth rag and inserted them into his nostrils. Annoyed by his non-serious wound, he shook his head as he gestured towards the location of the other battle, where the sprawled forms of the dead and injured were lying below the standing shapes of two of his armored men.

Walking over to the violent scene, Marius peered sympathetically down at his injured fighter. The soldier, Seneca was his name, was from a normal upbringing and had normal dreams of a place to call his own, as well as a generous pension and an accommodating wife to ease him into retirement.

Those dreams were denied for the moment, however, with his badly wounded head wrapped tightly in a dark cloth. His face, broken and swollen to an immense size, was so maimed and misshapen that only wheezing breaths could escape from his fractured airway.

Having seen innumerable wounds, Marius immediately decided the man would survive, but as Quintus indicated, hideous scarring from the wound would leave his face difficult to view for the remainder of his life. With a military existence, death was sometimes a result that could seem preferable for such a wounded soldier, even when a skilled surgeon and some thread could stitch much of his face back together.

Still, Marius would see to it that they would do their best to aid and restore the man, and with enough care, he could even hope to return to duty at some point in his hopefully long future. Part of the bond they shared was they would do, within reason, whatever was necessary to heal and take care of one another.

Shaking his head at this depressing thought, Marius peered towards the forest, where the other two soldiers were dragging a corpse back to their location.

The limp body, head banging across the ground, had apparently been slain just short of the forest. Nodding approvingly at the killing of the last scout, Marius at least had the success of this mission to offset the despair he felt for his seriously wounded man.

Crouching, Quintus took a moment to examine the body of one of the slain scouts. The pale man, the same one he had earlier hacked into, lay forward, his face turned away from the direction he was curled into as he bled out. Apparently, he had been kicked so hard in the skull that his shattered neck had bent his head the wrong way.

Digging through the man's pack, then quickly looking over the other dead, Quintus moved near to Marius, where he grimaced in frustration.

Having watched Quintus loot the body, Marius spoke the obvious aloud. "They have perhaps three days of rations. Their larger camp cannot be too far away. It would have been better to take a prisoner...at least we could have found more about the disposition of their incoming forces."

Quintus rolled his eyes. "Perhaps, just this one time, you could be happy with a mission done well? Maybe even relax a bit, appreciating your men's accomplishments?"

Looking around, Marius took the suggestion to heart. As the last two men brought up the wayward corpse of the enemy scout who had been caught short of the forest, Marius took the time to nod appreciatively at them, even taking the time to pat one soldier on the shoulder in a show of thankfulness. Such a display would have been frowned upon by many within the legion, but to Marius, it was merely the way a proper leader should act.

Quintus, getting in the mood of brotherly affection, a way of interaction that often overtook soldiers on the campaign trail when no other was there for support, went up to Cylas, who peered down at the corpses.

Cylas stared down at one of the men, the one he had so recently killed. Unlike Quintus, his lips were pulled tight in a frown, and he didn't appear overjoyed with the act of making this scout dead.

Raising his voice, Quintus kept his ecstatic disposition, and he leaned close to make his point. "Cylas, that was a job well done. You did what you had to, and we are all alive because of it."

Unconvinced, Cylas grinned a slight smile, but his eyes didn't match the gesture, moving apprehensively back down to the deceased adversary.

Quintus took the occasion to speak louder, addressing all his soldiers as he moved his gaze to each of them. "Remember this and take what I say very near to your hearts. These…beasts…would now be dancing with your heads removed if they had won. If the situation were reversed, your skulls would be planted on spikes, to be used as a battle celebration for their wicked religious…events."

Stepping in the middle of the circle of men that had formed, Quintus became mellow, his features becoming gentle, much like a kind family friend in some precious communal event. "We fight on the right side here. Never forget your role in visiting death on these…people. You do what must be done, and the empire only exists because of you. You will not receive the credit you deserve, but your place in our civilized world is essential. You are...heroic."

With that, some time passed, and the men grew happier, eventually taking on the smiles of people who had just faced death...and prevailed. The joy Quintus had sought from his men at last seemed to be a reality.

Marius watched the mood change, and he once again was impressed with the motivational skills of his second-in-command. Quintus was smart and shrewd, but he was also something more: full of faith in his cause and his men. When it came down to it, nothing more than that mattered in a leader, whatever they all had to face.

A genuine smile formed on Marius' own lips, and he moved into the circle, pivoting his head look over his...friends, not just subordinates. The love of a woman was a unique thing and obviously had physical benefits, but the love between brothers facing death was its own special occurrence, and nothing could quite replace it.

From the distance, far from where they stood but also entirely too close, the sound of a horn echoed through the night. The notes from the military implement, blown over and over in a haphazard manner, carried over the dark forest and meadow. It was not noise that suggested normal events; instead, the manic pace of the tone suggested acute trouble, as was its purpose.

His blood running cold, Marius' head jolted with each extended blast of the hurried sounds, flinching at each note and the unwelcome events they implied. All the men knew what it meant, of course, but to a person, each was afraid to confirm it openly.

With his expression now becoming cold and analytical, the recently happy Quintus finally broke the silence. Motioning to a litter the soldiers had prepared to carry their injured comrade back to the village, his tone was calm, but his severe features throbbed with anger. "The village, and the general alarm. We must get back…now."

Chapter Nineteen

A wide grin crossed Ballomar's face, his crinkly wrinkles expanding in conjunction with his good mood. Much like a spoiled child who expected and received the best gift on each celebration of his birth, the Marcomanni king appeared enchanted with himself, ready to open his present of conquest and domination to show the world.

Ballomar's demeanor was giddy at the prospect of sharing with his tribe an aggressive vision of military supremacy, a vision that would carry their armies far beyond their current borders and into the belly of that wealthy empire to their south.

These upstart and puny Romans from the sunny region on that distant southern sea had persecuted the forest tribes for too long, and the time for them to kneel and pay homage before the superior warriors of Germania was quickly approaching. That, or they would be utterly destroyed.

But even a despot had need for validation when it came to his aspirations, and to that end, Ballomar's mood pulsed with anticipation that his people would soon be witness to his geopolitical genius. True, many of these mindless tribesmen would also die to fulfill his ambitions, but that was the cost of greatness—for them, at least.

In front of him, in the clearing next to their sprawling war camp, Ballomar peered over a collection of his men and horses, where only the most capable of his tribe had been called together on his personal orders.

It was nighttime, and on this night, the moon provided abundant light. Illumination filled the expansive meadow, with an occasional bush or stunted tree visible between the boundaries of woods on either side. Presently arranged in the open area was an assortment of soldiers and their horses, looking restless as they stared up at Ballomar.

Ballomar stood on a wooden stage, which was put together with hewn branches and chopped portions of tree trunks. The rickety structure allowed him to stand above his men, making his presence easy to see from everywhere in the clearing.

Directly in front of the Marcomanni king was a large wagon, which consisted of two enormous wheels on either side that supported a huge storage area within the lumbering vehicle.

With a team of six oxen to pull it, the cavernous space within the wagon was covered by a large stitched-leather tarp that kept prying eyes from seeing what was carried inside.

Tethered behind the wagon were fifteen men, each of whom stood with deep frowns as they gazed up at the king. Their hands, chained in front of them with large locks to keep them in place, were connected to another chain that was linked to the back of the massive cart. In this way, they were obviously prisoners who would have to either walk or be dragged behind the wagon as it was driven to some as-yet-undisclosed destination.

Strangely, in spite of the fact they were prisoners of such a brutal leader, the chained men didn't appear harmed or overly afraid while they stood there. And neither were they underfed, as below their tattered clothing, they had muscular physiques.

Around the wagon were a protective force of seventy men, all heavily armed and looking intimidating as they waited. Additionally, twenty more cavalry milled near on horseback, but the majority merely stood close to the prisoners in a protective screen.

Ballomar took a while to speak, taking several seconds to clear his throat and panning his gaze to each point of the assembled group to let the tension of the moment build.

Finally nodding, looking entirely full of himself and convinced of the rightness of his intentions, he broke the silence with the obnoxious twang of his gruff voice. "My fellow conquerors, free men…friends, and most loyal followers," said Ballomar, his voice carrying easily to all of the assembled group. "We must do our part in this…time of weakness, a time of growing potential for Germania and our people."

He could have stated the time was also ripe for the glory of Ballomar, but that was something already understood by the large party of men before him. Many of the tribe exchanged glances to that effect, even if to say it aloud would have brought swift retribution.

"Now," continued Ballomar, flashing a frown at the undercurrent of distaste within the assembled tribe, "we move to our allies, the feared Verisi. After 'consulting' with them, we'll go collect our other allies, our other people—and all the tribes of Germania."

Pointing to the top of the wagon, Ballomar hopped down from the viewing stage. Moving to the front of the wagon, he pointed up to a flag mounted on a pole to its front. On it was the insignia of a raven, which, despite the lack of artistic talent of Ballomar's sewing aids, managed to look scary, with its red talons stitched over a black background.

Holding up the same likeness carved on an amulet, which hung from a long leather string around his neck, Ballomar raised his shout to a booming level, where there could be no missing his resonant power. "Alcis is with us. We'll drive the Roman dogs to their distant cities. Defile their women. Raise our standards above their pathetic monuments and palaces."

To this, a host of cheers arose. Clapping and shouts of *Ye* or *Argghh* echoed above the meadow. Even the prisoners seemed to appreciate the remarks, clapping and nodding in agreement.

"And you...my most valued followers...will join in my victories. Share in my wealth and power, rule without mercy as far as our victories will carry us, even to their wretched capital."

Wild cheers broke out further, and they continued for almost a minute. During that time, Ballomar smiled, taking in his moment—his time as supreme leader—with an overt and self-obsessed joy for the present. Men of power, men who changed the world, had to believe in themselves, and with this personality trait, Ballomar's confidence in himself knew no end.

Motioning to one of his guards, an enormous man of prodigious girth and a long beard, Ballomar pointed to the back of the cart. With a curt nod, the man moved toward the line of prisoners behind them.

When he came to each of the chained men, the guard produced an amulet from a large sack. Slipping another of the Alcis amulets over each of the men's necks, it wasn't long before they all were recipients of treasured talismans of their violent tribal god.

Continuing to nod and smile, Ballomar waved to his still-enthusiastic crowd. Walking to the front of the wagon, he pulled himself onto his enormous horse, which was covered in its own expensive suit of shiny metal armor.

Sitting fully erect atop the animal, he looked over to his assistant Alwin, who sat on his own steed alongside. The dour man, gaunt and without facial hair, appeared unhappy, clearly not liking something about the display of motivation and power.

Noticing this, Ballomar kept with his fake smile, continuing to wave at his men while speaking from the side of his mouth. "What is it? Spit it out."

Pursing his lips, Alwin spoke reluctantly. "I have heard from the Quadi. Much of their tribe is not happy."

"Nobody is ever happy in that cursed tribe. Why?"

Scanning nearby, Alwin spoke in a low voice, so that nobody else would hear him. "It seems Albrecht succeeded Ulrich on their war council, after Ulrich's 'accident.' Albrecht's deciding vote compelled the Quadi to join our cause against the Empire."

Staring over at Alwin, Ballomar flashed an innocent grin. "Sounds like normal politics. Nothing out of the ordinary, and it'll soon be forgotten when we march."

"Yes, my king, but Albrecht is now missing. Their entire tribe is in chaos."

Biting his lip, Ballomar considered the information. "Hmm…then it'll be easier for them to follow me, their REAL leader?"

Ballomar's subsequent gloating smile became infectious, and after a moment, Alwin also smiled, though more cryptically. Finally raising his eyes to meet his powerful leader, he bowed slightly. "As always, your actions are effective, King Ballomar. I'm just worried much of Germania will come to...hate you."

Unbothered, Ballomar shrugged. Motioning ahead with his hand, he kicked his horse and trotted toward a break in the forest, where a broad wagon trail awaited their impending travel into the dark cover of the surrounding woodlands. Behind him, the entirety of the mass of men, from the wagon drivers to the attached prisoners and their guards, moved into action, slowly picking up their pace to follow the king.

Confused, Alwin also got moving, hurrying his own horse to catch up with his impatient leader.

As Alwin pulled alongside him, Ballomar chuckled. Putting a skin of wine to his lips, he took a swig from its contents, then spat the dark liquid to the side before speaking. "Let them hate—so long as they fear."

Continuing to snicker, Ballomar moved his gaze towards the front. Contented with himself and his prospects, he became silent as the long retinue of his most effective soldiers got on its way.

Ahead, several scouts on horseback fanned out in front of the long caravan. Following at a plodding pace into the night, the war group commenced their long-awaited invasion of the Roman Empire.

Chapter Twenty

Fresh torches burned throughout the village, pushing away the darkness and making it easy to see clearly down cold alleyways and dusty pedestrian paths. On the perimeter walls, yet more torches were tethered to raised posts to provide enough light to look out into the surrounding countryside.

Wails of mourning and sobs of unrestrained despair echoed inside the confines of the town. The tempo of sad shrieking and pitiful clamors of anguish made it obvious the settlement's remaining citizens were locked in personal tragedy, the type formed by horrific, eternal loss.

Matching the intense gloominess, the figures of soldiers quietly shuffled from house to house. Carrying the forms of broken bodies between them, the various legionaries were in a baffled daze as they made their way to the main square.

Lined up on the ground across the stones of the square were now scores of bodies. Shriveled and black parents were some of the most common dead, but also evident were sprawled soldiers, town guards, and whomever else had come to their sudden end while confronting the village's deadly invaders.

Marius stood near the rows of dead, jaw set and eyes locked on many of these people he had known and liked during his time serving as the town's military protector. Sweeping his gaze over the husks of unidentifiable people and many of the soldiers he had looked at like his own sons, he was, for the moment, caught in a unique stage of both overwhelming grief and endless rage.

Not far away was Quintus, who went over the corpses of his fallen men, straightening their cloaks and smoothing out their death poses by adjusting the deceased fighters to lie straight on their backs. As if wanting them to pass the final inspection for their trip to the unknowable beyond, he moved efficiently, aligning each soldier to honor them for dying as a virtuous soldier of the legion.

Glancing back towards one of the stalls, Marius saw Julia, who leaned against a heavy table, her eyes lost and cheeks streaked with tears. Her puffy and terrified face was altered in that horrifying moment, her expression transformed into a shell of overt depression from her usual features of engaging kindness.

Stepping close to her and fighting back his own distressed thoughts, Marius tried to sound resolute. "We shall get him back. I swear by my very soul."

Looking up with eyes that didn't fully see him, Julia nodded. "I…was in the other room. I didn't…know anyone was there…."

Nearby, Quintus leaned near one of the villager's bodies. Snapping his fingers and uttering "Commander," he motioned Marius over. After patting Julia affectionately, Marius moved quickly to join him.

Brushing away the matted and bloody hair of the burly man below him, Quintus traced his fingers across huge holes in the man's neck, which were similar to the ones they had earlier seen from other victims. This man's skin, however, was relatively normal, not showing the blackened status of the other corpses.

"This isn't caused by a weapon, Marius," said Quintus, his voice sounding intrigued. "It's as if he's had thick nails driven into his flesh, yet he isn't black like the others, the 'Egyptians' we saw before."

Nodding, Marius stared for a time at the wound, then at the open mouth and shocked face of the unfortunate victim. He had seen wounds and death his whole adult life, but the dead people's expressions here were…somehow different, as if they saw something even worse than their oncoming mortality when they were killed.

Standing, Marius walked to his right, where one of his soldiers lay in permanent repose. Crouching over the man, he dispassionately nudged the soldier's head to the side, looking for similar wounds.

Instead of punctures, this man had the unmistakable gash of a sword blade into the lower part of his neck, at a point that could pierce downward without getting hung up on bone.

Death must have been quick, for the wound was deep and penetrated into his upper body, where his heart and organs would immediately have been sliced apart. Such a manner of attack was something administered by a professional, like a seasoned soldier or an assassin, someone with precise knowledge of how to kill instantly.

"This isn't the same," Marius said, his face forming into a confused expression. "It is as if he was struck by someone from behind. But…how did his killer get so close? Our man's sword is still in his scabbard. He must not have been expecting trouble."

Quintus stood fully erect from his inspection of the body, but his similar confusion and awkward silence indicated he had no answers to the mystery. Glancing around the town square, his displeased eyes looked for answers from the other dead splayed around them.

From behind, Julia spoke up, her haunted words breaking the temporary silence. "What do we…do?"

In answer, Marius walked over to embrace her. Hugging her briefly, his sympathy was obvious, but so too was his calculating manner. Gently stroking her hair, he disentangled himself after a moment of shared sorrow.

Breathing deeply, Marius raised his voice to address the huddled shapes of villagers over their dead. The strength of his words carried for some distance, breaking the sullen mood hanging over what was left of the town.

"Every citizen and soldier who remains is now to be issued a sword. We will now camp as a group in the square here. We will barricade the entrance to Avenio and survive here together. If you must relieve yourselves, you will do it here, within view of the rest of us. Nothing will be left to chance for the remainder of the night."

Sighing, Marius walked down a row of the dead, scanning over the earthly remains of the many people he had known amicably until just a few hours before.

Taking in the horrific sight, he nodded to himself, showing a temperament much like a gladiator who has accepted his fate in an unwinnable battle. "When the morning comes, we will discover what horrible enemy has done this."

#

When morning came, mist hovered on the surrounding fields, making visibility all the way to the wooded tree line somewhat spotty. The cloying fog, forever present in this forested region, always had the effect of making the mundane overgrowth appear mysterious, even as daylight became stronger.

In contrast to the horrific events that had occurred overnight, pleasant chirps from a variety of birds now echoed from the trees and across the grassy fields, evoking the beginning of what should have been an otherwise delightful day.

In time, as the sun rose over the eastern woods, its rays breeched through the canopy of spidery foliage, slowly burning away what remained of the night's misty remains.

In the town's main square, with only a few mumbles of hushed conversation around him, the mayor Ceres looked sadly up at Marius. His fleshy expression, normally whiny but kind, now had a distinct edge of trauma to it, and his wrinkled face was shrouded in gray hair and pointy whiskers that suddenly made him look ten years older than the day before.

Sounding lost, his voice was raspy and distant as he spoke. "There was panic, commander. Someone was killing everyone. There were shouts…and scared children…and this terrible clicking sound. Nobody knew what to do. The soldiers got us together and locked us inside the main tavern."

Dropping his head, the mayor's already weak resistance to his horrifying memories collapsed, and he began to blubber out his words. "We could hear the children crying…and the sounds of fighting. There…was also this shrieking sound…I never heard anything like it. And the little ones…why did they take away the innocent…?"

Marius peered down, his face taking on the appearance of a calculating surgeon who had to examine a ghastly wound. He was not the type to indulge weakness in others, except perhaps with the exception of distraught women, but the mayor's pathetic demeanor would have even made a ravenous lion in Rome's coliseum sympathetic.

Sighing, Marius patted him on the shoulder and nodded towards a cluttered table near the public well located in the middle of the square. Splayed on that table was a large breakfast of flat bread and boiled eggs, as well as some figs and dried meat. Standing near it were some soldiers and villagers, who, despite not appearing overly hungry, munched on portions of the food.

The mayor nodded and made his way toward the breakfast display. Normally such a presentation of tastiness would have caused a more hurried approach, but in these trying times, he ambled without obvious enthusiasm for the meal that awaited him.

At the lone entrance to the village, at the place formerly manned to prevent invasion of their settlement, several tables, crates, and other furniture were wedged in a makeshift barricade across the sealed gate. Five armed soldiers stood in front of it, looking happy that another defense of the town had not proved necessary for the remainder of the night.

Far to the side, in the area normally used for impromptu trade and weekend market activities, was the collection of corpses from the night before. Now arranged in respectful poses in three rows and covered by blankets, several of the deceased had family members crouched over them. Wails of acute sadness drifted from the distressed villagers, making for a sorrowful and overwrought background to the morning's evolving activities.

Shaking his head, Marius paced over to the former outdoor eating area. Quintus stood there, chewing on the remains of an apple and looking intently at the devastating scene around them. Behind him, Julia sat behind the counter, her scrunched-up face lost in her own tortured thoughts.

"How many?" asked Marius, his tone controlled, even as he fought the terror in his bones that forced his mind to return to Lucien every few seconds.

"Twenty-two dead from our detachment, and one missing. Thirty dead citizens, including the town guard, and fifteen children missing. There's…only a handful of the youth remaining. We are severely depleted."

Rubbing his unshaved whiskers with both hands, Marius nodded. "Who is missing?"

"Vitus. He must have chased the enemy into the night. When we are better organized, I'll get a patrol together. Whatever has happened, he deserves to be with his comrades…even if it means just finding his body."

Several seconds passed, and Marius scowled at the mention of losing a man. Falling in battle was a tragedy, but a man left on his own amongst their enemies was a fate much worse.

Walking to the counter, where bowls and wooden spoons were stacked haphazardly, Marius placed his hands on the stone surface. Staring down, he chewed on his lip, keeping his voice calm. "Who attacked? Were they tribesmen?"

Looking doubtful, Quintus shook his head. "Most of the survivors were in the tavern, where they heard the clamor of fighting and screams. Also, some sort of clicking sound and inhuman wails, like demons. Many of our scattered soldiers saw huge forms of…some robed figures, not looking like anything I've ever heard about. The ones who engaged them were slain. If these were the Marcomanni, they are like nothing I've seen in the past. I…fear we face something far worse than just those wretched barbarians."

Marius nodded, showing in his posture that the notion didn't surprise him. Collecting himself, he walked around the counter, where he gingerly approached Julia. Taking her into a hug, she didn't appear to notice his presence, even as he held her close.

After a moment, Marius released her, moving his eyes upward, as if hoping the faint twirls of clouds in the blue sky would give him answers. For some time, he stood there, and only the light sounds of crying or shuffles of armor around the square filled the void of conversation in the depressing environment.

Finally becoming aware, Marius' eyes lit up, and he gazed over at Quintus. "Have the men share their rations with the citizens, if needed. And have all but a few of both ours and any able-bodied citizen dig graves. Not one of these…people…are to be left to the buzzards."

Breathing deep, Quintus nodded. "That will take some time."

Stepping close to Quintus, Marius returned the nod. "And after, tell them all to pack their supplies, whatever they can carry for a march."

Coming out of her stupor, Julia's gaze shot over to Marius. Formerly lost and without speech, her intense expression was now openly defiant. Marius ignored her—for the moment.

"To Salvio, then?" asked Quintus, setting his jaw in expectation of the order for them to retreat from the doomed village.

Rubbing his face, Marius shook his head. "Not yet, my friend. For now, you and Julia will join me in the storeroom. We must get some answers before anyone leaves."

#

The mummified corpses still lay on the floor of the storehouse. With the door ajar, light from the morning flooded across the three bodies, while hosts of flies buzzed intermittently around the otherwise quiet room.

Standing over the dead, Marius motioned to the corpse that had earlier been brought by the merchant. Deep in thought, his words were precise. "Since Appius and his children went missing, we have been the subject of attack. Each…event that happens, we have had to react to. Even when we tried to take the fight to our enemies, this…massacre is the result. We are constantly on the defensive…and that is the certain way to lose this war."

Holding out a torch, Quintus crouched over the remains. After nodding his agreement, he still didn't use the moment to speak up. Instead, his gaze wandered over the fetid dead, visually examining their shrunken and wrinkled skin.

Frustrated, Quintus frowned at Marius' assertions, however true they might be. Looking up from the body, he fixed his stare on Marius, locking him with a serious expression and waiting for the reason Marius had brought him here.

To Quintus' other side, standing meekly in the vague rays of emerging daylight, Julia continued her sorrowful inner thoughts, but even in her case, there was a certain degree of morbid curiosity in her distraught features. Waiting, her glassy eyes moved carefully from the desiccated remains to Marius.

Acknowledging both Julia and Quintus with a raised eyebrow and a nod, Marius continued by pointing down. "The answer is here…it must be. What is causing this catastrophe? What is able to do these things, while we can do little to stop it?"

After a moment, Quintus moved as if to speak, but Julia cleared her throat, cutting him off. Using an emotionless tone, she talked in a dry voice, addressing both men with measured uncertainty. "I've lived around the forests of Germania my entire life. Whatever the tribe, there are certain ways they act and make war. Even the evil ones, such as Ballomar."

Stepping near the shriveled dead, she peered at each with some degree of horrified interest. Putting her hand on a necklace she wore, she massaged the lettering "⳨" on a copper ornament that hung from it. "This isn't the way of the tribes. This is...something more. The devil...or a demon."

Quintus finally broke from his solemn mood, his voice sounding incredulous. "Demon? What are you speaking of? Do you mean...dark magic, or something from the actual underworld?"

"Whatever you wish to call it. Someone...or some THING...has focused on us and this village. They won't stop until we're destroyed. And taking children...."

As Julia trailed off, stifled sobs crept into her breast, and she pulled her arms into a self-hug, containing the intense feelings of loss and worry that clearly racked her mind.

Holding up a hand for calm, hoping Julia wouldn't be offended, Marius spoke directly to Quintus. "Her religion is that of Chrestus, or the 'Christ' as he is called, which was spawned across the Mediterranean in the time of the Emperor Tiberius. In the past it has been persecuted, but for some time now, the worship of these 'Christians' has been tolerated by the empire."

Quintus raised an intrigued eyebrow, evidently not having met many who pursued this particular faith. But being a man of the world, meeting people who professed unusual beliefs—and these Christians were known for strange rituals of supposedly consuming the flesh of their God—was not too far from the ordinary. Shrugging, he returned his gaze to Marius.

"Anyway," said Marius, continuing with a glum smile, "all gods recognize this kind of evil. It is spawned in Hades, undoubtedly. What else can drain a man's blood and turn him into an ancient husk in little time? Nothing that is naturally of the world."

"That is true, Marius, nothing else can do such a thing," Julia responded, her voice suddenly forceful, even as she continued gently thumbing the Christian image of the Chi Rho on her necklace. "But to get Lucien back, we must find where the demons have retreated to...."

Seeking to control herself, Julia again fell into her personal tormented world. In response, the room grew silent, as both Marius and Quintus worked to avoid provoking her. This swelling moment of dread, with everyone contemplating what was to be done about Lucien's abduction, continued for some time.

Gazing at his dear woman, trying to strike the right balance between empathy and decisiveness, Marius finally stooped down to look at the body brought by the trader. Slipping a dagger from his belt, he turned the corpse over, looking for an answer he hoped would reveal itself.

For more than a minute he continued examining the body, replaying in his mind what he had done earlier and somehow missed. Taking his time, he prodded the skin in his search for something he knew must be there.

As if honing his skills as a field surgeon, Marius inserted the tip of the blade into the meatiest parts of the corpse's arm and lower back. But when he held up the weapon, no blood was streaked on the metal. Quizzically, it was almost as if its veins had not only been drained, but also that all moisture had somehow been sucked from the dead tissue. It appeared any approximation of life had been robbed from the flesh, with the body becoming an inconsequential and rather ugly doll from what had happened to it.

Frustrated, Marius sighed, and moving with some respect for the body, he gently began turning the corpse back over.

Quintus' arm shot out, his firm grip grabbing hold of Marius's wrist. Surprised, Marius peered up, his curious gaze fixed on his most trusted soldier.

Crouching, Quintus motioned to the upper part of the corpse's back. Holding out his torch, he illuminated a portion of the victim's sinewy shoulder blade, where there was a vague mark of a tattoo, just visible against the off-color background of dark skin.

Moving the torch next to the marking, the stenciled skin had the lettering "SPQR VITUS," followed underneath with "913 AB URBE CONDITA," which was precisely what was required for soldiers of the legion to designate themselves.

Such a mark both men knew well, as it was the primary means to designate a soldier in the legion, where men were required to obtain such a tattoo after joining. It was used to designate that a soldier was committed to twenty-five years of service, and it always had the start date of a legionnaire's service. In this circumstance, the second part of the tattoo indicated the soldier's beginning military date was in the Roman Consulship year of Atilius and Vibius, which was five years before the current time.

Staring, Marius' face, normally the image of restraint during moments of stress, grew shocked, then exasperated. Peering closer, Marius ran his index finger over the dry flesh, as if the tattoo could be removed by rubbing it away.

Gulping, Marius gazed at Quintus, and for the moment, they shared thoughts that could not quite be expressed. With each trying to process what this marking could mean, their response was to simply remain in the grips of their worries and most pronounced fears.

With wide-open and confused eyes, they studied one another, trying to understand how a man they had seen the day before could also have had his corpse recovered a few days ago from behind some random vegetation on the road to the provincial capital.

Like a forest wolf that had just encountered an elephant from the continent far to their south, coming face-to-face with an entity it had never known could exist, the only way to deal with a new reality required Marius and Quintus to reset their expectations about what was possible in their normal but sometimes violent lives. Even for men of action and fortitude, it was no easy feat to accept something completely unknown to them up until now. Something that was perhaps unknowable.

Thereafter, the storeroom's depressed atmosphere continued for an extended time in stunned silence, only now it was not merely Julia who was at a loss for words.

Chapter Twenty-One

T he interior of the woodlands was mostly shielded from the sun's light; only a few stray rays pierced the covering of spindly branches above the forest floor. These woods were impenetrably thick and undoubtedly full of birds, buzzing insects, and assorted creatures, but weirdly, no animal sounds or movements were currently evident.

A narrow trail led through the thickets of brush and trees, cutting through the dense foliage and leading to a hillside that was also shrouded in vegetation. Here the timber was more squat and the branches less thick, but encompassing the area was still a forbidding mismatch of undergrowth, making movement difficult for any but the most determined travelers.

On the hillside was a large cave entrance, wide and appearing as a blotch of darkness against a background of stunted greenery and thorny bushes. The cavern's opening appeared natural, but metal brackets affixed to the rock wall on either side of it, each holding an unlit torch, indicated the cave was recently occupied.

The children of Avenio, so recently kidnapped from their homes, filed listlessly behind Alia toward the cave entrance. Stepping with shoeless feet and aimless stares, they didn't slow down or seem overly worried as they approached the yawning cave. Much like they were otherwise asleep, their gazes were locked forward, unaware of what transpired around them.

A lone figure stepped from the entrance, his stocky frame revealing itself from the shadows. Unlike in the past, when Appius' formidable bearing and affable features identified him as a solid man of temperate character, he now looked unnervingly…foreign. As if his features could not quite contain an inner darkness, he peered ahead with dead-fish eyes and cocked his head at Alia.

"This will do, witch," said Appius, moving his lifeless gaze slowly behind her, letting his revolting eyes linger on each of her accompanying children. "Such a bounty of young flesh is…priceless."

Alia merely nodded, not eager to exchange pleasantries with the former soldier. When some time passed, she lowered her eyes, preferring to wait for what came next, feigning patience instead of the revulsion she felt growing inside her fluttering stomach.

With a deep breath, Appius reached into his robe and withdrew a handful of gems. Holding them out, he dropped them into her extended palm, where their black color shone strangely in the day's mild light. "For your efforts. You have brought us this treasure with remarkable skill."

In response, Alia smiled without emotion and stared into Appius' expressionless face. She had long been told that looking into the eyes of a person would reveal his soul, and a lifetime of evil had convinced her it was true, especially as she never felt in her own black heart the stirrings of kindness or loyalty to an honorable cause. Such was her own self-knowledge of wickedness that she usually grasped wrongful intentions from others rather quickly.

But taking in the glare of this...thing...reinforced to her that there were even worse—perhaps much worse—spirits in the world then the malevolent inclinations she herself harbored. She labored at the edge of an eternal darkness, taking from life what could give her power, but just because she constantly peered into that slum of evil did not yet mean she wished to bathe in the same despicable aura these creatures inhabited.

Waving her hand, Alia motioned the children to enter the cave, and as if they heard her silent order through their reduced perceptions, they moved obligingly and passed into the darkness of the inner cavern.

Tucking away the dark gemstones, she nodded at Appius and spun away. As she measured her steps, making sure not to seem too happy to be leaving, she angled toward another path, one that would take her toward the Verisi camp. It was a short distance from here, and taking her time would allow her to collect her thoughts and think through her options for the near future.

Walking sternly away from the cave, she paid no attention to the last child entering it. Lucien, wearing the impassive expression of a boy without concern for his surroundings, was quickly followed inside the dark tunnel by the frightfully changed Appius. After they entered the mountainside, the forest continued its unnatural silence.

#

The Verisi camp was calm in the midday light, and the huge tents containing its living quarters were spaced in an orderly grid across the flat, grassy meadow. At various points inside a fenced stockade-type barrier that ran along its exterior were numerous large fires, many of which had cauldrons suspended above their crackling flames.

The only noise in the wide area came from sporadic talking amongst scattered groups of spear-wielding guards. These strong men, who had thick beards and were dressed in heavy armor inside of long black cloaks, peered carefully at the trees surrounding the encampment, their wary eyes searching the shadowy woods for anything amiss.

Near one of the interior fires, which was located close to the camp's main tent, Alia gazed carefully upward, her expression doubtful and guarded. Glancing at the hunched-over outline of Magnir, she breathed deep, then swept her vision across the rest of the camp, clenching her jaw as she tried to remain calm.

"Are you…sure that is wise, Magnir?" asked Alia, continuing to hold her eyes away, avoiding his interrogating stare. "Hasn't your arrangement with Ballomar worked in your favor up until this point?"

Extending his rangy arms, which were hairless, pale, and jutted abnormally long from underneath his flowing robe, Magnir scraped his long and dark fingernails together as he clasped his hands in front of his pudgy belly. His face, pasty white and without lines, showed no emotion, but a vestige of impatience radiated from his bulging stature.

Peering down, Magnir waited until Alia looked back at him before speaking. When she did meet his eyes, his voice emerged in a genderless and raspy tone. "Ballomar is a…brute, Alia. He is a pathetic human whose worth to us is coming to an end. For too long we have been constrained by weak…people…such as he."

Forcing herself to meet Magnir's gaze, Alia nodded, making sure to appear not too subservient. She had long ago learned that weakness invited ridicule with these creatures, and potentially much worse—particularly if these beasts decided to cut all ties with their human partner in a very direct and deadly way.

With a measured voice, Alia continued. "But Ballomar provides the flesh you need, without the risk of feeding openly."

The Verisi leader chuckled, if the croaking sound he gave off could be considered evidence of humor. "We've fed without Ballomar's help for a pair of millennia, witch. We need no permission to do so. For this brief period of time, it was…merely in our interest to use him. We had urgent needs to keep our oldest members from aging. We are not eternal, and as centuries pass, more and more youthful sustenance is needed to prevent our own mortality."

Taking a step closer, Magnir's long fingers flashed out, his blackened nails held threateningly in front of her face. To her credit, she did not pull back, and Magnir pivoted to peer directly into her eyes.

Leaning down, he moved within inches of her face, and his distinctly sweet-smelling breath, almost like the odor of the common white flowers that bloomed throughout the Germanic forests, made her flinch at the sickly aroma he huffed out. "If you continue to use your witchcraft for our benefit…to hide our intentions from Ballomar, to let us see beyond the horizon with your vision, then you will have great allies in the Verisi. Your rewards will be many."

Pulling back, Magnir re-clasped his hands, but he didn't yet step back from her, instead using his bulky size to intimidate the petite woman as he loomed over her. "But if not, you can only imagine the results…."

For some time, silence passed between them, and Alia was not so stupid as to misunderstand his ill-concealed threat. Moving her gaze from Magnir's nightmare-inducing eyes, eyes that were inky black and soulless, she glanced at the nearby fire, wondering if her own remains might soon be boiling in the pot above it.

Gulping, Alia had a fleeting thought that the stew created from her insubstantial flesh would offer less nourishment than the Verisi were accustomed to. They seemed to enjoy the vitality of sturdy men as ingredients in their cannibalistic meals, which at least made her feel good about her chances to avoid such a fate.

Finally, Magnir moved on from his intimidating stance, turning away and swiveling his head to gaze into the surrounding woods. Sounding less predatory, he spoke with some measure of self-confidence. "Meanwhile, we will dispose of this vulgar savage Ballomar. We will use his face and power for our own ends. Food, from both the young and the old, will not be an issue when we control his empire. Our kind will take its place as the head of the world's species…and none will be the wiser that we are in their midst."

Moving her eyes back to engage Magnir, Alia could not quite hide her surprise at this sudden revelation. When dealing with the Verisi, she had known these ancients could be cagey in their dealings, but she had also thought their longevity was based on calculated and cautious decisions. This sudden proposal to assume strategic control of the Marcomanni tribe during a time of impending war appeared to be a beneficial move, but it was not without risks.

Magnir seemed to read her thoughts, and instead of acknowledging their apparently plain wisdom, a thin smile crossed his features, allowing sharp black teeth to momentarily protrude from between his tight lips.

With such a bevy of pointed teeth, it was little wonder his voice seemed to emanate from deep within his throat; speech from the front of that repulsive mouth would undoubtedly be more difficult to understand. She didn't physically comprehend how this beast was able to speak in such a neutral, breathy manner, but the reason for his odd pronunciation was now perfectly obvious.

The Verisi leader's wicked smile continued, keeping her unnerved, and Alia again looked back to the fire, seeking to avoid the arrogant gaze of her now-gloating and supremely confident host.

Meanwhile, around her, the camp's calm atmosphere continued in a mostly silent and unhurried manner. But below the seemingly calm edges of the extended clearing and the trappings of the ancients' bizarre power base, she could sense the very real presence of a sharpening dread. Its overwhelming intensity was raw and remorseless, and even if she were an otherwise normal woman, she still would have felt this unnerving presence of disquiet.

And, for a woman who practiced the darkest forms of evil with little conscience for most of her life, it actually surprised her that a sense of gloom filled her chest. For the briefest of moments, it was as if she really was an ordinary person after all.

Chapter Twenty-Two

The field outside Avenio, an accessible area of scrub brush and green grass, was silent at this time in the late afternoon. Twenty-four of Marius' men, more than half of what remained of his command, stood abreast in one lengthy line, all facing forward and at rigid attention.

They had cleaned themselves up from the disastrous night before, and now their red uniforms had been brushed to make them presentable. In keeping with the legion's rules, their faces were shaved to take away some of their haggard appearance, and their hair was combed to comport with expectations for proper military presentation.

But their darkened eyes peered ahead with various degrees of fatigue, as they hadn't slept much in at least a day, and their features, though disciplined, did not project self-assurance. Instead, they stared in equal numbers with worry or apathy for whatever was to come next in their traumatic lives. Strangely, they were unarmed as they awaited inspection.

Marius stood in front of them, his eyes roaming over their dress and bearing. As a man of strictness and the value it brought to campaign efforts, he would not let these latest tragedies they experienced distract from the need for his men to be disciplined. It was often the case that survival in combat hinged on efficient military movements, and to his way of thinking, success in battle could be quickly sabotaged due to lax rules or lazy soldiers.

Happy with what he saw, Marius nodded and cleared his throat. When he spoke, his voice was weary but firm. "We now stand at a crossroads, for both our duty and our people. Rome is in great danger, as a cruel adversary gathers to our north. The barbarians of the forests now move against us. They…are strong and ruthless, and they intend our utter destruction. Only the men of the legion stand between chaos and civilization."

As Marius spoke, Quintus walked behind the men. Stepping quietly, he reached forward to the first soldier, pulling back the uniform to reveal the back of the man's shoulder. Liking what he saw, he stared forward and met Marius' eyes, and giving his commander a nod, he moved to the next.

As Quintus made his way down the line, carefully checking each man in turn, none of the soldiers responded to his prodding. Being locked in a way of life that demanded absolute loyalty and no inclination to question orders, as well as having unquestioned trust for Quintus, they peered forward without concern for what he was doing.

Rubbing his now stubble-free face, Marius continued. "This wicked enemy who aims to destroy us has killed our comrades and friends. Men we've eaten with, trained with, laughed and shared good times with. Men who are now in the afterlife, enjoying their well-earned time of endless green fields in Elysium. As they were all faithful warriors to the end, we can be proud to have called them our fellow soldiers."

This got some attention from the legionnaires, and more than a few moved their gaze to Marius, their misty eyes growing sad at the thought of their lost brethren.

Behind them, for the moment out of mind, Quintus continued his slow inspection, checking each soldier carefully as he moved down the line. Methodical and with a grim expression, he looked up after each examination to nod at Marius.

Catching himself, Marius struggled with his own emotions. His worldview was not overly empathetic, but his bond with his men was undeniable. Shaking his head, he pushed away thoughts of mourning before continuing. "I want you to know that I grieve with you. Their deaths are like losing brothers to you, but like…sons to me. Each of them will be missed."

Stepping to the side, Marius reversed his course and paced in front of the men, taking great care to meet the eyes of each soldier, letting them feel his sincerity, even if his military bearing was still solid. "But their loss is not in vain, and the loss of these good citizens around us are also not without meaning…we will all face down this evil, fighting against those who would ruin life as we know it. Those that know only violence and fear, instead of the calming civilization of Rome."

Some murmurs of agreement met the increase in Marius' tone. With every pronouncement, the men's faces grew less dour, and now each of the soldiers seemed to stand taller, their bearing growing steelier, their determination stiffening.

Before he continued, Marius took a moment to let a smile play across his features, thinking now was the time for less strict interaction with his men. Breathing deep, he raised his voice. "We—."

The SCHIIK of Quintus' blade being pulled interrupted the speech. With a forceful stab, Quintus rammed his sword through the back of the soldier Cyprian's neck. The front tip of the blade ripped out the front of the man's throat, and blood surged from the hideous wound, spraying the grass in great gouts as the man stumbled forward from the sudden attack.

But Cyprian did not yet fall. His face, shocked and unsure of what was happening, was astonished, even as Quintus stabbed him once, twice more, with the mortal blows plunging through the tunic from behind and deep into his innards.

And still Cyprian did not collapse. The men around him shouted in alarm, trying to understand what was happening, their fearful eyes gaping at Quintus as they backed away from the slaughter of their fellow soldier.

Cyprian, unable to breathe, merely gurgled, but pushing away, he managed to pull himself off the blade and turn to confront his attacker.

Facing off with the mortally injured soldier, Quintus raised his blade in a fighting pose, getting ready to ram the sword directly through his neck from the front. His fierce eyes showed merciless disregard for his own soldier, as if the wounded man were the deadliest of foes.

But Cyprian was now changing. His face shuddered, and the muscles and bones of his head elongated and cracked in bizarre and forceful ways. His body, formally of a normal size, began to alter shape, growing bulbous and tearing through his clothes as his bulk became twice that of its former frame.

The air split with a bizarre scream, a horrid bellowing emerging from Cyprian's distended throat. The shriek was unlike a normal tone, even that of a dying person, because it reached a unique tone never witnessed by anyone who was present. It assaulted the ears with its high-pitched strangeness, much like it was an otherworldly animal who was lost in an unfamiliar land and sought help from a distant ally.

"Go, get your weapons," screamed Marius, drawing his own blade and rushing toward the hulking monstrosity.

The men scattered, some running towards the forest in terrible fear, while others sprinted toward the village, clearly responding to Marius' command to arm themselves.

Lunging forward, Quintus struck at the flank of the flailing monster, his blade slashing into what now looked like the thing's swollen right leg. The deep cut tore through the free-flowing flesh, and a chunk of thigh tissue flopped on the ground.

With a surge, the Verisi's lengthening arm struck out, smacking Quintus with a concussive backhand. Lifted off the ground, Quintus was flung for several yards, his whole body somersaulting and his weapon cast away from the vicious impact.

Landing in an awkward heap, he was momentarily in shock, and, trying to drag himself to his feet, Quintus could only grunt in pain. Unfortunately, mental commands to his limbs did not seem to immediately catch up with his physical ability to move, and he floundered in a contorted mass, momentarily unable to rise.

The looming monster, now taller than eight feet, raised itself to its full height. Still shrieking in spiteful agony, it faced Quintus, then moved to advance on him. Its clawed right hand, long and sharp, pulled back to deliver a cutting attack into the sprawled and disoriented man's face.

From behind, Marius crammed his short sword into the beast's lower back. Plunging the blade to the hilt, striking over and over with fanatical precision, gore erupted from the blade's lethal wounds, and the Verisi flailed back, spinning to strike at its new enemy.

Backing up, Marius ducked under a raking attack that careened over his head. Leaping away, he leaned back to avoid the other swiping hand from the monster, which came up short as it skimmed by his face.

Pressed back and being much smaller than the formidable creature, Marius stumbled, just catching himself and moving to the right to prevent being overwhelmed by the lumbering beast.

The sickening face of the monster, with a mouth full of black teeth and unblemished white skin, stopped and refocused on Marius, even as that pale skin seemed to bulge and flow with disturbances below its twitching surface. Peering at him with certainty, the confidence of a predator who knows it will prevail in pursuit of weak quarry, it stepped closer.

Looking to the right and the left, Marius searched for a method of defense, something that would give him a chance against the nightmare bearing down on him.

From the forest came a flitting sound, followed by the THUK of an impact in the Verisi's back. Several more arrows rapidly followed, each burying into the monster's thick flesh. With each impact, the ungainly creature squealed louder, its pain and frustration growing from the sudden long-range attacks.

For the first time, the Verisi appeared unsure of itself. As if estimating the chances for its survival, its dark eyes flitted around the clearing, gauging which direction or action were best for its prospects.

Turning towards the forest, facing where the missiles had just been shot from, it stopped. For several seconds it appeared to concentrate, and bizarrely, the deep wounds in its throat and back began to close, and blood stopped flowing as the skin appeared to stitch itself together. Around the projectiles protruding from its back, the skin tightened, and the deep arrowheads and shafts were pushed out, falling to the ground one-by-one, as if they were summarily being rejected by the thing's body.

His eyes growing wide, Marius stared at the spectacle of the beast healing itself. Nothing in his violent frame of reference prepared him for this, and for a moment he stared in amazement, almost like a child that couldn't comprehend its new place in the world.

From behind, Quintus screamed an *ARHHH* and leaped onto the beast's back. Holding a dagger in each hand, he punctuated several successive thrusts of his knives with more battle cries as he plunged them into the creature's neck. As the Verisi spun in a circle, trying vainly to get the bothersome man off, Quintus held on and continually struck down, stabbing the creature with more deadly jabs of his long, bloody blades into the thick flesh of its shoulders and upper torso.

The wounds were deep, and in seconds, the beast slowed its flailing defense. Dropping to one misshapen knee, it clawed behind it, trying to cast off the determined attacker. In seconds, its movements were slower, and it grew less able to move, even as its hateful shrieks echoed across the meadow.

Grimacing and covered in the creature's dark blood, Quintus continued plunging the blades, drawing more and more gashes into its inhuman flesh.

Falling to both knees, the Verisi's shrieks lessened, but arching forward, it slung Quintus forward, flipping him over and slamming him with a ghastly crunch onto the firm ground.

Stunned, Quintus was now completely exposed below the fearsome monster. Raising one of its taloned hands, moving slowly and apparently at the end its strength, the beast flexed its sharp, conical claws as it prepared to eviscerate the upstart soldier.

The flash of a sword, the mighty swing of a blade with all the strength that could be mustered, swung down and tore through the Verisi's neck, decapitating it in one swift slash. The beast, formerly so menacing, crumpled to the ground without further efforts or noise. Behind it, Marius huffed, breathing in great gasps as he stared down at the headless creature.

Gripping his sword, Marius peered at the result of his attack, as if evaluating whether the beast could recover from such an obviously fatal wound. Given the nature of its condition and what the monster had just survived, such a worry was perhaps wise.

From the distance, several legionaries rushed from the village. Holding spears and bows, they hurried toward the battle scene, faces determined and confused at what just happened. Others, those who had made for the safety of nearby trees, also returned, though some had sheepish looks due to their unarmed tactical retreat in the face of the horrific creature.

Running up, the frantic men stopped short of Marius, who resheathed his sword and moved to check on the condition of Quintus. Bending over his sergeant,

Marius used a rag to wipe blood from Quintus' face. The man was a mess, but although covered in the detritus of the creature, the blood was mostly not his own, and his swollen face was quickly exposed as the Verisi's gore was wiped away.

Mumbling to himself, Quintus blinked several times as he struggled to make sense of the world around him. With a lulling head, he took some time to fight through the effects of being thrown about the clearing and slammed into the earth. His dulled senses made efforts at recovery slow, and he grunted inaudibly while waiting for the fuzzy environment to come back into focus.

Finally, breathing deep and shaking his head, Quintus responded to the first aid attempts by brushing away Marius. Bringing himself to his knees, he rose to his feet, barely kept himself from pitching over, then somehow managed to maintain his balance. As he finally got hold of his physical faculties, he hoarsely mumbled, "It's not serious."

With the remaining soldiers returning to stand around the scene, it became quiet, which was in great contrast to the raging madness of the recent fight. Disbelieving men stared at the body on the ground, coming to grips with the fact that their former comrade had somehow become an enormous half-naked creature.

The extent of the confusion was experienced by all who were present, so much so that they didn't notice a figure walking from the nearby trees until he was almost upon them. Tarquin, Julia's brother, strode across the field with an almost playful grin, carrying his bow at his side, the same weapon he had so effectively used to skewer the Verisi with arrows during the recent melee.

When Tarquin came close, he met the gaze of the collected soldiers, then moved to stare specifically at Marius. For some time, neither said anything, and Tarquin dropped his eyes to the horrific gore-covered monster on the ground, indicating it with a shrug.

Apparently not too surprised by the fight, Tarquin spoke with some irony in his calm voice. "I had feared you would never believe me, so this at least makes what I have to say more credible. Otherwise, you would have thought me insane."

#

Later, the village's communal square was largely empty. The victims of the beasts' recent attack had been dragged away, and only pools of dried blood remained where many of the dead had lain just hours before.

The sun was receding, but generous light still flooded from the cloudy western sky, allowing clear visibility in the now-dreary town. From within its shaded streets, occasional bursts of sorrow continued, as fitful wails from distraught villagers erupted from several homes, maintaining a heartbroken mood throughout the traumatized settlement.

Marius, Quintus, Julia, and Tarquin stood in a group near the square's central fountain. Below them, in the middle of their standing circle, the body of the slain Verisi lay on a stitched animal-skin tarp. Moving their eyes over its grotesque outlines, they shared looks of revulsion and disbelief.

Sighing and shaking his head, Marius spoke, his voice faint and disturbed. "These…beasts are eating children? Why would anyone…anything commit such an atrocity? Even for the Marcomanni, that is too far. The barbarians must be in league with these creatures, but even they must have limits to their depredations."

Tarquin carefully nodded, but having dealt firsthand with that dishonorable tribe for much of his life, he didn't appear surprised at their enemy's choice of allies, even horrific and supernatural ones.

Considering the question of why these strange monsters would need youthful bodies, Tarquin offered a stark opinion. "It is for their survival, I fear. I've seen them make a fetid stew from the remains. Perhaps this process is what allows them to alter their appearance?"

Crouching down, Quintus peered closely at the hacked form of the monster. Shaking his head, he pointed to the outstretched talons of the creature, which had significant channels within its claws to allow blood to be quickly drawn from victims to nourish the gorging predator. "They suck living adults dry with little effort. What do they need children for, and why in a kind of soup?"

This got a brief cry of despair from Julia, who cringed at the mention of children. Feeling abashed, Quintus went quiet, avoiding for the moment further mention of the village's now-missing youth.

Appearing preoccupied, Marius shook his head. "We cannot know why denizens of Hades perform the rituals they do. Their evil is unknowable, but we must face it. They can assume the forms of people we know and trust, so they must have infiltrated the village while we skirmished with the Marcomanni scouts. The wounds we found on some of the men were from behind, where only trusted comrades could have come so close to inflict the mortal blows."

Standing, Quintus nodded his agreement. His face was swollen, but he seemed to have recovered well from the recent fight with the monster. The bruising on his features was mostly formed over his right eye, which had taken the brunt of the creature's powerful strike.

Putting his hands on his hips, Quintus let his gaze lock on Tarquin, then Marius, and finally, Julia. When he spoke, his words were expectant, almost painfully so. "What are…we to do next?"

Julia's eyes flashed, as she was clearly ready with an answer. "If I have to go alone, I'll get my son back, or die trying. I…won't live without Lucien."

Julia's committed words moved the conversation to silence, and the four people, each for different reasons, gazed quietly at one another for several long moments. Tarquin, sensing his sister's distress and feeling of loss, stepped near and comforted her with a gentle hand on her shoulder.

Julia's appreciative eyes quickly filled with tears, and she smiled in thanks, absorbing his empathy with sincere appreciation. Emotionally she was plainly in a tattered state, but her determination to absorb such a personal shock without a mental breakdown was impressive.

Marius and Quintus were no less caring, but each struggled to put into words an action for their future that could coexist with their roles as soldiers of the empire. Like specialized students in an elite school with a math problem that no one knew how to solve, they were simply at a loss with the vexing problem of *what to do?*

Taking a calming breath, Marius let his eyes move to the ground, as if mulling over his options was warring for his inner core, making finding a reasonable decision incomprehensibly difficult.

After a painful wait, with his tormented thoughts forcing his mind to consider many heretical possibilities, Marius raised his eyes, his decision suddenly made.

"I shall fetch the boy, along with all the missing youth, dear Julia," Marius said, intently staring at Julia. "No matter the cost, I will bring him back to you."

Quintus' eyes shot open, his face suddenly flushing. None who were present had ever seen the alarm and intense anger that currently filled Quintus' shocked features, as he was always the one in control and not prone to rapid emotional shifts. For several seconds he stood still, locked in an irate posture and looking unsure of what to say.

With a hurried motion of his hand, Quintus pointed to a nearby abandoned building, one that had formerly stored supplies used in the constant markets that the village had held up until the current crisis.

With a reluctant sigh, Marius got the intent of Quintus. Knowing they needed to speak privately, he paced toward the structure, where he pulled open the door and stepped inside.

While Tarquin and Julia watched, they exchanged confused glances, unsure of the reasons for the serious conversation the soldiers were soon to have. They continued their bewildered stares as Quintus stepped in behind Marius and slammed the door.

Inside the mud-brick structure, which had rays of light leaking through joints in the wall and around the door frame, Quintus faced his commander, his expression full of hostility. With a clear attempt at self-control, he stepped close to Marius, keeping his voice low, even while his eyes bulged with resentment.

"Have you lost your mind, Marius?" asked Quintus, his voice rising with each word. "Are you thinking to desert your post in the face of the enemy? You are a COMMANDER in the legion."

Nodding, Marius kept his eyes down, appearing like a child who had been caught stealing candy by his law-abiding mother. "I know this, Quintus; you need not point it out. But…what would you have me do? We both know there is little chance for her, even with Tarquin, to retrieve the boy without my help."

"Yes, and your concern is real and justified. I also care for the fate of the boy. But will your getting killed and betraying Rome fix the situation? You have never shirked your duty over the five years we have served together. Never."

Raising his eyes to his friend, Marius was not offended. Instead, he nodded. "I'm not avoiding my responsibility. I will face this despicable enemy, find out what I can—."

"—You're making excuses," interrupted Quintus, and his tone rose further, becoming openly angry, "for your own personal efforts, efforts that lie outside your commitment to your men and Rome. My mother is alone in Carnuntum, which is in danger from a Marcomanni invasion. Am I to leave our men to their fates so I can go check on her condition? Is it my sacred duty to throw away my responsibilities when they are inconvenient?"

Lowering his voice, Quintus got hold of his emotions. After a pause, he spoke sincerely. "You are better than this, old friend."

Now, Marius' own eyes grew angry, and his reserved nature melted into a seething distress at his current circumstance. "Do not dare to tell me of my duties, Quintus. I've given my life to Rome. I have fought its enemies around the known empire, killing and watching my comrades be killed by the score. Over decades. And I never questioned what needed to be done."

Lowering his tone, Marius continued. "I have missed out on family…on love, on children, all for the empire. What good is any of it if I cannot save the family I have finally found time to…protect?"

Quintus' anger, formerly bordering on violence, came down in tempo. Nodding, he found room for a bitter smile. "It's good you have finally found the courage to call Lucien and Julia family, Marius. But this is the price of what we do…what all military men must do. Commitments mean nothing if we throw them away for our own personal ends."

Peering down again, Marius thought over his options. The passage of the next moments in silence cooled the mood, and when Marius finally found his resolve, he patted his friend on the shoulder, speaking in a respectful manner. "I shall not involve anyone in it. I'll go north with Tarquin and Julia. We will find a way to get the children back…and when we return, it shall be as before."

In response, Quintus's face relaxed, but his voice was exasperated. "Tarquin will be a wanted man the moment he doesn't assist Rome. What do you think the legion will do to me if they find I knew any of this? Am I to be sacrificed as well? Will your selfishness lead to my demise, even if we survive the invasion?"

Shaking his head, Marius' doubt about such an outcome was obvious. He had seen examples of cowardice and personal motives throughout his time in the legion, and they rarely ended in poor outcomes for those who were not involved. As a matter of policy, Rome did not punish soldiers who should have known better, even when they would be justified in assigning blame.

Still, just because he felt his friend was safe did not mean Quintus's position was without risk. Whatever the likely outcome, Marius couldn't deny he was putting the man in a delicate predicament.

Speaking slowly, Marius nodded towards the outside, where the rest of their lives waited for him to make a decision. "I shall leave without the men seeing. I'll rendezvous with you in a week's time here. In the meantime, send the civilians back to Salvio with most of the men as a guard, and be certain to send our injured man from the fight in the clearing with them. You must warn the cohort about everything, including these demons who are allied with the Marcomanni. We can't even be sure Vitus arrived to tell them the first time we needed help. Make sure the commanders know these beasts are real by sending the corpse of the creature. Have your men tell them to use scars or tattoos to determine everyone is who they say there are. These beasts cannot mimic what they do not know is there."

Acknowledging the order, Quintus focused on Marius. With a slow shake of his head, he spoke quietly. "This is not a decision you will be able to undo, old friend. This may lead to your ruin—or mine."

With the choice for their future made, Marius stepped back and glanced down to assess his readiness in the meager light. Taking the time to ensure his uniform was arranged properly, he ran his hands along the seams of the red tunic, pulling it in line to be sure of his ordered appearance. Feeling the proper weight and distribution of his breastplate, he tugged on the attached leather ties to ensure it allowed easy and balanced movement when engaged in close combat. Carefully, he adjusted his sheathed sword to the optimal direction for drawing it.

With these small preparations, Marius had often found that a soldier could make his own luck when confronting an uncertain future—either in actual fighting or by being of a sound mindset to face the unknown. Coming out on top, either in a confrontation or in everyday interactions, required a man to condition himself in all ways, not just physically.

And with an awakening sense of what he had to do, he grew certain of the correct path forward: *The boy must be saved.*

Now fully determined, Marius looked up and showed Quintus a supportive smile. Trying to put a positive spin on his decision, he spoke with confidence he wasn't really sure he possessed. "You may be right, but for this one time, I must do what is right for those that matter most. Just…this once."

Chapter Twenty-Three

The clear moon glowed in the night sky, its rays radiating through a cluster of clouds hovering high above the wide river. The Danube, seemingly an eternal force of nature, was but a few kilometers from the village of Avenio, and with a constant surge of its watery volume, it flowed briskly between thick forests into the calm darkness.

Long used as a natural barrier between the Romans and the tribes of Germania, the river was an appropriate symbol of the gulf between cultures lying on either side of it. On one side was the often-violent culture of warring tribes that made up a loose confederation of forest clans, while on the other stood the outer border of a colossal empire that dominated and administered much of the known world.

Pushing into the current, Marius hopped into the back of the small boat and peered across the placid surface of the water. Tarquin crouched at the front of the craft, pointing toward a faraway gap in the woods that appeared best for landing, while Julia sat between them, pulling her cloak tight to keep the night chill out.

"We must be cautious," whispered Marius, "yet also hurry to their camp. It is not an easy task, I fear, with enemies all around."

Glancing back, Tarquin acknowledged Marius' thoughts with a quick nod. "The way is not far, perhaps three days travel, but we must hurry if we are to have a chance at success."

Scowling, Marius glanced all around their small boat, his eyes searching for threats, and then began using his oar in firm swooshes through the water. At the front, Tarquin joined with vigorous paddles with his own, and in little time they steered with increasing speed toward their intended destination on the opposite bank.

As they picked up their pace over the river's gentle eddies, Marius spoke in an ironic tone. "I think in this game we are playing, the winner will be the one who plans well in advance. The…problem is, I do not yet know our first move, much less several more that will be necessary for success."

Marius punctuated his half-humor with a grin, but the effect on Julia, at least, wasn't successful. She frowned at his smile and returned her anxious gaze to the approaching shoreline.

Tarquin broke the awkward silence by leaning backwards. "How did you know your soldier was the creature? That is a big risk you took to kill something— or someone—without being certain."

"Our men are tattooed with a mark that denotes their name and date of service when they commence their time with the legion. It is known by all soldiers, but it is not readily visible, as it is marked on a portion of the body covered by clothing or armor."

Running his hand through his close-cropped hair, Marius' tone became intensely sad, sounding wispy over the rippling water. "A corpse that was found on the road to Salvio had this mark, even though that same man Vitus had already returned from bringing a message to the cohort several days before. And even though Vitus came up 'missing' after the attack on the village, we could only assume a new impostor had taken his place somewhere in the ranks of the remaining men. We are lucky these demons did not take notice of the tattoo."

Tarquin raised an eyebrow, impressed with the soldiers' investigative technique and daring. "So, they cannot precisely copy everything? We can also hope they also do not know the thoughts of their new identities. Finding their true identity if they transferred the knowledge of those they copied would be difficult…perhaps, impossible."

Marius grunted in agreement, leaning into the oar as the small sandy area they aimed for loomed closer.

"Are you able to obtain help from your people?" asked Marius, changing the subject, raising an idea that offered some hope for assistance in their current effort.

Shaking his head, Tarquin didn't look back. "None, I'm afraid. Ballomar has raided and destroyed much of our tribe's living areas, killing some of our scouts and burning what he can. I sent…my people west."

The suddenness of the admission caught Marius unaware, and he cocked his head in surprise.

After a moment of awkward silence, when Julia came awake and glanced worriedly between her brother and Marius, Tarquin acknowledged the obvious implications with his next tentative words. "A tribe in the mountains to the west has agreed to take us in. Also being a small group, we'll combine our limited numbers to become more formidable. They are also beyond Rome's influence—and that of Ballomar. We shall start anew...and be free of this impending war...a war we have little chance to survive."

Subtlety nodding, Julia moved her gaze to her longtime partner. Watching Marius closely, she examined his weathered face to see how he would reply. Knowing Marius had just witnessed the equivalent of treason from her brother, she held her breath, anxiously waiting.

When Marius didn't quickly respond, merely lowering his head to consider the situation, she spoke carefully, trying to focus on his shadowy eyes as the craft sloshed through the current. "And I will be with them, Marius. It is my hope...and the hope of Lucien when we rescue him...that you will join us?"

With all her intentions and hopes laid bare, Julia waited. Over an extended pause, no immediate answer was forthcoming from Marius, and her hopeful expression waned into dread.

For several moments more, the boat drifted ahead, propelled along with even stronger paddles by Marius' now-trembling hands. As a man with nervous energy to be burned, he pressed the boat even faster through the current, driving the wood with great paddles as he ignored both Julia and her brother.

Eventually, the vessel thunked into the narrow shoreline, precisely where they had planned to complete their crossing of the river. After waiting a moment, Marius was silent and still, then collected his supplies for the journey into enemy territory. Ahead, Tarquin jumped onto the bank and dragged the boat more fully onto the pebbled shore.

For the moment, either by design or because he had not yet decided his final actions, Marius didn't respond to Julia's question. And as time passed, with Marius purposely not making eye contact, it was obvious there wouldn't be a reply in the near future.

#

That night, the group slept in nearby woods, where they rested without making a fire in a thick copse of dense spruce trees. Focusing on getting sufficient energy for the trek to the Verisi camp, the companions munched on supplies of salted beef and dried fruit while they gathered their strength.

After six hours of fitful sleep, they departed by a local game trail that threaded through tightly packed bushes and trees towards their distant goal. With resolute faces, they continued hiking quietly for several hours, ensuring they took each step lightly to avoid excessive noise.

Eventually, they came upon a larger trail, one that was wider and allowed for several men to walk abreast at the same time. Here, the dirt-packed ground was upturned with marks of frequent travel, indicating people had recently passed through the area. The enemy was undoubtedly close.

Taking an extended rest, the party waited for several minutes, and in time, they heard the commotion of a group of loud men, all of whom were speaking in the harsh language of the Marcomanni. The incoming cadre of a war party, with hard-leather and metal-studded sandals kicking the ground in concerted steps, was not silent, and they could easily be heard from around a bend in the forest trail as they approached.

Shuffling to the side, the group quickly covered themselves within piles of pine needles and leaves amongst nearby brush. Controlling their breathing, they waited silently for a glimpse of their long-hated enemies.

Thoroughly hidden, only their eyes were visible when a column of twenty soldiers, all carrying sharp spears and armored in thick leather, came near their location.

The rough appearance and stout bearing of the tribal warriors were common expressions of their warlike society, and the barbarian men carried themselves in confident if irregular strides. With scraggy beards, scarred armor, and heavily tattooed limbs lugging their long weapons, they were an intimidating sight, even to the war-hardened perception of Marius.

In testament to the group's skill at hiding, none of the clever enemies, who were themselves experts at seeing anything out of place in the forest, noticed the party sprawled so close to the well-used path.

After they had passed, Tarquin took again to the trail and led the way for the rest of the day, moving in spurts and scouting ahead as they worked their way north and east.

Eventually they arrived at a thick swamp full of runt trees and twisting vines, where the main path through it meant they could be easily detected if they used the trail the entire time. Gesturing to the side, Tarquin frowned and picked his way into the shabby undergrowth before the marshes, where they would camp for the night in anticipation of crossing it the following day.

After getting an early start the next morning, each time they heard more soldiers coming from the misty path ahead, the group was forced to depart from the trail. As a result of avoiding their traveling enemies, the three found themselves wading in the muck of putrid water and fighting off waves of buzzing and hungry pests.

The physical misery of their way forward was not new to any of them, but the thought of finding Lucien and the other children kept away worries of discomfort from the foul environment. Determined, they pressed on, drawing calming breaths as they carefully trod along the muddy swamp floor.

In one particular area, where the water was deep and where they had to hold their bags above their heads to prevent being inundated by fetid sludge, Marius found himself last to cross a particular stretch of brackish water. Deciding to take a more direct path to a stand of trees than either Tarquin or Julia had already done, he suddenly found one foot tangled in a root below the water, while his other was suspended in front of him, finding no ground underneath on which to take his next step.

The hole in the dark pool's bottom, unknowably deep and full of slugs and other impediments that threatened to pull him down, yawned before him, and for a moment Marius teetered on the edge, fearing for his very life that he wouldn't be able to recover from this odd situation.

From the side, Tarquin extended a thick branch, which poked Marius in the shoulder just as he feared he would lose his footing and flail about in the deep water.

Grabbing hold of the offered help, Marius pulled himself to the safety of solid ground, and breathing in great relief, he met Tarquin's grinning face with an appreciative smile of his own. And even though Julia and Marius had not recently spoken much about their future, she also flashed an approving grin, glad that she and her brother did not have to fish the mighty Roman commander from the noxious water, as if they were fetching a waterlogged child.

The following day, after another miserable night of cold and fire-free slumber, the party emerged from the swamp, where most of the time they had managed to stay off the sometimes-busy trail leading through it. Though free of the buggy marsh, they were now sweaty, stinky and fatigued, conditions that were often typical for travelers and tribesmen within such a wild environment.

Directly in front of them was a series of grass-topped hills, surrounded by extensive woods, while in the distance, a substantial mountain loomed on the horizon, which was draped with dark and dense clouds around it. A vast belt of forest lay between them and the imposing peak, filled in between with various interruptions of open meadows and difficult-to-cross ridges.

Pointing to the left, at a place where the trail descended into a green valley, Tarquin strode with some confidence for their successful arrival at their goal.

Farther to their left, at an area that extended to the north towards the far interior of Germania, a wide wagon path became visible. Merging with the current trail, it was clear the joined path could soon host even more enemy soldiers from the other tribes within the fractured interior domain of the barbarians.

Worried, Marius understood they would have to be even more cautious as they approached their objective. They faced two forms of evil now, one of this earth and the other from some unknown and hideous origin. At this point, he had fought both, and he wasn't sure which was more dangerous to his intentions for the future.

Whatever his prospects, either as an individual or on behalf of Rome, Marius would perform his tasks one at a time, obsessing over the best means with which he would wrench Lucien back from their enemy's malignant purposes. Then he could...consider his next options with a clear head. *One thing at a time.*

As Tarquin stepped onward, preparing for another day of scouting and staying concealed from their ever-present foes, the trees around them came alive with rustling birds, which gathered in a great flock amongst the abundant undergrowth of the surrounding forest.

Chirping and shrieking in equal measure, it was as if the loud birds were an anointed chorus to greet the group, providing a bizarre welcome for their desperate mission to save the kidnapped children.

Chapter Twenty-Four

The encampment was once again quiet and unremarkable in the calm light of late afternoon. Its attentive guards continued to roam the perimeter, while the campfires still licked at pots of bubbling mush at several points between the arrangement of tents.

But the Verisi were not to be seen. The wide area was clearly meant as their main staging area for whatever plans they pursued, but the mysterious enemy weren't currently visible outside the heavy material of their sloping canopy walls.

Lying on a hill slightly above the line of the camp, Julia, Tarquin, and Marius lay firmly on their stomachs. Their view was not all-encompassing, but it allowed for an excellent vantage point to see most of the enormous location.

All three of the wayward rescuers had their faces pasted with a black, tar-like substance. Supplied by Tarquin, they each had liberally smeared the paint-like substance across their faces, making it hard for their white skin to be noticeable among the brush as they peered anxiously over the camp.

Leaning close to Marius, Tarquin whispered carefully. "They spend most of their time in those tents.

When we move on the children, we must be sure they don't rally and reinforce from here."

Glancing over, Julia met eyes with Marius, who nodded his understanding at their problem of being so close to Lucien, yet unable to effectively do anything about it. Taking time to assuage her litany of worries, he offered her a quick smile.

Looking back at Tarquin, Marius spoke softly. "We'll need a distraction, then. And the darkness to mask our intentions. The only path to save the children will mean going unnoticed within this host of beasts. Where are...the children?"

Nodding, Tarquin motioned with his eyes behind them, from where they had just scooted to ascend a sloping ridge to their current location. With barely a sound, he reversed course, gingerly picking his way back through the cover of dense bushes clogging the hillside.

Meeting her eyes, Marius gestured for Julia to follow her brother. Gulping, she scowled and wriggled carefully behind Tarquin, shifting her weight on her elbows with manic attention to avoid the noisy twigs that might snap with the slightest wrong move.

Taking a last glance at the vast site of the Verisi base, Marius soon crawled after her into the growing shadows of early evening. Not being a religious man, he nevertheless recited an internal prayer to whichever God would best offer them an opportunity for success.

#

A while later, the trio had maneuvered close to the nearby mountain. Here, they had likewise arranged themselves with a hidden view of the cave. Around them, the cover of brush was less thick, but using the drooping branches of several trees, they managed to stay concealed from easy view of their target.

The dark opening to the interior of the mountain, at the place where the children had earlier been led by Alia, was currently unoccupied. But now torches burned hotly to either side of the entrance, casting spotty light into the encroaching darkness.

After several minutes of silence, Julia frowned, her impatience growing. Shifting forward, she made to rise, but Marius cut her off with a gentle grasp of her shoulder. "Not yet. We'll get him, but we must wait for the right time. If we are dead, it will all be for nothing."

Gazing at her brother, as if looking for an ally for a quick assault on the cave complex, Julia implored him with his eyes.

Tarquin responded with a shake of his head, clearly agreeing with Marius to wait for the proper moment to move. With a doubtful grimace, Julia went limp, allowing her restless muscles to lower herself back to the cold earth.

Some time passed in this way, with successive moments of anxious anticipation making the venture more torturous as nighttime enveloped the surrounding forest. Constantly looking at her companions for permission to rescue her child, Julia's rigid eyes and agitated disposition seemed to pressure both her brother and Marius, making them progressively uneasy.

Finally, Marius tensed himself to rise, but as he locked his hand on the hilt of his sheathed sword, as if preparing to wade into hell itself to save the boy, an alert figure strolled from the cave mouth.

Looking healthy but oddly out of place, Appius stopped at the edge of the torchlight. Dressed in a simple white robe that hung loosely on his powerful frame, he placed his hands on his hips, staring into the night and searching the darkness.

It was almost as if Appius could sense the interlopers' presence, and he swept his gaze several times over the group's hiding place, each time hovering his eyes with probing intensity.

Confused, as if peering at some disembodied spirit that had just been made flesh, Marius scrunched his face up, grappling with the idea that Appius could have somehow joined these monsters in their pursuit of youthful flesh. This man, long a friend and confidante even after he had retired from the legion, looked very normal, even in the limited glow of the flames.

The problem was that, until just now, he had believed Appius had been killed by the Marcomanni in a raid, with his children abducted to be raised by the barbarians. *How could he be here, except for in service to some wicked intention of their enemy?*

But Tarquin got Marius' attention with a curt shake of his head. Holding up his hand, Tarquin pointed to his ring finger, then gestured back to the backlit figure of Appius.

It took a moment for Marius to get his intent, but when he focused on Appius, he quickly understood: the ruby ring of the Roman army, something that a retired Legionnaire would never take off, was missing from his hand, which was now extended at his side as Appius stared into the darkness.

That Tarquin had noticed such a small thing in the limited light was testament to his skills at observation, and Marius had to remind himself that Julia's brother was leader of the Naristi for a well-founded reason.

Impressed, Marius relaxed, trying to calculate his chances to easily kill the monster that was dressed up in his friend's likeness. In reality, he would have found it exceedingly difficult to slay the normal man in a common fight, much less in the form of whatever Appius had become.

To move now would be risky, especially as Appius looked completely aware of his surroundings. As events now stood, Marius didn't like his odds to overcome what had to be a formidable creature, and he had lived a long time in his dangerous profession by avoiding situations that were not in his favor. Courage as an ideal did not mean one had to act stupidly.

A flutter of birds from the direction of the camp came unexpectedly, and Appius, like the party itself, peered into the darkness, taking sharp notice of something from the direction of the Verisi camp.

After a pause, next came the distant sound of a methodical clanking. The obvious creaking of heavy wheels was not a noise either Appius or the group had expected to hear so far in the forest.

Leaning close, so that both Marius and Julia could hear, Tarquin whispered. "Something is happening at the camp. I'll investigate and return. Do not do anything unless necessary. I won't be long. The children are within the cave, and that is where we will fetch them— together."

With that, Tarquin rose and scampered into the night, melting into the darkness without a sound.

Nodding in unison, Julia and Marius watched him go, then reverted their stare back to Appius. Regrettably, the former pensioner had since disappeared from view, apparently retreating into the cavern.

Disturbed by the appearance of one of their own, even if Appius had nothing left of his old personality,

Marius and Julia collected and readied themselves for their upcoming moment of action.

The effect of their painted faces in the disappearing light lent a sense of foreboding to their preparations, making both of them more distressed, like they were now reluctant ghosts waiting to swoop in to fight a battle that simply could not be won. Their odds of reclaiming the children, never high when they set out on this mission, grew less likely with every additional minute they waited.

In his role as a mentor throughout his service, Marius had often used the common Latin expression of making your own luck, *Faber est suae quisque fortunae,* directly meaning that a man was an artisan of his own fortune. It was an appropriate saying for most of his exploits in the legion, as it encouraged he and his men to not count on others to win the day, instead relying purely on their own ingenuity to fulfill a mission.

Unfortunately, Marius' time for exploiting the current situation was now short, as was their opportunity to remain unknown among their numerous enemies. Worse, the price for not achieving their goal would mean a horrible death for every person who was dear to him in his shrinking world.

Chapter Twenty-Five

T he clank of the ponderous wagon proceeded slowly toward the Verisi camp, its wheels moving in a lunging tempo as they were pulled in spurts by the hulking shapes of huffing oxen. The combined sounds of animal and cart were loud, resounding over the subdued backdrop of the open meadow.

Ballomar canted in front of the wagon on his armored horse, while several of his cavalrymen ranged farther ahead, shielding his advance on equally large steeds. The fresh breaths of the animals spewed condensation into the brisk night air, marking their movements in measured trots across the clearing's moist grass.

Ahead, the opening to the encampment, which allowed a wagon-size entry through stockade fortifications, was becoming very busy. A detachment of fifteen men, each holding the long shafts of metal-edged polearms, blocked the way into the camp. Behind them, several more groups of soldiers, obviously moving with some urgency, emerged from tents and rushed from various points to face the incoming Marcomanni party.

After an extended period of slow movement, the tribal party, stretched out around and behind the enormous cart, gradually came to the perimeter of the camp. Magnir, holding his spindly arms within his long robe, waited for them between the break in the camp's barricade.

The character and mood of Magnir was not easily discernible under the firelight, but that would have been the case at any time, even if the group's arrival had occurred in the brightness of mid-afternoon.

Still, some malice was evident in Magnir's brooding dark eyes. Striking a hostile pose, he stared intently up, just as Ballomar brought his horse to a stop in front of the entrance.

Smiling down, Ballomar did not say anything, merely motioning behind himself toward the retinue of prisoners attached to the wagon, then gesturing with a disrespectful smirk for permission to enter the camp.

For several moments Magnir's gaze moved over the extent of his visitor's forces, evaluating their size and capabilities with the eyes of one who had made such calculations for a very long time. Obviously liking what he saw, he offered a nod towards his nearby guard commander, making it clear they were to be allowed inside.

Over the next several minutes, the Marcomanni group trundled into the sprawling interior of the camp. Moving slowly, the group of twenty cavalry, the wagon with fifteen prisoners tied to it, and the accompanying force of seventy foot soldiers moved incautiously to an extensive clearing near the largest tents, where sufficient space allowed them to assemble in a vestige of parade-ground order.

By the time they had stopped, the group was surrounded by icy guards who were perhaps three times their own number. And this collection of camp soldiers did not appear to be without martial experience; indeed, even in comparison to the seasoned veterans of the Marcomanni, their cool features suggested they were ready for any violent eventualities.

Alia, who had stood to the side during the arrival, stepped from a wedge of the guards just as Magnir made his way to stand in front of Ballomar and his horse. Peering up at the Marcomanni king, she kept her expression cold, even while her unsteady eyes revealed discomfort in the tense surroundings.

Dragging his legs over his horse, Ballomar hopped down, his armor clinking as he drew himself to his full height. Two of his largest men, brawny and with the openly malicious scowls of his personal enforcers, moved dutifully behind their leader, trailing Ballomar as he strode up to Magnir and Alia. When Ballomar pulled up short of his hosts, they stopped directly behind him, both within easy reach and holding ready hands on the warm pommels of their well-oiled swords.

Leaning forward, Ballomar kept his eyes solely on Alia, moving to embrace her in a show of camaraderie. The effect of a man who probably had never shown respect to a woman, much less a female who was openly well-connected and powerful in her own right, made the effort appear unserious, even odd. Alia tilted her head to the side as the beefy man's stench made her recoil from the fake hug.

"Witch, so...great see you," muttered Ballomar, backing up and using the moment to flash his best diplomatic smile, then motioning casually to Magnir and his large force of stone-faced fighters. "And my other...friends."

Pivoting towards Magnir, Ballomar extended his callused hand to shake with the leader of the Verisi.

As if surprised by the offer, Magnir peered carefully down, fixating on the filthy hand with undisguised revulsion. As if Ballomar himself was an incurable disease, he did not extend his own hand, nor did he show an inclination to greet the tribal king on anything like equal terms.

And from the hillside to the north, where Marius and his group had earlier watched over the encampment, Tarquin now crouched behind a tree, secretly watching the whole spectacle unfold.

Unsure of what any of it meant, Tarquin focused on the belligerent form of Ballomar, a man he had only seen from a distance on one occasion in the distant past. The obnoxious bearing and unequaled arrogance of the Marcomanni leader was hard to miss, even in the reduced light of the camp's campfires and pole-suspended torches.

Raising a lip in disgust, Tarquin waited to learn what he could, hoping the unexpected arrival of his archenemy would not doom the small party's efforts to take back the children.

#

Twisting his leg behind him, Marius grimaced and stifled a groan of pain. Finally able to reach the source of his agony, he massaged his calf, trying to drive away a cramp that had formed deep within the muscle.

To his side, Julia frowned. Unlike Marius, she appeared at ease and reasonably comfortable within the covering foliage of the heavily limbed trees.

Speaking in a whisper, she rolled her eyes at Marius. "I thought you were a soldier of the empire. You look more like a bug stuck in tree sap."

Gently straightening his leg, Marius managed a grin. "Your observation is correct. A bug would be more comfortable than I, unfortunately."

Hearing her playful words for the first time in a few days, Marius felt heartened, even considering their difficult circumstance. After hesitating, he pushed away his doubts and forged ahead, feeling the time was right to speak, however quietly, with his long-time partner. "When were you going to inform me of your intentions with your brother?"

Peering towards the cave, Julia didn't meet his eyes in response. "When I could safely do so—without others finding out."

Looking back at Marius, Julia finally offered him a genuine smile, one that had been missing since Lucien was abducted. Over several moments, however, the smile drifted way, replaced by a more serious inflection in her features. "Marius, I truly tell you that you are my life and world—along with Lucien. But you and my brother would surely die in Ballomar's war. You're not a stupid man, and it would take an imbecile to not see this simple fact."

Focusing on her dark outline, Marius nodded. "You could be right, but you ask too much, dear Julia. My whole life has been devoted to my profession…and men. You would really have me abandon them? Not only would that be dishonorable, but the punishment for such a transgression would be death. Even to suggest such a thing is a crime."

Undaunted, Julia stared directly at him. "I only know what is right for me and mine, and you are mine, Marius. A woman has to hack her happiness from life. It's the only choice I have, and the only one that makes any sense."

Reaching her hand back through the leaves, she let her fingers fall on Marius' hand, entangling them within his moist grip. Leaning closer to him, where he could still smell her sweet scent underneath the pungent sweat of their travels, she spoke with some conviction. "If you stand in front of Ballomar, nothing will stop the flood that carries you away. In time, someone else will surely bring that evil dog to his well-deserved death, but that event will not be witnessed by you…or Tarquin. We are small beings that must find a way to survive. Sometimes the best course in life is to strike out anew, to find another way than you have in the past."

Silence overtook the discussion, and for the next moments, neither had something else to add. She had made her point, and try as he might, Marius could not easily refute her logic. Even taking into account his own inviolable trust in the empire and his duties, the truth that each individual had to find a way to live, to carve out happiness in an often-cruel world, was beyond dispute, even if he didn't want to admit it to himself.

Holding her hand, Marius looked down, tracing over her thin fingers with his palm. He was not angry with her, and neither did he begrudge her desires for the future, but for the moment, he remained unconvinced.

Mulling over her words, he took several deep breaths to work through his thoughts and plans. His future…or more properly, *their* future, if such a thing were going to be possible, required everything to happen in a precise way, in a manner that would somehow allow them to pursue a life unencumbered by needless death and war.

Raising his eyes, Marius didn't return Julia's stare, instead moving his gaze to the unoccupied cave entrance, and now it was he who became untalkative.

Chapter Twenty-Six

Hesitantly, Alia glanced first at Magnir, then towards Ballomar. As she tried to keep her voice firm, she spoke in a tentative tone, ensuring she could not be viewed as disrespectful. "King Ballomar, this is a surprise. You never indicated you would visit us here, and I never told you of this location."

Ballomar responded with a hearty chuckle. Pointing to his men tethered to the wagon, who peered back stoically, he offered both Alia and Magnir a rotten-toothed grin. "My entire army, numbering in the countless thousands, will march on Rome in the coming weeks. We'll soon smash their pathetic cities and make them slaves in their own homes...so, I thought I would stop in and check on my cherished allies."

Magnir tilted his head, eyeing Ballomar with overt disdain. Glancing at the collection of soldiers and prisoners behind the Marcomanni leader, he rasped out his words in a curt, snappy tone. "Before you stand in our presence, Ballomar, you must request an audience. Alia should have made you aware of this requirement. This visit is unacceptable."

Moving his gaze to Alia, Magnir's sub-context to Alia was equally obvious: she was also responsible for

Ballomar being here, whether she denied helping him or not.

From another of the massive tents to the back of the clearing, an orderly rank of soldiers filed out and took up position, completing the formations now surrounding Ballomar's forces. The comparative numbers for any potential hostilities were rapidly approaching the status of an obvious massacre of the Marcomanni—should that become necessary.

Shrugging, Ballomar didn't appear in the least bothered. Gesturing to his tied-up men, he grinned at Magnir. "I've brought you some of my strongest men. Don't you need them for a feast? What kind of ally would you be to insult such a generous gift?"

Visually inspecting the prisoners, Magnir let his eyes linger on the strong and vigorous warriors for several seconds. Perhaps unintentionally, he flexed his lips, as if anticipating their taste.

After a moment of hesitation, Magnir appeared to make his mind up on some inner point, and facing Ballomar, he continued in his strange breathless voice. "You…really are in for more than you could ever know, Ballomar. Such a pitiful creature you are. Your end will be swift and satisfying."

Meeting Magnir's stare, Ballomar showed no fear. In fact, his demeanor bordered on the absurdly confident, like he had no worries whatsoever about his men's vastly inferior tactical situation.

Smiling, Ballomar turned away from Alia and Magnir. Pacing back toward his horse and wagon, he shouted over his shoulder. "I've heard that before, you arrogant mongrel. But the result…is always the same."

Thirty of Ballomar's men, who before had seemed bored and listless, suddenly formed a line of shields, then marched in precise order to set up a position around their leader, aligning themselves in a wedge to defend him. Crouching behind their shields, they held out their spears in preparation for any attack.

As the tribe's numbers were small compared to the camp soldiers they faced, Magnir merely gloated, flashing the black incisor-teeth that stuck at strange angles from his mouth. Around him and Alia, the clearing and camp grew surprisingly silent, which was odd considering the incendiary nature of interactions up to this point.

Turning slowly around to face his hosts, Ballomar was readily visible through a gap between the rank of men protecting him. But now he did not look the same: his eyes were as black as the Verisi's, and his face appeared to swell under the flow of blood, with veins bulging in his neck and protruding from his temples. Grunting a beastly cry, as if struggling to control some complex physical eruption, only one word was understandable in his gruff voice. "Now."

With that command, events moved quickly. The remainder of Ballomar's soldiers and cavalry rushed back in precise formation around the wagon and prisoners, clearly moving in a defensive fashion that must have been planned in advance.

Peering over at Alia, Magnir lost some of his arrogance, and he hesitated as he made eye contact with Ballomar, wondering what he was now facing and sensing that something was woefully wrong. Scowling, such that his smooth skin appeared to pinch into a distorted image of an even more unpleasant creature, he made a firm movement of his hand.

In rapid response to the motion, phalanxes of armed soldiers throughout the camp, all wielding pike-like weapons, began to march towards the group of Marcomanni, pressing forward with great numbers to exterminate their guests. As they closed the distance to the island of tribal fighters, the sounds of armor and weapons, along with thumping feet, brought a strong reverberation across the formerly calm base.

To the back of the wagon, where the "prisoners" had been quietly waiting, the warriors threw off their fake bonds of chains and rushed to the back of the cart. With eyes black and faces pulsing with power, the men were no longer recognizable for what they had been.

Pulling long and thick swords, each more than the length of a man, from the wagon's covered storage area, the men rushed to the side of the nearest tribal warriors.

When there soon came a clash of spears and shield between the first camp guards and the Marcomanni defenders, the tribesmen were immediately under duress, pushed backward by the superior numbers of their enemy.

But then the heightened fighters, each holding their thick, long swords and moving impossibly fast, tore into the ranks of the Verisi's soldiers. With ferocious bellows they swung their weapons in great, sweeping arcs, first cutting through the shafts of their opponents, then through armor, and finally through limbs and torsos. Bodies were quickly caved in by the wide strikes, heads were cleaved from shoulders, and cries of fear, dismay, and outright terror soon broke out over the guards.

In little time, dismembered bodies littered the ground, shrieks of pain filled the battle, and what soldiers were able tried to fight off the attack.

But as they turned to meet the collection of nightmarish adversaries, the block of soldiers quickly lost cohesion. In spite of a score of spears tearing into the advancing madmen, and two being slain by the camp fighters, the normal Marcomanni warriors also pressed ahead, ramming their long weapons into the rapidly disintegrating enemy.

It was a rout, and it didn't take long for the panicking men to lose their nerve. As that large group of fighters pulled back, screaming and trying to survive the encounter, the other side of the clearing became alarmed. Not knowing precisely what was happening, they could only hear screams from their side and see their comrades running in fear from the clamor of the pitched battle.

Turning to their other side, the remaining thirteen berserker fighters, those that had the amulets of Alcis bestowed on them by Ballomar, now turned to another of the marching phalanxes.

Accompanied by a group of other normal warriors, they fought in tandem, performing their tactics in the same way as before. As the common tribal fighters advanced and engaged their enemies, the black-eyed berserkers, appearing like demons in the melee, quickly cleaved into the guards' flanks, slicing through their defenses and purging the formerly tough soldiers of the will to fight.

For purposes of the set battle, the fight appeared as if it were already over, and now it was merely a question of how many of the camp's defenders would make it out alive. Many cast down their weapons, and the defeat soon became a slaughter, with tribesmen finishing off individual soldiers, while cavalry rode down and hacked apart those who fled for the exit of the camp. Only a lucky few of the guards were able to hop onto horses and ride with frantic gallops into the night.

Next, the fevered and relentless fighters, bodies covered in splattered gore from their overmatched foes, peered at the enormous tent of the main Verisi. Here, Magnir and Alia, ducking behind a group of soldiers who had not yet retreated, moved through the structure's opening and into the dark interior.

Charging after Magnir, Ballomar heaved his blade and cleaved into the first of the soldiers, the swipe crashing through the man's shocked face and flinging his facial bones into the darkness, while his follow-up slash carved through the girdle armor of another man, severing his leg and leaving the soldier screaming in agony as he collapsed into the mud.

Ballomar was soon joined by more of his tribesmen, and the arriving spearmen quickly converged on the remaining soldiers, plunging the sharp tips of their weapons into their exposed flanks as the fighters tried backing up.

Outnumbered and pursued by ruthless and seasoned fighters, the Verisi's rearguard were cut down in a hail of vicious stabs, slain piecemeal as they tried to retreat, only making it a few feet before crumpling under their pursuers' merciless thrusts.

Now the way was clear to the enormous main tent. Approaching the entrance, Ballomar kicked aside the slumped remains of two defenders, then called out in a guttural shout to his chosen aggressors, those who had already annihilated so many of the camp's defenders.

From around the clearing, these animalistic fighters rushed to Ballomar's side. As they collected around him, eyes wide and lungs huffing from the effort of slaughtering so many men, Ballomar's supernatural brethren awaited his orders.

Only nine of the fifteen remained, but with a nod, Ballomar clearly thought they were enough. Motioning them ahead, he used his sword to move aside the flap. Stepping inside the tent, Ballomar and his demonic men looked up with expectant, almost hungry features. Before them was a wide interior, which was supported by tent poles for more than fifty yards ahead of them.

Torches hung at intervals, illuminating a vast assortment of deep wooden baths that were laid out in rows across the leather-covered floor. The soft lighting of the flames cast spotty illumination over the strange vessels, making them appear almost cozy in their precise arrangement.

The baths, numbering more than fifty, held Verisi in great numbers. The awkward, puffy creatures were suspended in yellow liquid, apparently sleeping as they bathed in a vile-looking liquid that had the appearance of a bubbling pus-like concoction.

Scattered throughout the array of bizarre sleeping pods were the remaining guards. Dressed in full chain mail, these ten men were obviously above the proficiency level that had already been decimated in the Marcomanni assault. Peering at the invaders with hatred from under metal helms, they stood in three groups, awaiting Ballomar's attack.

Clearly these practiced and competent soldiers were prepared to die for the Verisi, and in that, Ballomar appeared enthusiastic to accommodate their wishes.

Beyond them, in a central area that was raised on a platform, appearing almost like a shrine with tables and various collections of dark decanters arranged in meticulous order, stood Magnir and two more Verisi.

Transformed, the monsters were now tall and grotesque, with enormous, clawed arms extended and flexed, waiting for Ballomar's men. No word or challenge came from the group of beasts, but with their defensive posture, it was clear they were not accustomed to the effect of impending violence within their sacred area.

Looking like a child behind them was Alia, who stood off to the side and didn't seem like she wished to be there at all. Glancing first at the Verisi and then at Ballomar and his obscene enforcers, she apparently wasn't certain which side winning the fight would be more beneficial for her own purposes.

Around the ten Marcomanni, some of the bathing Verisi appeared to be waking up, as their limbs began twitching, and some of their arms began to struggle, trying to extricate themselves from their strange slumber.

Flashing his grin, the one he always wore when teaching his enemies a lesson, which was something that seemed to happen often in his life, Ballomar pointed down a row of the tubs, to the waiting Magnir and his lieutenants. "Kill the live ones first, then put the rest to the sword."

With that, his maniacal men rushed forward, throwing themselves into a fight with the last of their enemies. While the few human guards hurried to intercept them, the meat of the battle would clearly play out between the enhanced warriors and the horrible beasts that awaited them.

Little time had passed since Ballomar had first entered the Verisi camp, but one way or another, an outcome of either a crushing defeat against the monsters or a successful defense of the base was soon to play out in this remote forest outpost.

Away from the chaos, kneeling in the tree line that gave him such a good overview of the hostilities, Tarquin had been watching everything unfold. Witnessing the butchery, he was in awe, with his mouth open and eyes locked on the unmerciful killing of so many formidable soldiers.

In contrast to his expectations, Tarquin saw that very few of the Marcomanni warriors were slain by the camp guards, and as a result, the engagement shifted from a fight between well-matched enemies to an extended struggle for personal survival by the defenders.

None of it made sense. Tarquin had battled with numerous other tribes during his time as a leader of his people, but he had never seen a group like these specific berserker tribesman fight with such speed and power. It was simply unfathomable to see men cut so easily through groups of opposing fighters, with so few of them being killed or maimed in the process.

Unfortunately, Tarquin was flooded with mixed feelings from the entire episode of brutality. The fight provoked a mix of happiness from the Verisi being destroyed with a feeling of sadness that the wretched Ballomar was winning the battle.

While it was true that the killing of one side was a benefit to all that was good, the developing result also left a hideous winner in the person of Ballomar. Whatever brought the powerful forest king to destroy his beastly allies could only make him stronger, further endangering anyone else who stood in his way.

Lost in his thoughts, Tarquin could only hope he would live to see a day when the Marcomanni would be similarly destroyed.

#

The distant sounds of battle, with the echoing screams of dying men and the punctuated clanging of weapons off armor and shields, were unmistakable. Beginning as a far-off surge of strident fighting, in little time it grew to a conflagration of widespread combat, and the sound of the struggle soon assumed its own tempo of nasty carnage.

Glancing at each other, Marius and Julia shared looks of worry, not least of which because of their knowledge that fighting, even from some distance away, meant that the children's captors would no longer be unaware of hostilities around them. It would be exceedingly hard to conduct a rescue when their local adversaries were mobilized for war.

As if in agreement with their fears, it didn't take long for the inhabitants of the cave to take notice of the sounds of open conflict. Rushing from the mouth of the cavern, Appius was first to investigate the loud evidence of ongoing hostilities.

Striding quickly towards the trail that led toward the camp, Appius held tightly to a long sword and shield, but his face, just visible in the vague firelight, appeared to swim, with its structure reforming in rapid stretches, like he was unsure of which likeness to assume in confronting whatever calamity was befalling the Verisi base.

Behind him, four other soldiers, appearing to be normal men armed with their own swords and hefty shields, also hurried from the cave. Following Appius to the edge of the clearing, their clean-shaven faces showed shock and worry, as if they didn't know how or what could be happening in the safety of their forest redoubt.

For several seconds the group stood there, with Appius, the four soldiers, and even Julia and Marius unsure of the smartest way to proceed. In the meantime, the battle continued, and the increase in sound portended an ongoing fight that wasn't a mild affair. The distant engagement was obviously serious and could be something that would endanger their base's very existence.

Finally, Appius spoke forcefully, pointing with his sword down the trail and shouting, "go." Moving carefully, the soldiers followed his instructions, though they rushed toward the sounds of battle with the weariness of men who did not relish what was next to come.

Looking after them, Appius stopped, and as if again sensing the eyes of his hidden observers, took several seconds to search over the dark collections of trees that encircled the mouth of the cave.

Satisfied, Appius ran after his men, hurrying down the trail towards the main camp.

Left alone, Marius didn't take long to act. Standing, he motioned toward the cave, urging Julia to join him. "This is our opportunity. Let us make our move."

Gathering themselves from their cramped time of being silent and still, they shook out their limbs and approached the dark cave opening. As they moved close, no sounds emanated from the passage, and creeping cautiously, Marius held out his short sword, readying himself for what lay beyond.

Behind him, Julia crept with her hunting bow held close. Having prepared an arrow on the bow's string, it would be difficult for her to operate the missile weapon effectively in the confines of a cave, but her fierce expression, full of both hope and anger, showed it was better than nothing.

Reaching up, Marius took the torch from the sconce to the right of the opening, and holding it in front of himself, made slow and silent steps into the mountain's dark interior.

Inside, the passage ahead went for forty yards, which chisel marks on the rock walls showing it was not a natural creation. Breathing deep, the fetid stench of death and excrement assaulted Marius' nostrils, and he cringed as he moved ahead, preparing himself for the worst result imaginable. He was a man that had seen the worst the world could offer, but for the moment, the thought of finding Lucien already dead and eaten made everything else appear as mere sidelights to that appalling possibility.

Ahead and to the left, a door was set in the wall. Of thick and sturdy construction, Marius grabbed its metal knob, and pulling quickly, hurried inside.

The small chamber beyond was obviously used by guards of the cave complex. Bowls of porridge, fresh and half eaten, still lay on a table in the middle of the room, while on some pegs on the wall were various personal items and animal skins for ready use by the room's inhabitants. The rest of the chamber was filled with weapons and equipment, making it the likely duty station of the guards who just ran to the main camp.

Shaking his head at Julia, Marius nodded toward the passageway they had yet to see, and reassuming his role as point man, he sneaked farther down the tunnel. Creeping ahead, there were multiple torches lining the walls, so he gently set aside his own, propping it in a niche in the rock wall.

A cough ahead made both of them twitch, and Marius and Julia abruptly stopped their advance. Waiting a few more seconds, another cough told them the location of whoever was located up the corridor, and Marius began walking more slowly, ready to ram his sword into whatever person might be found in this foul place.

Rounding a slight bend in the rough-hewn corridor, Marius saw an entrance that had a strong source of light from an area outside of his sight. Against the far wall of this room as a small cell, which had metal bars in front of an alcove in the solid rock.

Marius saw what he hoped for. Three children sat in the grime and filth of the area, appearing miserable and horribly afraid. As one of them caught sight of Marius, his eyes went wide, and Marius could see that he would soon speak up. Marius recognized the boy and the two girls next to him as being from the village, and he held a finger to his lips to encourage their silence.

Nodding, first the boy and then the girls agreed with enthusiastic nods, and pointing toward the area farther inside, held up one finger each to indicate someone was there. The fear in their eyes made it obvious the unseen person was not friendly, but at this point, Marius had no delusions about finding allies in this wicked environment.

Peeking his head around the stone corner, Marius got a full view of the room's confines in the short glimpse. Several more cells were ·spaced along the opposite wall, and a desk of sorts, stacked with keys and various implements of a resident jailer, was set against the far wall, in a place that would allow easy view of the captives.

The jailer himself, middle-aged and as dirty as one could be expected to live in such a place, was stooped in front of one of the cells. For that brief gaze into the area, he had not yet seen Marius.

Speaking in a deep, drawly voice, the jailer muttered to the disheveled and scared children, who sat in the dim light beyond the bars. "Your turn will come soon, you wretches. For once in your miserable lives, you'll be worth something. The masters will enjoy the delicate meat on your pathetic bones."

The language the jailer used allowed only Julia to understand, but the manner of speech and the location of this hideous wretch left little doubt to Marius about the man's intentions or value as a person.

After quietly sheathing his sword, Marius moved quickly, and in three long strides he grabbed the fumbling guard, twisted his neck, and held a shiny dagger to his throat. Shocked, the unshaven jailer, with wide eyes and quivering throat, put up little resistance.

Holding him against the wall, Marius' eyes communicated a rather direct message: one peep and he would soon be quite dead.

Moving behind Marius, Julia quickly searched the total of five cells, and with joy in her exasperated features, saw that one of the sixteen children inside was her dear Lucien. All of them were alive, and with various degrees of hope in their eyes, they peered expectantly at her, like she was a heavenly angel sent to rescue them.

Pointing at his desk with a shaking hand, the jailer indicated a series of keys, and after snatching them, Julia quickly unlocked the cells, allowing the mewling children to gradually emerge.

Shushing the other children to be quiet, Julia embraced Lucien, whose eyes were clear and appreciative, especially as he saw Marius holding the jailer against the wall. Hugging him close, Julia prayed, whispering, "praise God," several times.

For several moments, even amidst their difficult circumstance and surrounded by so many other children, Julia held her son tight, even while sounds of the other youth rose from their lack of attention and due to their own fears.

Snapping out of her intense thankfulness, Julia moved near the jailer, whom Marius still held fast against the wall. Speaking in the language of her tribe, she addressed the terrified man. "Where are the other children? Lie to us, and your death will be slow."

The jailer could never be accused of being brave. Pointing hysterically towards the room's door, his words came out in panicked gasps. "There aren't any more...I promise. I just work for them. They'd kill me for even talking...uchhh—."

With surprising quickness, Julia plunged her skinning knife, a long and thin blade, into the jailer's throat. Thrusting it upwards, she pierced deep into his interior skull. As the sharp tip hung up on some portion of the man's brain, his eyes went wide, and they quickly filled with blood due to rupturing arteries inside his head.

Surprised by the brutal act, Marius raised his eyebrows at Julia, while also letting the now-expiring jailer collapse to the ground below them. Meeting eyes, he grew impressed and gave her an approving nod. He had supervised many soldiers in his time who had been unable to exhibit such ruthlessness, which caused him to feel a certain degree of pride for her actions. But, of course, those men were not mothers taking revenge for the kidnapping of their son.

Peering down at the evil lump of flesh below them, Marius then followed up with a triumphant kick to the dead man's quivering corpse. Smiling, he now hugged the woman he loved, using the awkward moment of her dispatching a depraved enemy to solidify his feelings for her. Romance was sometimes a very odd thing, and emotions attached to the taking of human life brought out strange inclinations in everybody, even seasoned soldiers.

After a moment, Marius came to his senses, then reached over to pull Lucien close. Holding onto the boy, he whispered, "Be silent," to him and the other children. Carefully, he began herding the large group toward the door and a hurried exit from the cave.

Whatever time they had left was not plentiful, and they needed to get their bearings and focus on a rapid return to the village of Avenio. Traveling with children would not be easy, and doing so in complete silence would be immeasurably more difficult.

With only half their task done, performing their other duty—surviving the trip home—meant they could waste no time in fleeing this horrible area.

#

Tarquin focused on the main tent from the safety of his hiding place in the thick vegetation. On his knees, he perched himself behind a single trunk, allowing for glimpses to either side of the thick tree without being exposed.

A horrid crash, along with a thick clack of swords on armor, emerged from the tent. Followed by chaotic shuffling, crashing bodies and beastly snarls, the combat taking place inside was explosive, keeping Tarquin's attention solely on the outlines of the loose structure.

For more than five minutes, the raucous fight continued inside, punctuated by more grunts, growls, thuds of bodies slamming into furniture, and screeches of pain.

Taking a moment to look away, he observed the rest of the camp. Most of the active fighting had died down, with only a few groups of Verisi guards trying to hold off the parties of Marcomanni from finishing them off. Elsewhere, in places where some guards were injured and vainly dragging themselves toward…anywhere else but the camp, a few of the tribesmen went from body to body, finishing them off with a deep stab into their torso or a quick slit of their throats.

Having retrieved the information he came for, which was primarily to see the disposition of their enemies, Tarquin raised himself from the moist earth, preparing to return to the cave and his sister.

Stopping cold, he looked over to see Appius and the four Verisi soldiers, who were crouching behind thick brush no more than twenty yards away. Also staring at the spectacle of their base and wiped-out comrades, they had not yet noticed Tarquin in his nearby overwatch.

Shocked, Tarquin held himself perfectly still, realizing he had little chance of surviving an encounter with such a party. Keeping his breathing quiet, he waited for them to run to the defense of their largely destroyed compatriots, to make a play to save the day for their species.

But they didn't move. It may have been the desolate nature of their odds, or simply waiting for the right time to make their move, but Appius and the stooping soldiers were not quick to leave their own hiding spot.

And just then, one of the soldiers took notice of Tarquin. Surprised, but also not being overly loud about his unexpected discovery, the man reached over and shook Appius' shoulder. The remaining Verisi leader, turning his quizzical gaze on Tarquin, spent several moments observing him, taking his time to evaluate the man and his intentions.

After a considerable time, Appius shook his head, then peered back to the main camp, where most of the creatures he was acquainted with over his immense lifespan must already have been slain. No sadness registered on the creature's human face, but his slow, wide-eyed stare revealed a sense of melancholy from the recent loss of his supernatural family.

Turning his head, Appius gazed into the forest behind him, and after motioning to his men, withdrew quietly into the night. Crouching and scurrying through the tightly packed trees, it didn't take long for them to disappear because, like Tarquin, they spent a lifetime making their way silently throughout the dense woods of Germania. In seconds, all that was left of the Verisi was gone, along with the impending threat they had so acutely posed to humanity.

Watching them leave, Tarquin realized with a stress-relieving sigh that it was not only people who struggled to survive in dangerous times. Even monsters knew when the time was right to retreat.

Chapter Twenty-Seven

Night was quickly approaching, and the skinny and filthy children stood and sat along the forest trail. Looking haggard and sad, they formed groups, using each other's close proximity to make the incoming night less intimidating.

Walking between them, Marius spoke slowly, trying to keep their minds from dwelling on what they had seen or what they would need to do in order to be free of the horrific memories they had experienced. Handing out small treats of dried meats and figs, he sought to buttress what strength they had with some quick energy for their travels.

Running low on food to hand out, Marius frowned and moved near Julia, who was comforting Lucien and inspecting the boy for injuries.

Keeping his voice low, Marius spoke earnestly, showing some worry with his harried features. "You have to go, dear Julia. Whatever is happening, the young ones will prevent our fast escape if you wait."

Julia kept her eyes on Lucien, checking the boy's hairline for cuts as she responded. "We can take them to the west—towards the mountains."

Shaking his head, Marius pointed the way she just mentioned. "Some of the children have family that still lives, and they are being taken south, towards the interior of the province. Others, even if we avoided the Marcomanni, would die from a lack of food."

"But Tarquin…."

"I'll wait for him. If we're pursued by this route around the swamp, I'll lead them away from you. Wait for us in three days' time by the meadow—."

"—That won't be necessary, Marius," said Tarquin, stepping from the dark brush to the front of the group.

Emerging from the darkness with his customary swagger, Tarquin stepped quickly to Julia. Giving her a quick embrace, he next moved to hug Lucien, whom he viewed with the undisguised adoration of a long-missing family member.

Disengaging from the smiling boy, Tarquin moved to youngest of the children, and lifting the toddler from the ground, placed him on his shoulders. The youth, formerly stuck in a sour mood, brightened with the attention, smiling from his tall perch.

Mouth open, Marius merely stared, trying to keep his composure at Tarquin's sudden appearance. "What…is happening…how…?"

"I'll tell you on the way from this cursed area," responded Tarquin, his pleasant eyes flashing in the lessening daylight. "There are now even worse things to fear than eaters of children. Things that are coming our way."

Leading the party down the trail, which was narrow and vague as it twisted through patches of grass and tall bushes, Tarquin spoke plainly over his shoulder, making sure they didn't waste time. "And we must avoid them at all costs."

\#

After a few hours of travel, the party of tired children and even more exhausted adults diverted south, avoiding the swamp that they traversed on the way to the Verisi camp.

Mercifully, the night provided ample light from a radiant moon and constellations of shining stars. The way across a wide meadow, bordered by bulky trees and heavy grass, was open and easy to see across.

Walking to the front, Tarquin still held the small and sickly child on his shoulders, focusing his tired eyes on the bends in the trail and depressions in the uneven ground. He was a man renowned for his ability to scout and avoid trouble, but currently, the most important aspect of their travel was to hurry, neither pausing nor being particularly careful in their rapid progress.

After Tarquin came Julia, who walked protectively in front of her son, who was immediately followed by the other fourteen children. Their pace was not great, and at times they slowed to a veritable crawl every time a child stumbled or slowed to stop.

At the back of the line came Marius, who continually peered behind them to offer protection from their back. Holding a line of twine that was tied around each of the children in the party, he carefully guided them by offering support and caring as they struggled to stay on their feet.

From above, this flight to safety became visible from a concentrated and fuzzy view. The ground, formerly dark and hazy, became sharper with the passing of seconds, and the entirety of the region around them opened into a wider perspective, one that easily indicated their position and path of travel.

Now the group was entirely visible and trackable, with nothing to stop them from being hunted down.

Chapter Twenty-Eight

Sweating intensely, such that her eyebrows were dripping and her vision blurry, Alia returned to her senses. Sitting up, her head swam to awareness of the area around her.

Sitting next to a barrel near the main Verisi tent, she finally came fully awake. Tied with rough ropes to the barrel and a nearby post, she was held fast, and after a few exhaustive tugs, she gave up on pulling herself free.

To her left was one of the campfires, one that formerly held the black goop that was used by the Verisi to nourish themselves. Now it was overturned, its disgusting contents spilled over the fire below. The smoke from the extinguished blaze leaked gently from inside the ring of stones, and its pervasive odor, a mix of sweetness and death, wafted over the entire area.

A guard peered down at her, holding a long spear shaft and grinning broadly. It did not take any of her black magic to see the man viewed her as a tasty treat, one to be enjoyed without regard to permission or mutual satisfaction.

SPLAT.

With some suddenness, the decapitated head of Magnir was dropped in front of her.

While never a handsome being, the Verisi leader looked eminently worse now, as jagged cuts showed where his head had been torn off, leaving his maw, half angry and half surprised, to stare straight ahead. Worse, his death seemed to have occurred during a transition to one or another of his identities, as his left eyebrow was elongated and stuck in mid-transition.

Looking down, Ballomar grinned. His eyes, still all black, made his malignant sneer even worse, and his voice, brusque and deep, was worse yet. "Surprised, witch? This bastard killed two of my men, even when we had him where we wanted 'em. He was as tough as he was ugly."

Gulping, trying to force moisture into her mouth, Alia peered for a moment longer at Magnir, then looked to the side, avoiding Ballomar's gaze. Anything was better than Ballomar's invasive stare, especially in his present state.

With a flash of his impossibly strong hand, Ballomar grabbed her chin, wrenching it back to look directly into his eyes. "I killed my first man when I was eight, witch. A man my father owed money."

Releasing her, Ballomar stood, but he kept his lurid focus on her, teasing her with his frightful presence. "And my dear father died by my own hand when I was fifteen. I never did get a proper thank-you for erasing his debt."

Alia, shocked and caught unprepared, merely opened and shut her eyes, trying to come to a semblance of order in her thoughts and feelings. Gulping, she didn't say anything more, merely nodding at the Marcomanni butcher.

This seemed to cool Ballomar's aggression. Reaching down, he pulled his amulet from his leather necklace. His eyes became normal again, and his pulsing temples and neck receded from their former swollen appearance.

Now speaking calmer, Ballomar continued. "The point is, everyone has always underestimated me…Alia. They've always thought my love for violence means I'm stupid."

Looking over at his guard, Ballomar motioned for the man to get lost. Nodding, the suddenly unsure tribesman hurried from the area.

Leaning near Alia, Ballomar's words were clear, even though they pulsed with hostility. "I knew your moves before you ever made them, witch. Did you think I'd be stupid enough to let your ugly friends live? What would have prevented them from killing me if I allowed them to exist…in my kingdom?"

"King…Ballomar," said Alia, her words rasping in her dry throat. "I never approved of the Verisi's intentions. They—."

"Drop it, your lies no longer matter—they never did. Did you really think you're the only one to have magic? I've been favored by Alcis since before you were squirted from your mom's womb."

Dropping his voice lower, Ballomar leaned closer. "And I knew when you were watching me. I controlled when and what you saw. What you sensed. That's real power, witch."

As if slapped by the news, Alia dropped her eyes. It was like finding that a longtime confidante has always understood an exotic language that was supposedly secret. Full of dread, she felt dejection fill her stomach.

Cackling with a bizarre laugh, Ballomar addressed her with what passed for humility. "Don't feel bad. You're not the first to lose to me, and you won't be the last. You never had a chance. But I ask myself: what can you do for me? What's the life of a lecherous witch worth in my kingdom?"

Peering up, Alia's eyes were without emotion. "You tell me, King Ballomar."

Taking a moment to consider, Ballomar paced two steps away. Stopping, he rubbed his blood-stained beard with a filthy hand.

Nodding, he turned back to her. "You will serve me. Tell me everything I want to know about my enemies. You'll see them from beyond the horizon, telling me where and how many they are."

"King Ballomar, I can't…"

"And I'll know when you're hiding something, because I'm chosen, witch—to rule the known world."

Growing inquisitive, Ballomar's grin lessened. "Like right now, you've seen something. Just tell me what it is. Is it that weakling Roman commander? He'll be dead soon enough, but just tell me the location of their forces and I'll let you live. You'll be my favorite toy. Every ruler needs a consistent wench, and you'll be my favorite."

Looking down at her hands, Alia evaluated the offer. Rubbing several of the black gems in her hands, the ones she had just used to witness the location of Marius and his group, she stared for several long moments. As time passed, Ballomar grew impatient, leering closer at her from above.

Finally making a decision, Alia slowly shook her head, then stared directly into Ballomar's manic eyes. "I don't think so, Ballomar. I think my time in this world has come to an end, but I will tell you what I've seen about your future."

Intrigued, Ballomar lowered himself to her level. "Well, spit it out."

"You'll die an embittered and petty tyrant, Ballomar. Killed by your own adoring soldiers, your corpse will be thrown into a cesspit. You will never be the great ruler you pretend."

For just a second, Ballomar's confidence melted, and his eyes glimpsed to the side, like the prediction could come true at any moment. Then, a reassuring grin formed, and the moment of uncertainty melted away from the forest king's expression.

Motioning to a distant guard, Ballomar stood and waited for the man. When he came close, Ballomar spoke loudly, so that Alia could know what fate was coming her way. "Put her in my tent tonight. I'll slit her throat after having her. She should be worth a roll—or two."

With that, rough hands grabbed Alia. As she was untied from her bindings to be hauled away, a mix of both fear and ironic satisfaction came over her features.

Chapter Twenty-Nine

The day was bright, with the sounds of birds filling the calm background of the forest around Avenio. The flutter of the birds, flapping from one tree to another, filled the otherwise silent morning with a trace of life.

Ahead, a trail of smoke drifted from the collection of houses that made up the small village. No sounds of living people emerged from the settlement, and at present, no soldiers manned the gate at its entrance.

Marius led the way to the town. Tellingly, though he still wore his breastplate, his clothes had been changed to that of a common citizen. Behind him, the line of children walked slowly, with Julia holding Lucien's hand to her left while also grasping the fingers of another child to the right. The pace was slow, with both the children and their chaperons fatigued due to their hectic flight from the Verisi camp.

Walking carefully through the town's main entrance, Marius squinted, peering at the smoke billowing from the remains of the bonfire that was lit to keep the area illuminated during the night.

Next to the smoke, just visible against the backdrop of deserted buildings, Quintus stood. Looking calm and controlled, he watched Marius approach, appearing as if he knew the precise time and place of his commander's arrival.

Striding up to his subordinate, Marius eschewed a common salute, instead briefly embracing him. Talking in a serious tone, he met Quintus' eyes directly. "Good to see you, old friend."

Grinning, Quintus shook his head. "It's only been a few days. We have many more together, if the Gods are kind."

Looking behind Marius, Quintus grinned at Julia, Lucien, and the remaining children of Avenio. "Did you dispose of Rome's enemies? All on your own initiative?"

Not answering, Marius avoided Quintus' kind eyes. Pointing to the children, he spoke with some effort, as if emotions were warring for control of his vocal cords. "See to it that the children are taken care of. Perhaps family can be found for some of them."

Nodding, Quintus put his fingers to his mouth and forced an ear-splitting whistle across the settlement. From the interior of the village, several of the detachment's remaining soldiers, apparently just having awoken, emerged from its empty streets. Nodding at Marius, they led all the youth except Lucien towards the location of their camp.

In moments, only Quintus, Julia, Marius, and Lucien remained. Noting the odd atmosphere of their interaction, Julia led Lucien to the side, using the moment to get him some food and drink and leave the soldiers to their own discussion.

Returning his gaze to Quintus, Marius spoke in a soft voice, as if each word were dreaded. "You're ready, I think."

Quintus responded with a sorrowful look. For once in his military life, he showed empathy and understanding, even though the military situation called for something quite different. "So, you will really do this, Marius? You need not leave; we will be quite able to cover for your prior absence. From what the scouts tell me, we will have other things to worry about in the near future."

Marius nodded at the sentiment but said nothing.

Quintus continued. "You will never get the chance to retire to Rome. To live the decadent life we always planned."

From the distance, a new sound emerged. Coming from the interior road to the capital, the marching of feet, broad and in proper step, grew louder over the next moments. To the ears of a professional, the sound announced the obvious: an army on the move.

Still remaining quiet, Marius kept his eyes down. With a firm jaw, he held his silence. Only a single tear, the first that Quintus ever witnessed, ran down his cheek.

Clearing his throat, Quintus spoke without reservation. "Marius, I've never had, nor will ever have, a friend better than you. You will always be with me. Your wisdom will always inform my actions. Your friendship will be eternal."

Extending hands, the longtime soldiers shook, grasping each other with a firmness and fidelity that could only occur between brothers.

From the distant trail, the sound of marching grew louder. With it, the neighing of horses and the creaking of wagon wheels also became clearer. Their arrival would be soon.

Collecting himself, Marius spoke clearly. "I believe the creatures we have faced were decimated, if not completely destroyed. But be careful of Ballomar. He is something more than human, I fear."

Quintus nodded in understanding.

Smiling with a bittersweet grin, Marius met Quintus's gaze. "Someday you will make the greatest of centurions, Quintus. I will have the chance to read of your exploits."

Bending down, Marius reached into his pack. Pulling out his red uniform, he dropped it into the fire pit. After a few moments, flames caught on the cloth, slowly incinerating his cherished symbol, severing the connection he had built over a lifetime of service.

"Pax Romana," shouted Marius, and saluting his friend, he turned and went to Julia and Lucien. Moving with some urgency, they linked hands and hurried out the gate to the western woods. Ducking under limbs and dodging thick bushes in that direction of rarely traveled forest, they were soon out of view.

Behind them, Quintus watched them go, a pained expression forming over his face.

Soon, from down the road, the first columns of Roman soldiers emerged. Marching five abreast and in perfect sync, reinforcements had finally arrived at the backwater village of Avenio.

From far overhead, a view of the surrounding countryside offered a vision of green trees, plush grass, and rolling hills. On the road that stretched from the provincial capital, thousands more soldiers marched toward the village, with red uniforms stretching in a snake-like column over several miles.

From far in front of village, the glistening artery of the Danube River was also visible, and the sky and weather were beautiful, standing in stark contrast to the storm of conflict that was soon to arrive.

THE END

Epilogue

Ballomar invaded Roman territory soon thereafter, igniting a conflict that lasted more than a decade and threatened Rome's very survival. Like much that happened during the time of Imperial Rome, the soldiers and families that felt the impact of such devastation were lost to history, their specific names either buried in the ground where they were interred or their bones left to the elements, where they would be bleached white in time and similarly forgotten.

The Marcomannic Wars developed as a brutal conflict in an era of especially deadly wars, with several hundred thousand soldiers and tribesmen dying in an area that stretched from Central Europe to portions of modern-day Northern Italy. When invading Germanic tribes were finally expelled from its borders, Rome persevered as a great empire for three centuries longer.

To this day, elements of civilization from that distant time, assiduously nourished under Roman tutelage, are felt in the structures and religion we see all around us. To all those anonymous people, from peasants who tilled the fields of the frontier to the soldiers who imposed the peace of an empire on a reluctant, chaotic world, much is owed.

With a little effort of imagination, they will not be forgotten.

About the Author

Tim lives in Nevada, where he makes a life enjoying all things horror and thriller-related, from films to books, and even the occasional convention. He has three children, three cats, and sincerely enjoys providing reading entertainment for the monster and creature-loving masses.

If you like this novel, he would appreciate a review or a follow on Facebook:

https://www.facebook.com/Horrorthrillerguy

Also by Timothy Bryan:

Chindi
books2read.com/u/mlAJ7Z

The Huntsman of Corvinus
books2read.com/u/mVRyr5

Despicable
books2read.com/u/49k0ak

Core Ruleset
books2read.com/u/mqXyQ6

By Their Cold Fingers
books2read.com/u/bPgMKr

Prisoners of a Dark Night
books2read.com/u/mllzqW